*"I—I don't know ...
from me,"* Michelle whispered.

Tony sighed and rested his forehead against hers. "You really have a problem with trust, don't you?"

"I've had reason to."

"Men who said they wanted you, when what they really wanted was the Trent money?"

Michelle nodded stiffly.

"I could tell you I couldn't care less about your money. That it's only you I want—very badly. But I know it's going to take time for you to believe those things. I won't rush you."

Michelle cleared her throat of a large, painful lump. "Thank you."

Tony smiled crookedly, and then he kissed her again, until her knees were weak and her lungs were burning from lack of oxygen. When he finally released her, she clung to the doorknob, not sure her legs would support her without assistance.

"That was just to hold me over," he said, smiling with a mixture of satisfaction and frustration, then he loped toward his Jeep.

Dear Reader,

Welcome to Silhouette **Special Edition** . . . welcome to romance. Each month Silhouette **Special Edition** publishes six novels with you in mind—stories of love and life, tales that you can identify with—as well as dream about.

This Valentine's Day month has plenty in store for you. THAT SPECIAL WOMAN!, Silhouette **Special Edition**'s new series that salutes women, features a warm, wonderful story about Clare Gilroy and bad-boy hero Reed Tonasket. Don't miss their romance in *Hasty Wedding* by Debbie Macomber.

THAT SPECIAL WOMAN! is a selection each month that pays tribute to women—to us. The heroine is a friend, a wife, a mother—a striver, a nurturer, a pursuer of goals—she's the best in every woman. And it takes a very special man to win that special woman!

Also in store for you this month is the first book in the series FAMILY FOUND by Gina Ferris. This book, *Full of Grace,* brings together Michelle Trent and Tony D'Allessandro in a search for a family lost . . . and now found.

Rounding out this month are books from other favorite writers: Christine Rimmer, Maggi Charles, Pat Warren and Terry Essig (with her first Silhouette Special Edition).

I hope that you enjoy this book and all the stories to come. Happy St. Valentine's Day!

Sincerely,

Tara Gavin
Senior Editor

GINA FERRIS
FULL OF GRACE

Silhouette®

SPECIAL EDITION®

Published by Silhouette Books New York
America's Publisher of Contemporary Romance

SILHOUETTE BOOKS
300 East 42nd St., New York, N.Y. 10017

FULL OF GRACE

Copyright © 1993 by Gina Wilkins

ISBN: 0-373-09793-X

First Silhouette Books printing February 1993

All the characters in this book have no existence outside the
imagination of the author and have no relation whatsoever to
anyone bearing the same name or names. They are not even
distantly inspired by any individual known or unknown to the
author, and all incidents are pure invention.

®: Trademark used under license and registered in the United
States Patent and Trademark Office and in other countries.

Printed in the U.S.A.

Books by Gina Ferris

Silhouette Special Edition

Healing Sympathy #496
Lady Beware #549
In From the Rain #677
Prodigal Father #711
*Full of Grace #793

*Family Found

GINA FERRIS

declares that she is Southern by birth and by choice, and she has chosen to set many of her books in the South, where she finds a rich treasury of characters and settings. She particularly loves the Ozark mountain region of northern Arkansas and southern Missouri, and the proudly unique people who reside there. She and her husband, John, live in Arkansas, with their three children, Courtney, Kerry and David.

Monday's child is fair of face.
Tuesday's child is full of grace.
Wednesday's child is full of woe.
Thursday's child has far to go.
Friday's child is loving and giving.
Saturday's child has to work hard for its living.
But the child that is born on the Sabbath Day
is fair and wise and good and gay.
                                        —Anon.

Prologue

My dearest Michelle,

I want to take this chance to tell you one last time that you have blessed my life in so many ways. I could never have imagined the joy and pride I would find in the little girl who was given to me in answer to years of prayers.

Your father and I loved you from the moment we saw you. You were so small and frightened and vulnerable. You looked up at us with your big blue eyes filled with tears and your tiny mouth trembling and we knew our lives would never be the same.

Now your daddy has been gone for three years and I will be joining him soon. I know how lonely you will be, how empty this big house will seem to you. And I feel compelled to tell you something I have withheld until now because I couldn't bear to share you with those who may have had reason to feel you belonged more to them than to your father and me.

We told you that your real parents were dead and that you had no adult relatives who could have taken you in. I'm sorry, darling, but we kept one important bit of information from you. You do have a family, four brothers and two sisters, to be exact. All are older than you except one, a little girl only a few months old when your mother died when you were two.

I don't know what happened to any of them, but I will tell you that the last name was Walker. Your biological father was Hank Walker, your mother's name was Hazel. You lived in a rural area near Texarkana, Texas. You were born in Texarkana and given the name Shelley Marie Walker. Hank died while your mother was pregnant with your younger sister. When Hazel died so tragically soon afterward, there was no one else to provide for seven small children, so the decision was made to split you up and find homes for you. Perhaps a bad decision, but had a different one been made, your father and I would never have had you. I can't even bear to think of that.

Please forgive us for not telling you these things sooner, and try to understand our fears. We loved you so much. You were our life. We almost lost you once. We couldn't bear to risk losing you again. Remember us only with love, darling, and know that no child, no young woman, has ever been loved more than we loved you.

                                                            Mother

Chapter One

Tony D'Alessandro looked up from the letter in his hand to the young woman sitting absolutely still in a worn leather chair on the other side of his desk. With her rich brown hair swept into a neat coil, her blue eyes focused intently on his face, her seductive mouth unsmiling, her slender body clad in a suit that probably cost more than his monthly food allowance, the woman could have passed as a mannequin for a Rodeo Drive boutique.

When his secretary, Bonnie, had escorted Michelle Trent into his office less than ten minutes earlier, Tony had been struck speechless by the woman's beauty. Only after he'd closed his mouth and self-consciously cleared his throat had he become aware of the icy shell she maintained around her—invisible, but unarguably real.

He'd wondered if her lovely, porcelain-fair face ever warmed with a smile, ever softened with emotion. Now he knew that at least one person had loved Michelle Trent with an almost neurotic intensity—her adoptive mother, Alicia Culverton Trent, the late widow of immensely wealthy, near-legendary Dallas business tycoon Harrison Ellington Trent III. Tony knew of the family, of course, in the same way everyone else heard about them—through newspapers, magazines, gossip and rumors.

So what was wealthy, reclusive, incredibly beautiful Michelle Trent doing in the office of a low-profile, ex-cop-turned-private-investigator? With his usual straightforward approach to mysteries, Tony decided the only way to find the answer was to ask. "Why are you here, Ms. Trent? Why did you want me to read this letter?"

Her voice was as cultured and alluring as the rest of her. "I would think the answer is obvious, Mr. D'Alessandro. I want you to locate my brothers and sisters."

His left eyebrow rose as it always did when something intrigued him. "Why me?" he asked bluntly. "Surely you have attorneys who could initiate this search as easily as I can."

She inclined her head in an annoyingly regal gesture. "I have attorneys, of course, but I've chosen not to involve them. To be completely honest, you're the only one other than myself who has seen this letter or who knows about my search. I've been told that you are an honest, discreet investigator. I trust that your business ethics will ensure strict confidentiality in my case."

Piqued by the undercurrents of doubt in her voice, Tony scowled. "I've never gossiped about a client in my entire career, Ms. Trent, and I can assure you that won't change with you. I'm only trying to determine why you came to me with this."

She moistened her artfully tinted lips with the tip of her tongue, for the first time looking somewhat less imperturbable. "Eighteen years ago my father hired your father for an assignment that was highly sensitive and even involved physical danger to your father. It was important that the case be handled quickly, efficiently—and privately. My father was always grateful to yours for the skillful way he handled the job, and he told me that if I ever needed help, I should contact Vincent D'Alessandro."

"Who retired in '86," Tony finished for her. "I started the business back up two years ago."

She nodded. "So I found out."

Tony tried not to look surprised that his father had once handled a "highly sensitive" assignment for one of the wealthiest, most powerful men in Texas. He wasn't at all surprised, however, that the mysterious case had been handled well, or that it had apparently been kept utterly private. Vinnie D'Alessandro had never, in some thirty years in the business, broken client confidence, a record Tony had every intention of maintaining.

Michelle Trent crossed her long, silk-covered legs and subjected Tony to a thorough scrutiny. "Are you as good at your job as your father was, Mr. D'Alessandro?"

He crossed his arms over his chest and met her eyes, knowing if he looked down at those luscious legs he'd find himself stammering. "No one's as good as my father was, Ms. Trent. But I'm damn close."

It was a calculated risk, of course. If this insouciant attitude offended her, he'd lose what could turn out to be a profitable assignment. On the other hand, he intended to let her know that he didn't particularly care to be treated like a menial subordinate during their association, should there be one.

Her lips twitched in what he would have sworn was the beginning of a smile, and he felt his left eyebrow rising again. But she quickly suppressed the expression and nodded in response to his words. "I can depend on you to keep my business completely private?"

"You can trust me," he replied, too curtly.

"I trust very few people." Her tone was cool. Some might have called it icy. "Your father was one of them. I'm taking a risk that he trained you to be as honorable as he is."

Tony couldn't help but soften at her praise of his father. After all, his dad was a hell of a great guy. "I've always tried to be as much like my father as possible," he admitted grudgingly.

"Then consider yourself hired," she said. "I'll pay your usual rates, plus expenses, of course. I'd like to handle the transaction in cash, if that's agreeable to you. How much do you want up front?"

She opened the small leather bag resting in her lap.

Tony held up a hand, palm outward. "Now hold on a minute," he said quickly. "I haven't agreed to take the case yet. There are a few things I'd like to know first."

Michelle looked surprised that he wasn't jumping to take her money. "What things?"

He glanced back down at the letter. "This is dated five months ago."

"Yes. My mother wrote it six weeks before she—before she died," Michelle said, quickly masking the slight break in her voice. "I found it among her things the day after her funeral."

"And this was the first you knew of your brothers and sisters?"

"Yes. I'd always assumed that I was an only child for my biological parents, as well as my adopted ones."

Tony studied her shuttered expression, wondering if he'd imagined a note of longing in her words. He'd had cool customers before, had dealt with masters at concealing emotions and facts, but Michelle Trent confused him as few people had before her. Outwardly, she was cool, reserved, aloof. But there'd been something in her eyes when she'd talked about his father, something in that slight break when she'd mentioned her mother's death, something in her voice when she talked about her unknown brothers and sisters.

He couldn't help wondering if there was much more to Michelle than she allowed him—or anyone else, perhaps—to see. A veritable storm of emotions concealed behind a bank of impenetrable clouds.

It had been years since a woman had rattled his composure the way this one did, years since he'd felt as though all it would take was a fleeting touch to reduce him to tongue-tied incoherence. His reactions to her greatly annoyed him.

"Why are you so concerned with privacy?" he asked, though he suspected he already knew—the answer had to do with her money.

She proved his guess to be correct. "I'm a very wealthy woman, as I'm sure you know. Through unpleasant experience I've learned that there are many unscrupulous people who would leap at the chance to take advantage of me. Should word get out that I'm searching for my long-lost family, I'm sure I'd find impostors by the dozens lined up at my door."

Tony nodded. "Quite probably. Which explains, of course, why you want to keep your search out of the newspapers. But you said I'm the only one other than you who has seen this letter or who knows about your siblings. You haven't told your friends? Family? Your attorneys?''

She shook her head, avoiding his eyes for the first time since she'd entered his office. ''I have only a few close friends, and I haven't seen the need to discuss this with them as yet. Not many of my adoptive family are left now that my parents are gone. Some distant relatives on my mother's side, my father's older brother and his son, both of whom live in California and whom I see only rarely. My attorney also happens to be my godfather. He tends to be overly protective, having known me ever since he handled the legal details of my adoption. He would be concerned about the financial risks of finding family members about whom I know nothing.''

Tony wondered if such an attractive, obviously intelligent young woman could really be happy living as reclusively as Michelle apparently did. Her experiences must have been unpleasant, indeed, to make her this distrustful.

He scanned her mother's letter a third time. ''How old are you now?''

''Twenty-six.''

''So it's been twenty-four years since your family was separated.''

''Yes.''

''You don't remember anything about them?'' He looked up at her as he asked the question.

She opened her mouth to answer immediately. But then she paused, frowned a bit and looked down at her lap before answering more slowly. ''No, I don't remember.''

''You started to say something else. What was it?''

In response to his tone—the one he'd used for interrogation back in his police officer days—she looked up quickly, her eyes widening. ''I don't remember anything," she repeated. "I was only two. How could I remember?"

He didn't think she was being entirely straight with him, though he, too, wondered how she could possibly remember anything from that young age. Still, there'd been something in her voice when she'd answered....

Deciding to come back to that later, he nodded and changed the subject. "Your mother said the family was split up. I must assume that they were widely scattered, perhaps adopted, as you were. Most likely, their names will have been changed, as yours was. The younger ones, anyway. They're grown now, and the chances are slim they're all still living in Texas."

"I realize I haven't given you an easy assignment, Mr. D'Alessandro."

He gave her a cool, utterly confident smile. "I'll find them, Ms. Trent. Don't you doubt that."

Her answering smile was tentative, as though it was something she didn't do often enough. "I'm beginning to believe you will."

He cleared his throat abruptly, forcefully. "Which leads to the next question. What do you want me to do when I find them? Do you want to contact them yourself or would you like for me to make the initial contact on your behalf?"

"No!" She spoke too hastily, her knuckles going white from her tightened grip on her purse. Realizing her vehemence had startled him, Michelle took a deep breath and tried visibly to relax. "I don't want you to contact them. All I want is a list of their names and locations, if possible."

"So you intend to contact them yourself?" he asked carefully, still watching her face.

She hesitated only a split second before nodding. "Yes."

She's lying. Tony didn't know why, but he suspected that Michelle Trent had no intention whatever of meeting her long-lost brothers and sisters. So why was she hiring him to find them? Baffled, he stared at her in frowning silence until she squirmed in her chair.

"You'll take the case?" she asked.

What the hell. "Yeah, I'll take it."

If she was pleased or relieved, she hid it just as she hid her other emotions. With a brisk nod, she opened her purse and extracted a plain white envelope. "This contains a thousand dollars in cash," she told him, holding the packet out to him. "Will that be enough to get you started?"

"More than enough," he assured her, hesitating to take the money for some reason he couldn't quite understand.

When he didn't immediately reach out for it, she set the envelope on his desk and rose gracefully from her chair. "I'll call you in two weeks for a report, around the first of May. Will that give you enough time to gather some preliminary information?"

"Well, yes, but why don't I call you if I—"

"No," she broke in coolly. "I'll call you. Good day, Mr. D'Alessandro."

Damn, the woman's attitude irritated him. Almost as much as her sexy walk aroused him. "Good day, Ms. Trent," he muttered, his gaze following the sway of her slender hips as she left.

He sighed rather wistfully when he was alone. And then he picked up the letter she'd left with him and read it one more time, slowly and thoroughly.

* * *

"Pat-a-cake, pat-a-cake, baker's man! Clap your hands, Shelley."

"Look, Shelley, Jerry's a horsey. Can you say horsey?"

Still hearing a distant echo of children's voices, Michelle woke with a start and peered blearily around her bedroom. The room was dark and quiet and, except for her, empty, just as it always was when she awoke.

She'd heard the voices again. Those laughing, high-pitched children's voices that had invaded her dreams for as far back as she could remember. Occasionally she heard them saying names—Shelley, most often, and Jerry and Layla. The dream voices, strange names, had never made sense to her, never seemed to have meaning. Since reading her mother's letter—and learning, to her great shock, that she'd been called Shelley for the first two years of her life—Michelle suspected that the voices weren't truly dreams, but snatches of memory.

She'd never told anyone about those dreams—memories—just as she hadn't told Tony D'Alessandro earlier that day when he'd asked if she had any memory of her brothers and sisters. She hadn't really thought he'd believe her. It had all happened so very long ago.

Her brothers and sisters. "Oh, God," she whispered, staring blindly into the shadows of her big, elegantly furnished bedroom.

So many years she'd longed for brothers and sisters. Gazed wistfully through the looming fences surrounding the fortress of a mansion in which she'd grown up, pampered and adored and so very lonely at times. Feeling as though she were the only child in the world. And all the time—all those years—she'd had four brothers and two sisters growing up without her.

Did they know about her? Did they, too, have bits of memory of playing together, laughing together? Had any of them ever looked for her, asked about her?

"Dammit," she whispered, rolling over to gather her pillow into her arms as though to comfort herself. "Why did she have to tell me? Why couldn't she have told me sooner?"

A week after her visit to the private investigator's office, Michelle threw open the door to her home in response to the doorbell, too eager to wait for her housekeeper to answer the summons. Only after opening the door did she mask her broad grin, turning it into a cool smile. "Hello, Taylor. Back in town so soon?"

A dark-haired beauty in khaki slacks and a multi-pocketed safari shirt sauntered past her into the entryway. "I've been gone four weeks, Trent."

Michelle lifted an expressive eyebrow. "That long? I hardly noticed you were away."

Taylor Simmons grinned and lightly punched Michelle's arm. "Yeah, right. So how are you?"

Michelle dropped the phony hauteur, knowing Taylor meant the question seriously. "I miss Mother, of course," she answered candidly, "but I'm fine. You know me. I'm always all right."

"And even if you weren't, you wouldn't tell anyone," Taylor added with exaggerated exasperation.

"I'd tell *you*."

Pleased with the admission, Taylor smiled. "Yeah, I guess you're right. I wouldn't give you any other choice, would I?"

Michelle laughed and shook her head. "No." Taking Taylor's arm, she led her into the den. "Can I get you anything? Betty made your favorite cookies, of course.

She started baking them the minute I told her you'd be here today.''

Taylor groaned. "And I just managed to lose the two pounds I gained from the last batch of her cookies. Oh, well, it's back to grapefruit and cottage cheese tomorrow.''

"Does that mean you want cookies?''

"Of course I want cookies. Dozens of them.''

Amused, Michelle waved Taylor to a couch and pressed a discreetly placed button beside the wet bar in one corner of the large, pecan-paneled room. On the other side of the fifteen-thousand-square-foot Tudor house, a bell chimed in an enormous kitchen. After twenty-four years of such luxury, Michelle didn't doubt that the efficient Betty would respond almost immediately with refreshments.

"How'd the shoot go?'' she asked, crossing the room to the couch where Taylor lounged with the ease of one who'd spent many hours in this same den. Michelle sat sideways on the opposite end of the couch, one elbow propped on the low-cushioned back, one leg tucked comfortably beneath her. For her friend's visit, she'd worn a short-sleeved peach sweater and ivory slacks, her chocolate-brown hair loose around her shoulders. Her peach flats lay now on the floor beside the couch, leaving her feet bare. There were very few people with whom Michelle could feel so comfortable. But Taylor had been her best friend since their first year of high school when Taylor's parents had moved to Dallas and into the exclusive social circle to which Michelle's family had belonged.

"The shoot went okay,'' Taylor answered in response to Michelle's question about her work as a much-sought-after professional photographer. "The usual hassles.

Whining models, uncooperative weather, clothes that got misplaced or soiled, a few equipment problems. Other than that, I had no complaints."

Michelle laughed. "Oh, is that all?"

"Yeah. Same old stuff. And how about you? What've you done to stay busy for the past month? Lounge on satin pillows? Nibble bonbons? Foreclose on a few widows and orphans?"

"And don't forget my daily manicures," Michelle reminded her with a wave of one peach-polished hand. Polish she'd applied herself.

"That's understood, of course," Taylor replied gravely.

Her right elbow still propped on the back of the couch, Michelle rested her cheek against her right fist and fondly examined her friend. As she always did when hurried or in deep thought, Taylor had been running her hands through her short, almost-black hair, leaving it ruffled in spikes around her face. Not just anyone could get away with the style; Taylor's big, long-lashed eyes and classic bone structure made her a natural for the short, casual cut. "I'm going to say something sentimental."

Taylor sighed deeply and rolled her eyes. "Oh, Trent, do you really have to?"

"Yes. I'm glad you're back, Taylor. I've missed you."

Taylor's smoke-gray eyes warmed and softened. "I missed you, too. You're sure you're okay?"

"I'm sure." Michelle nibbled her lower lip, wondering whether she should tell Taylor about the letter from Alicia, and about her visit to the private investigator. She really hadn't intended to tell anyone about her quiet search for her lost family. For one thing, she didn't know how she would explain that she felt driven to locate her siblings, but wasn't at all sure she ever intended to do anything with the information once she obtained it. How could she explain to anyone else what she couldn't understand herself?

She should have known she wouldn't be able to keep anything so momentous from Taylor. After one look at Michelle's expression, Taylor straightened abruptly. "What is it?"

Michelle blinked in surprise at the sharp question. "I—uh—what do you mean?"

"I want to know whatever it is you're debating telling me about," Taylor replied bluntly. "Something's happened, hasn't it?"

She really should have known. Sighing lightly, Michelle shook her head. "Why did I ever think I'd be able to keep it from you?"

"Keep *what* from me? What's wrong?" Taylor was beginning to sound worried. Like the others who cared most for Michelle, Taylor tended to be overprotective, despite her habitually brusque teasing. It had always touched Michelle almost as much as it exasperated her that her friends considered her fragile and vulnerable, just because of a couple of unpleasant experiences in her past.

Before Michelle could reassure Taylor that nothing was wrong, a heavyset woman in a red blouse and navy slacks wheeled in a serving cart loaded with a variety of refreshments, her famous raspberry-jam cookies taking the place of honor in the center of the cart. "Here you are, Miss Taylor. I made a double batch for you today since you've been gone so long."

"Betty, you shameless woman, you're going to turn me into a blimp yet, aren't you?" But Taylor was already reaching for a cookie even as she affectionately scolded the longtime Trent family employee.

"Hmmph." Betty eyed Taylor's figure with frank skepticism. "You and Michelle are both thin as rails. You think a man wants to cuddle a bundle of bones? No, ma'am. A man wants to know there's a woman in his arms."

Looking at Taylor's full bustline with unconcealed envy, Michelle murmured, "I don't think any man would mistake Taylor for another guy, Betty. No matter how she may be dressed," she added for Taylor's benefit, turning up her nose at Taylor's favorite army-surplus ensemble.

Unperturbed, Taylor laughed and shook her head, causing the soft indirect lighting to glimmer in her dark hair. "And no one could doubt that Michelle, here, is anything but a lady all the way down to her little peach toenails."

"That may be," Betty replied slyly, "but I notice that neither of you has a diamond on your left hand. No immediate prospects, either."

Taylor frowned as if in deep consideration of the older woman's words. "That's true, of course. You really think your raspberry-jam cookies would help us land Prince Charming?"

Betty tried without much success to mask a smile. Taylor had always been her favorite of Michelle's friends. "My cookies couldn't hurt."

Grinning, Taylor reached for one of the two Wedgwood dessert plates on the cart. "That just gives me even more of an excuse to pig out on them," she said cheerfully. "C'mon, Trent, dig in. Betty's cookies are going to bring us eternal love and devotion."

"Not to mention cellulite."

"No, let's not mention that," Taylor grumbled, defiantly adding another cookie to her plate.

"Want me to pour the tea, Michelle?"

Michelle shook her head and reached for the teapot. "No, thanks, Betty, we'll serve ourselves."

"All right. You just ring if you need me now, you hear? Good to have you back, Miss Taylor."

"Thanks, Betty. It's nice to be back." Taylor waited until they were alone again, an aromatic cup of tea resting on the low table in front of her, before turning determinedly back to Michelle. "Okay, spill it."

Michelle lifted a brow and glanced pointedly at the teacup in her hand.

Taylor sighed impatiently. "Not the tea, you airhead. What was it you were about to tell me when Betty came in?"

After only a momentary hesitation, Michelle set her teacup down, clasped her hands in her lap, and told Taylor everything from the moment she'd found the letter in her mother's possessions to the time she'd left Tony D'Alessandro's office. Characteristically, Taylor listened with intent concentration, nibbling on her cookies and sipping her tea without once interrupting or taking her gaze from Michelle's face. Only when Michelle had finished did Taylor finally speak. "You have six brothers and sisters."

Michelle swallowed and nodded. "Yes."

"Wow."

"I guess that's one way of putting it."

Taylor pulled thoughtfully at her lower lip. "You think this P.I. can find them?"

"He assured me that if it's possible, he'll find them."

"What are you going to do when he does? Are you going to try to meet them?"

Michelle looked down at her hands, which were clenched so tightly in her lap that her knuckles shone stark white. "I—I don't know," she admitted. "I don't think so."

"I see."

Risking a peek at her friend's unrevealing face, Michelle asked, "Do you think I should meet them?"

Taylor shrugged. "I don't know. I can see where you'd want to, of course, especially now that your folks are gone. But—"

"But," Michelle broke in, "I'm a very rich woman and I don't know these people from Adam. They came from a presumably poor background, we have no idea how they've been raised, what sort of lives they live. I could be opening myself up to all kinds of trouble by acknowledging them as family."

Taylor nodded slowly, reluctantly. "As cold and cynical as that sounds when you say it, you're right, of course. I'd hate to see a bunch of strangers suddenly show up and start trying to sponge off you. It's not as though you haven't had reason to be cautious of the motives of others."

Bleakly, Michelle thought back to being a frightened, heartbroken eight-year-old crying for her mother in a dark, locked closet while a man she'd trusted wrote a ransom note to her father. And thirteen years later, at twenty-one, finding out that the first man she'd loved was much more deeply attracted to her wealth than her mind. "Yes, I definitely have reason to be cautious," she agreed, trying very hard not to sound bitter.

Taylor started to speak, hesitated, then changed the subject. "So tell me about this P.I. you hired. How'd you find out about him?"

"His father was the man who rescued me when I was— taken," Michelle answered. She'd never been able to say the word *kidnapped.* Taylor was one of the few people still living who even knew about the incident. Vincent D'Alessandro, Tony's father, was another. "I thought I'd be hiring the father, but he's retired. The son, Tony, started the business back up a few years ago. I understand he worked as a policeman before that."

"Tony?"

"Yes. Short for Anthony, according to his business card."

"Age?"

Michelle shrugged. "Early thirties, I think."

"Good-looking?"

It wasn't at all hard for Michelle to picture glittering dark eyes, a shock of jet-black hair, a bright smile and a sexy cleft chin, even a week after her brief meeting with Tony D'Alessandro. "Yes, he's quite attractive."

"Married?"

Michelle made a face at Taylor's increasingly avid questions. "Now, how would I know that? I hired him, I didn't date him."

"*Yet.* Here, eat a few more of Betty's cookies."

Michelle giggled—as Taylor had known she would. And felt incredibly better for it. "You idiot," she said mildly, but reached for her first cookie, anyway.

Looking entirely relaxed and accepting, Taylor lounged lazily against the cushions behind her. Only her eyes indicated she was at all concerned with Michelle's state of mind. "Do you want to meet your brothers and sisters?" she asked casually, sounding no more serious than she had when she'd asked about Tony's looks and marital status.

Fully aware that the question hadn't been in the least frivolous, Michelle took a moment before answering honestly. "I think—maybe—I do. But it scares me, Taylor."

"Then wait until you're ready, if ever," Taylor answered logically. "It's been twenty-four years, after all. There's no reason to rush now, is there?"

"No, of course not," Michelle answered. And even as she spoke, a niggling little voice inside her murmured that it might already be too late. The search had already been set into motion, and her safe, secure life might be changed irrevocably whether she wanted those changes or not.

Chapter Two

Michelle Culverton Trent was annoyed and she made no effort to conceal it as she took a seat in Tony's office and arranged the full skirt to her demure dress primly around her knees. Tony watched appreciatively, thinking again what fine legs she had, until Michelle cleared her throat abruptly to regain his attention.

"All right, Mr. D'Alessandro, you insisted on giving me information in person rather than over the telephone. Now that I'm here, perhaps we could get on with it?"

Because her snooty attitude brought out the worst in him, Tony leaned back in his creaky chair and slung his crossed feet onto his desk, his hands clasped behind his head, elbows out. He knew he was the very picture of lazy insolence, yet did nothing to counteract that impression. Damned if he was going to sit here and let Her Highness walk all over him just because she had more money than

God and he happened to be working for her at the moment. "In a hurry, Ms. Trent?"

"I have other obligations."

"Oh? What is it today? A meeting of one of the many charity boards you belong to? An executive session at Trent Enterprises? Or is it your day to rock babies in the intensive-care nursery?"

Her reaction was satisfying; he'd wanted to see her lose a bit of that cool poise. Her blue eyes widening, she tightened her grip on the purse in her lap and leaned slightly forward. "I hired you to locate my brothers and sisters, not to snoop into my personal affairs."

He shrugged. "I like to know something about the people I do business with."

He'd been pleasantly surprised to discover that she was one of the favorite baby-rockers at Memorial Hospital. Somehow, she hadn't seemed the type to possess maternal instincts. Yet he'd learned that she'd been volunteering at that particular job for nearly five years, and that she refused any media credit or glory for doing so. He liked that.

Her eyes narrowing, she stuck her purse under her arm and rose from the chair. "Consider our business association terminated. Good day, Mr. D'Alessandro."

With that, she turned and headed for the door, slowly, decorously, not once looking back. And it was obvious that it took every ounce of willpower she possessed not to stamp out in fury.

Tony chuckled beneath his breath. So she had a temper. Maybe there was hope for Michelle Culverton Trent, after all. "Ms. Trent—"

She reached for the doorknob without turning to look at him. "I said good day, Mr. D'Alessandro."

"I have information about your brothers and sisters."

She became still, her hand remaining on the tarnished brass knob. Though she didn't turn, he knew he had her full attention. "Why don't you sit back down and I'll tell you what I found out," he suggested enticingly.

She gave him a long, considering look over her shoulder, obviously tempted but just as obviously still mad at him. "Exactly what did you find out about me? And why *did* you snoop into my personal affairs?"

He came very close to retorting that if she'd been having any affairs, she was damned discreet about them, since he hadn't gotten a hint of a serious relationship in her life. He knew that if he did say that, she'd be gone and he'd have seen the last of her. And he wasn't quite ready for that.

"I simply wanted to find out exactly how vulnerable you are to claims of relationship by impostors," he said soothingly, dropping his feet from the desk to sit straight in his seat and make an effort to look more professional. "As you pointed out, this is a very sensitive situation and I have to be careful, for your sake. All I've learned about you is the routine you've maintained for the past year or so. That gives me an idea of who you might come into daily contact with, in case word of the search gets out and anyone tries pulling a scam on us."

Okay, so it wasn't exactly the truth. It wasn't exactly a lie, either, he assured himself. And it *sounded* damned good.

Evidently she thought so, too. Looking half-convinced, she dropped her hand from the doorknob and turned to face him, though she didn't yet return to her seat. "You've found my brothers and sisters?" she asked warily. "All of them? Already?"

"I didn't say that," he reminded her, reaching for a file. "I said I have information about them. I can tell you all their birth names and their ages when you were split up. And I can give you current information about two of them.''

Michelle moistened her lips, her eyes on the typed pages in front of Tony. He couldn't tell if her expression held more eagerness or dread. Perhaps an equal mixture. He tried to imagine how it would feel to be told that he had six brothers and sisters he'd never known about, to be given their names, details about a life with them of which he had no memory. He had to admit he wasn't sure how he'd feel about meeting those strangers who shared his genes.

''Why don't you sit down, Mich—uh, Ms. Trent.'' Damn, but it was getting harder to remember that he was her employee for the time being. He was all too eager to get beyond that ethical barrier. Not that he had a snowball's chance with her, anyway, he conceded fatalistically. But he'd never know until he tried, would he? And, for reasons he couldn't have explained had he made the effort, he seemed hell-bent to try.

He watched as she slowly crossed the room—oh, could this woman *walk!*—and sank gracefully back into her chair. ''All right, Mr. D'Alessandro,'' she said, her voice only slightly less confident than usual, ''I'm ready. What have you found out?''

Calling on years of professional experience, he kept his own tone brusque and impersonal as he began, knowing it would be easier for her if he did so. ''Your biological parents had very little money and far too many problems. Your father, Henry 'Hank' Walker, had a hard time keeping a job during his twenties. At thirty-one, he died in an industrial accident in Texarkana when your mother, Hazel, was pregnant with your youngest sister. Accident reports said that he'd been drinking when the incident occurred, and it was believed that he'd been an alcoholic for years."

Michelle winced but said nothing. Tony noted sympathetically that her fair complexion had gone paler than usual.

"Your father had no family and your mother's family disowned her when she'd married him—she was seventeen and pregnant at the time—so there was no one for her to turn to after your father's death. Money was painfully tight, since the insurance companies weren't overly generous with an accident involving alcohol. She worked as a waitress as long as she was physically capable, just to pay rent on the one-bedroom apartment she'd moved you all into, and to put food on the table. Her prenatal care was almost nonexistent and she simply didn't recover quickly after your younger sister's birth just after you turned two. Eight months later she caught pneumonia and died."

"How old was she?" Michelle asked quietly.

"She'd just turned twenty-nine."

Michelle made a slight strangled sound, then fell silent again, waiting for him to continue. He took a deep breath, forcefully resisting the urge to walk around the desk and take her into his arms. Not in a sexual way, but simply to comfort her during what had to be a painful moment. She'd probably take his head off if he tried. Instead, he focused grimly on the notes in front of him.

"As you know, your parents left seven children. The oldest was a son, Jared, who was eleven when your mother died."

Michelle started, drawing his gaze back to her colorless face. "Jerry," she whispered, the word hardly audible.

Tony's left eyebrow rose sharply. "You remember him?" he demanded, though it hardly seemed possible that she would.

She shook her head, a bit too emphatically. "No, of course not. It's just—the name sounds familiar. Go on, please."

Skeptically, Tony nodded. "I was able to trace Jared through a series of foster homes until his graduation from a high school in Houston seventeen years ago, at which time he entered the military—the Navy, we think. It's going to take me a bit longer to find out where he is now."

"Did you—" She paused to clear her throat. "Did you find out anything in particular about him during those years? Was he happy? Did he get into trouble?"

"No. As far as I can determine, he was well-behaved, a good student, but quiet and very withdrawn. According to the principal of his high school, Jared refused to allow anyone to get too close to him, had very few friends. After being separated from his family at eleven and then living in a number of foster homes, I can certainly understand why he'd be reluctant to get attached to anyone," Tony added pensively.

Her lower lip caught between her teeth, Michelle nodded for him to go on.

"Next was a sister, Layla, age ten." Again, he noted that Michelle seemed to react to the name, though this time he didn't question her.

"Like Jared, Layla was never adopted. She was, however, raised in only one foster home until her high school graduation and she seemed to be happy enough there, though she, too, was reported to be very introverted during her school years. She was also the easiest to find now. Ten years ago, she registered with a service that reunites families separated by adoption or other legal action, so that she could be traced if any of her siblings chose to initiate a search."

"I wonder why she didn't do so herself," Michelle murmured, almost as if to herself.

"Maybe you should ask her that," Tony answered gently. "Her married name is Layla Walker Samples, she's thirty-four, and she has three children, ages eight, five and two. I have their names here if you're interested. The family lives in Fort Worth, where her husband's an accountant and she sells real estate."

"You're very thorough, Mr. D'Alessandro," she said faintly.

"You're paying me to be, Ms. Trent."

She nodded. "Go on, please."

"Next in birth order was a brother, Miles, who was two years younger than Layla. Miles died in a car accident on his eighteenth birthday. He and his friends had been drinking beer to celebrate the occasion and three of them were killed in a head-on collision with another car."

Though he wouldn't have thought it possible, Michelle's face seemed to bleach even whiter. "He's—dead?" she repeated.

Seeing the stricken look in her eyes, Tony cursed himself for breaking the news so bluntly. It was just that he hadn't expected her to grieve for a young man she couldn't possibly remember. It seemed he'd lost sight of the fact that poor Miles had still been her brother, whether she remembered him or not.

"I'm sorry, Michelle." Her first name slipped out before he could stop it.

If she noticed, she didn't comment. "I'm fine. I'm just sorry to hear that he died so young, and so senselessly. Please continue."

"The five-year-old twins, Joseph and Robert—Joey and Bobby—were kept together. They went first to an orphanage and then into a foster home, where they got into some minor trouble at the age of nine and were sent back to the institution. They stayed in and out of trouble—nothing criminal, just reckless mischief—until they were sixteen."

"And what happened then?"

"They disappeared. They ran away from the foster home in which they'd been placed a few weeks before and they haven't been heard from since. I have inquiries out, of course, but so far I haven't turned up anything on them."

Michelle digested that news in silence for a few long moments, then took a shaky breath and looked back up at him. "That leaves only one. The baby."

"Lindsay was eight months old when your mother died. She was adopted, possibly by a family somewhere in Arkansas. She'd be twenty-four now. I haven't located her yet, but I've got quite a few inquiries out. There's a very good chance we'll find her."

Michelle straightened in her seat, raising one hand to brush a nonexistent stray strand into her neatly upswept dark hair. "You've been very efficient, Mr. D'Alessandro. And in such a short time. I'm impressed."

"Because I do my job well? Don't be." He closed the folder and extended it to her. "This file contains duplicates of everything I've learned to this point. I'll keep the original material here until the investigation is completed. You'll find the latest available addresses, the current information on your sister Layla, juvenile records on the twins."

Michelle took the file and held it gingerly, as though it might be explosive, he noted with a quick flash of sympathetic amusement. "Is that all for today?" she asked, on her feet once again.

He nodded, though he was tempted to stall for just a few more minutes with her. This interlude had convinced him that there was more to Michelle Culverton Trent—née Shelley Marie Walker—than she had allowed him to see before. Now he found himself irresistibly curious to discover more about her. But then, curiosity had always been his major weakness—or strength, depending on how one looked at it.

"You want me to continue with the investigation, then?" he asked carefully, not forgetting that she'd fired him earlier.

"I want you to find my family, Mr. D'Alessandro," she answered from the doorway. This time she turned the knob and opened the door. "I'll call you again in two weeks to find out what you've discovered. Oh . . . do you need any more money at this point?" she asked.

Shifting restlessly in his chair at the thought of taking more of her money—though he *was* working for her, he reminded himself impatiently—he shook his head. "No. Not now," he answered gruffly. "And I *will* find your family, though I can't promise I'll have all the information we need in the next two weeks."

"All I expect is your best effort. Good day, Mr. D'Alessandro."

"Ms. Trent," he muttered in resignation, damned tired of the way she continued to address him so formally, almost as if the "Mr." erected a physical barrier between them. But she'd already closed the door behind her, so he had no opportunity to ask her to call him Tony. Not yet.

Jared Mitchell. Layla Renee. Miles Daniel. Joseph Brian. Robert Ryan. Shelley Marie. Lindsay Nicole.

Seven children. Seven double names carefully chosen by
a young woman living in poverty with the alcoholic husband she'd chosen over her family, a woman who'd
driven herself so relentlessly that she died at twenty-nine.
Had she fought to live, wanting to provide a future for
her children? Or had she been too worn-out and defeated to care, perhaps thinking that they would be better off without her?

Swiping at an escaping tear, Michelle looked up from
the file in front of her and thought with reluctant guilt of
the luxury in which she'd been raised, the money she'd so
often taken for granted because, for as far back as she
could remember, it had always been there. Money that
could easily have fed six more children.

As much as she'd loved her adoptive parents, Michelle couldn't help wondering why she'd been the one
brought into this home. Why not the twins, or the baby?
Why not all of them?

How she would have loved having brothers and sisters. She remembered childhood fantasies of having a big
brother to watch out for her, play with her.

Jared. Eleven when they'd been separated. He'd remember their time together, perhaps, remember a little
sister named Shelley. *"Look at Jerry, Shelley. He's a
horsey,"* the dream voices had said. Had Jared given her
rides on his back, loved her and grieved for her when
they'd been separated?

Layla. At ten, she would have been the little mother for
her younger siblings. *"Play pat-a-cake, Shelley."* Had
Michelle clung to her big sister as they'd been swept in
opposite directions? Had they cried and futilely protested the separation?

Miles. Dead at eighteen. Had he been a reckless, mischievous boy? Had he had dark hair and blue eyes like

her? Had he died missing the family he'd known until he was eight?

Joseph and Robert—Joey and Bobby. Five-year-old twins. Had they been identical? Closer to her age, had they tumbled and roughhoused with her, held her hands between them as she'd learned to walk?

And the baby. Lindsay. Had she been no more than another mouth to feed, another burden on an already-desperate situation? Or had she been welcomed with a wistful, hopeful love?

Michelle hid her face in her hands, thinking of the five children now grown to adulthood, as far as she knew, anyway. Would any of them want to see her again, want to be reminded of that troubled time in their young lives? Lindsay wouldn't remember that time, not even as much as Michelle did through her vague, haunting dreams. Would she want to meet a sister she'd never even known she had?

And did Michelle really want to meet these strangers who may share her hair color, her nose, her eyes? Who may well have come into her life much too late, and for no real reason?

Her deep sigh seemed to echo through the depths of the big, carefully guarded house surrounding her, empty except for her and the two employees who went about their jobs in other rooms. Would finding her lost family ease the loneliness she'd lived with so much of her life? Or only make it worse?

She really needed to talk to the one person who'd always been there for her, always cared about her, the only one who'd never let her down.

Taylor avidly studied the file spread out in front of her on Michelle's dining room table. ''So you have at least two nieces and a nephew,'' she commented, reading from the top page. "Dawne, Keith and Brittany. I wonder if they look like you.''

When Michelle didn't immediately answer, Taylor looked up from the file. "Michelle?''

Blinking at the sound of her name, Michelle focused on her friend, who sat across the table from her, sipping coffee and reading the file Tony had provided two days earlier. It had taken that long for Michelle to decide to share the file's contents with Taylor. "I'm sorry, Taylor, what did you say?''

"I was just wondering about your nieces and nephew. Where were *you?*''

Michelle cleared her throat and brushed busily at a nonexistent bit of lint on her dark skirt. "Just—thinking,'' she answered vaguely.

"Did you ever find out if he's married?''

"I don't think he—Wait a minute.'' Michelle looked up abruptly, suspiciously. "If *who's* married?''

Taylor's smile was decidedly smug. "The guy you were just thinking about. The P.I. Tony, right?''

"How did you know I was thinking about him?''

"I didn't. It was a guess. You just confirmed it.''

Michelle sighed. "All right, so I was thinking about him. Don't read anything into it. I was simply wondering if he's found out anything else since he gave me this information.''

"It's only been two days, hasn't it?''

Michelle shrugged, trying to look nonchalant. "He got all this information—and more—in two weeks.'' The "more,'' of course, being the personal information he'd obtained on her. Why? she asked herself yet again. Why had he wanted to know more about her before beginning his search for her siblings?

"He sounds very good," Taylor murmured. "At his job, of course," she added mischievously.

"You can be such a juvenile at times," Michelle accused, falling into their habitual teasing insults to distract Taylor from the direction the conversation had taken.

"Honey, when it comes to attractive men I'm a full-grown woman," Taylor taunted with a toss of her dark head.

"Yeah, right. And if you've been on more than two dates with any particular guy in the past year, I'll eat a bug," Michelle retorted.

Taylor smiled. "Yuck. Lucky for you I haven't run into any Prince Charmings in the past year, isn't it?"

"How would you know if you had? You're still comparing all the men you meet to a memory of perfection." Michelle wasn't teasing now. Instead, her words were spoken with warm sympathy.

Growing abruptly serious in response, Taylor sighed faintly. "I guess I am. But it's not as if I haven't tried to get over Dylan. You know that."

"I know." Michelle wondered pensively if both she and Taylor had been fated to be unlucky at romance. Taylor had tumbled head over heels during a whirlwind Caribbean affair she'd been swept into while on a three-week photo assignment. And then her lover had been run down in the street by a hit-and-run driver. Taylor would have shared his fate had he not heroically pushed her out of the way at the last possible moment.

She'd spent a desperate night in a hospital waiting room, only to be told the next morning that Dylan had not survived his injuries. His body had been returned to his family, whom Taylor had never met; Taylor had gone on with her life. But, Michelle thought sadly, Taylor had never been quite the same as before. Though she'd known Dylan less than a month, Taylor had truly loved him. Since then, she'd dated but, as she'd recently asked Michelle, what ordinary man could compare to a memory of a dream lover who'd given his life for hers?

Taylor swiftly turned the offensive back at Michelle. "What about you? Have you given any guy a fair shake since Geoff the Gigolo broke your heart?"

"He didn't break it, he only dented it a little. And I haven't met any man who interested me enough to take the risk that he's not like Geoff," Michelle admitted.

"So this Tony D'Alessandro doesn't interest you?"

Michelle couldn't answer that one. The problem was that Tony D'Alessandro interested her all too much. But why? Because he held the key to finding out about her long-hidden past? Or because she liked his smile and the spark of interest in his beautiful dark eyes? And *could* he be trusted?

She thought of his plain, functional office furniture and his neat, department-store clothing. It had been quite obvious that he wasn't exactly rolling in money. Was the interest he'd shown in her due to a mutual attraction or was he anticipating more reward than a one time fee for a temporary assignment?

Taylor began to look rather concerned at Michelle's hesitation. "Is he a nice guy?" she asked, making an unsuccessful attempt to mask the protectiveness in her expression.

Michelle thought of Tony's reaction to her unexpected distress at the news of her brother's death. His sincerely spoken promise that he'd find her family. "He seems very nice," she said. "But of course I hardly know him."

"Want me to go with you next time you meet with him? I could check him out for you, give you an objective opinion."

Michelle made a face. "Objective? I don't think so. And no, I don't need you to check him out for me. I'm quite capable of doing that myself, thank you."

Taylor grinned. "Are you politely telling me to butt out, Trent?"

"You got it, Simmons."

"Okay," Taylor agreed with a deep sigh. "But I surely would love to get a look at this Italian stud that has you so flustered."

"Why don't we change the subject," Michelle suggested uncomfortably.

"If you insist. Let's talk about your sister Layla, instead. She lives less than an hour's drive from here and she's made it clear that she'd like to be reunited with her family. Are you going to call her?"

Again, Michelle found herself at a loss for a definite answer. "I don't know."

Taylor propped her chin on her hand and studied Michelle thoughtfully. "I know we agreed you should be careful, but this woman sounds pretty respectable. A real-estate agent married to an accountant, living in suburbia with their three children. How dangerous could she be?"

Michelle automatically started to remind Taylor of the precautions inherent in wealth, but stopped because even she was aware what a shallow and mercenary excuse that was. She would have to start being honest sometime— with herself, if no one else.

It wasn't fear of losing her money that held Michelle back from contacting her siblings. It was fear of being hurt again. Taking the risks of caring, reaching out, needing someone again in the safe, comfortable routine she'd built for herself.

She'd have liked so much to see her nieces and nephew. Dawne, Keith and little Brittany. She knew their names, of course. During the past two days she'd studied the file Tony had provided her until the edges of the pages had begun to crumple from handling. Just as she'd studied the names of her brothers and sisters, straining to remember any details to accompany those distant, barely remembered voices.

Jerry. Layla. "Play pat-a-cake, Shelley."

"I'm scared, Taylor," she said, hardly aware of speaking aloud.

Taylor's face softened sympathetically. "I know, Michelle. I know."

Tony was immersed in the computer research of Michelle's case late the next afternoon when Bonnie appeared in the open doorway to his office. A tall, beautiful black woman, Bonnie walked with a natural grace that inevitably reminded Tony of Michelle. But then, everything seemed to remind him of Michelle Trent these days, he thought with a faint sigh as he turned from the computer screen.

"The call on line one is for you, Tony," Bonnie said, setting a stack of correspondence on one corner of his desk. "He wouldn't give a name. I'm out of here for the day unless you need me for anything else."

"You go home and feed your family," Tony urged with a smile, one hand resting on his telephone.

"Hmmph. Today was Mick's day off. He'd darned well better have dinner on the table when I get home," Bonnie retorted, "or he might as well resign himself to eating out tonight."

Tony laughed. "You're a tough wife, Bonnie Kennedy."

She smiled brightly. "You should be so lucky to have one just like me."

Tony wasn't at all opposed to the idea of marriage and family. His happily married parents were the perfect example of how a loving partnership could enrich one's life. The problem was that Vincent and Carla D'Alessandro set a pretty high standard. Tony hadn't yet met a woman he thought he could love for the rest of his life with the same unfaltering devotion Vinnie had always given Carla. "I *would* be lucky to find someone like you," he assured Bonnie.

Both embarrassed and pleased, she shrugged him off. "If you think flattery will make me forget it's time for my annual raise, you're entirely wrong. But you'd better take your call now. I'll see you in the morning."

"Good night, Bonnie." Half his attention on her as she waved on her way out, Tony lifted the receiver. "D'Alessandro."

"I understand you've been looking into the background of Michelle Culverton Trent."

Frowning at the blunt, unprefaced remark, Tony automatically reached for a pencil to make notes if necessary. "Who is this?"

"My name is Carter Powell. I've been the attorney for the Trent family for over thirty years. Who are you working for, Mr. D'Alessandro? Who hired you to find her biological family?"

His eyes narrowing, Tony frowned at the hostility in the caller's voice, determined not to confirm anything without his client's permission. "If you're so convinced that I am working toward that goal, I'm surprised you don't already know who hired me."

Powell ignored him. "Did Michelle hire you herself? If so, how did she find out? Her adoptive parents never told her about her biological siblings."

"As an attorney, I'm sure you know all about client privilege, Mr. Powell. Surely you understand that I'm not at liberty to discuss my cases with you."

The attorney growled in frustration. "If you're working for someone else, someone hoping to capitalize on her wealth, do your client a favor and tell him to forget it. Ms. Trent and her money are well-protected against opportunists. It won't work."

"I repeat, I cannot discuss my cases or my clients with you. Now, if there's nothing else—"

"Take a little friendly advice. Drop this case. If you *are* working for Ms. Trent, tell her you are unable to find out anything about her long-lost family and that you doubt anyone else could, either. Got that?"

Tensing in response to the barely veiled threat, Tony gripped the receiver more tightly. "Even if I were working on the case you've described, why would I want to take your advice?" he asked carefully, wanting the implicit warning spelled out. His pencil was poised to take the words down verbatim.

"I have some influence in this state, D'Alessandro, as I'm sure you'll find out if you ask around. Your own operation, on the other hand, is only two years old and still not firmly established in the business community. You would be wise not to work against me."

"Suppose I *am* working on the case you've mentioned. Suppose Ms. Trent is my client. How do you think she'd react if I mention this call to her?"

"I've known Ms. Trent for twenty-four years. You've known her a few weeks. I'm not worried about anything you have to say to her. Michelle knows that I have her best interests at heart, just as I always have. But for your own best interest, Mr. D'Alessandro, I suggest you tell her that the case is closed for lack of information. There's no need to make this any more unpleasant than necessary, is there?''

"Look, Powell, I—"

A firm click and a dial tone broke into Tony's angry retort. He slammed his own receiver into its cradle. Nothing made him more furious than threats, veiled or otherwise. Damned if he'd stand for being treated that way.

He snatched the phone back up and dialed a familiar number. "Dad?" he said a moment later. "I need to ask you a few questions about a former client of yours. Michelle Trent."

Chapter Three

Humming beneath her breath, Michelle cradled the tiny pink-blanketed bundle in her arms, stroking a downy soft head with her fingers. Her slow movements of the wooden rocker calmed her as well as the tiny infant she held.

Lakeisha was one of Michelle's favorite little patients in the intensive-care nursery. Three months old, the child still weighed less than five pounds, having been born nearly three months prematurely. Lakeisha's mother lived some distance from the hospital and wasn't able to make the trip more than twice a month, so Michelle was one of the volunteers who, along with the loving, caring hospital staff, made sure the infant didn't lack affectionate human contact.

Michelle had discovered the baby-rockers while investigating charity programs for contributions from Trent Enterprises. After the first session, she'd been hooked.

Only in this busy, beeping, noisy nursery could she feel at peace, quietly content.

At first it had surprised her just how bright and noisy the nursery could be. Had she thought about it, she probably would have imagined the room to be shushed, dimly lit. Nothing could have proven farther from the truth. Babies cried, monitors beeped, crib alarms went off periodically, nurses worked, talked, laughed, visitors streamed in and out, doctors rushed in with orders and procedures, the janitorial staff mopped and scrubbed.

Somehow the babies had adapted to the carefully controlled confusion, learning to sleep through almost anything. Just as Michelle had learned to block out the noise and movements around her and concentrate totally on whichever fragile infant needed her attention at the moment.

Taylor couldn't understand Michelle's pleasure in the rocking program. "I'd get too attached," she'd admitted candidly. "It would devastate me to get close to one and then have it go home—or, worse, to have something bad happen to it."

Michelle had tried to explain that, yes, those were valid points, and yes, it hurt when babies she'd grown to love left her life forever, devastated her when a tiny infant lost its battle to live. But there were always other babies needing to be cuddled, crying for attention. Babies who needed Michelle's loving care as much as she needed to offer it.

With these babies, as with so few people, Michelle could freely offer the affection dammed up inside her without fear that her vulnerability would be exploited, her generosity abused.

Fifteen minutes later she carefully placed the sleeping Lakeisha in her constantly monitored high-tech bassi-

net, exchanged a few words with a smiling nurse, and
headed for the scrub room to remove the sterile hospital
gown she was required to wear over her street clothes
when visiting the nursery. The gown halfway down her
arms, she stopped in utter astonishment when she saw the
man who leaned against a near wall, arms crossed carelessly over his chest, smiling at her. It wasn't hard to guess
that he'd been watching her through the large observation window—but for how long?

"Mr. D'Alessandro," she greeted him warily, slowly
removing the gown and tossing it into a nearby hamper.
"What are you doing here?"

"We need to talk." He watched as she opened a small
locker and pulled out her purse. "You look very nice today," he surprised her by saying then, his dark eyes ap-
praising her thoroughly.

Still wondering what was so important that he'd had to
track her down here, Michelle cleared her throat self-
consciously at the personal observation. "Um—thank
you," she murmured. She'd dressed professionally, almost sternly, for her two appointments with Tony. Now
he was seeing her on a Saturday afternoon with her hair
swinging soft to the shoulders of the pale pink sweater
she'd worn with a full floral skirt and comfortable pink
flats. It was obvious that he preferred this more casual
look.

Trying to mask the awkwardness she felt at this unexpected encounter, she cleared her throat and spoke in a
cool, brisk voice. "I still don't understand why you're
here. I said I'd call you for news. Surely you haven't
found anything so earth-shattering that it required you to
track me down to tell me immediately."

"We need to talk," Tony repeated, not at all intimi-
dated by her tone. He looked around, stepping aside for

a scrubbed-and-gowned young father who was on his way into the intensive-care nursery. "But not here. Let's go someplace more private."

"Mr. D'Alessandro, I—"

"Michelle," he broke in firmly, his gaze holding hers. Startled by his use of her first name, she stared at him in silence when he continued. "I wouldn't be here if it wasn't important. Something's come up and I need to talk to you. Now. So cut me some slack, will you?"

She flushed at the unconcealed amusement lurking beneath the latter words. Perhaps she was overreacting to his sudden appearance. Maybe she *should* listen to what he had to tell her before reprimanding him. "All right, we'll talk. Where would you like to meet?"

He smiled. "I was sort of hoping you'd offer me a ride. I came here in a cab."

Since she was quite sure he owned a car, she couldn't help wondering why he'd arranged it so that he'd be riding with her when they left the hospital. Something else she intended to ask him when she found out exactly what it was that had brought him here. "Very well. We'll take my car."

His smile deepened. A passing nurse gave Tony a long, speculative look, then glanced at Michelle with obvious approval mirrored in her expression. Since Michelle was having a difficult time ignoring her own decidedly physical response to Tony D'Alessandro's sexy smile and knowing dark eyes, she quickly looked away from the other woman and headed briskly for the exit doors.

Michelle waited only until she'd navigated her two-year-old gray Lexus out of the hospital parking lot before glancing at the attractive man belted into the passenger seat. He seemed perfectly at ease as he lounged against the pale gray leather, giving her a smile that made her throat tighten. She cleared it abruptly. "So what was it you wanted to tell me?" she demanded, needing very badly to get back on a professional basis with him.

"I'd rather not discuss it in the car. I'll want your full attention. Take a right at the next intersection, okay?"

She sighed soundlessly. "Where are we going?"

"Someplace where we can talk without worrying about being overheard. I like your car."

Her eyebrows lifted at the change of topic. "Thank you."

"I've got a four-wheel drive. A Jeep Cherokee. Not as luxurious as this, of course, but it comes in handy when a case takes me onto country roads—or into places where there are no roads at all."

"Does that happen often?" she asked, intrigued despite herself.

"Often enough."

"Your job must be quite—interesting," she ventured carefully.

He laughed. "Yeah, sometimes. Other times it seems more like an endless stream of paperwork and computer research. I pawn as much of that off on the other guys as possible, but being the boss, I end up with most of it."

"The other guys?" she repeated curiously. During her two visits to his offices, she'd seen only Bonnie, his secretary.

"I have two full-time operatives. Bob and Chuck. Great guys. And one part-time employee, Cassie Browning. She's a bit overeager at times, but she shows a lot of potential. They do most of the legwork, while I concentrate on the computer and customer relations end of the business."

Michelle was rapidly revising her opinion of Tony's business as a low-level operation. Though he certainly wasn't in the big leagues of private investigation firms, he must be doing okay to employ three full-time employees and one part-time. She doubted that Tony made what most people would consider a fortune, but she was beginning to believe that he wasn't exactly penurious, either. Maybe he just liked wearing off-the-rack department store clothing—or jeans and knit shirts, as he was wearing today. Not that he didn't look wonderful in them.

She brought her thoughts sternly under control when he pointed out another turn. Obligingly, she followed his directions.

"So you like babies, do you?" he asked, catching her off-guard with another casual change of topic. "You looked very natural at the hospital. That was a tiny one you were rocking, wasn't it?"

Still bothered that he'd watched her without her knowledge, and at a time when she was admittedly more vulnerable than usual, she squirmed in her seat. "I enjoy the volunteer work I do at the hospital," she answered noncommittally. "It's quite satisfying."

"Quite satisfying," he repeated, that faint trace of amusement back in his voice.

"Did I say something funny, Mr. D'Alessandro?" she challenged.

"Forget it, Michelle. And by the way, could you drop the 'Mr.' stuff? The name's Tony."

Her fingers tightening on the steering wheel, she came very close to retorting that she hadn't given him permission to use her first name. Only the knowledge that the words would probably come out huffy and priggish— thereby providing him further entertainment at her ex-

pense—kept her from voicing them. "How much farther to where we're going?" she asked instead, ignoring
his suggestion altogether.

"Turn right at the next traffic light. After that, it's only
four blocks."

Since they had entered a middle-class residential
neighborhood, Michelle suspected he was taking her to
his home. She moistened suddenly dry lips and wondered if she should insist that they go to his office instead. And then she told herself that she could handle
Tony D'Alessandro. Even trust him, to an extent. After
all, he was a reputable businessman, a former policeman, the son of a man who'd once saved her life. The
problem was, she wasn't entirely sure she could trust
herself to continue to ignore her growing attraction to
him.

The house Tony directed her to wasn't exactly what
she'd expected. A sprawling red-brick ranch-style with
white shutters and a neatly trimmed lawn, it looked too
sedate, too average for the dynamic, wickedly attractive
man beside her. "You live here?" she asked curiously,
glancing at him as she parked in the driveway and turned
off the engine.

"I did for fifteen years," he answered, already climbing out of the car.

So who lived here now? Puzzled, she followed him to
the front door. He grinned at her as he pressed the bell.
"Got you wondering, don't I?"

She frowned repressively at him, asking herself what
had happened to the comfortable employer-employee relationship she'd established during their two former en-
counters.

The door opened before she could answer her own
question.

An older man with weathered olive skin and steel-gray hair stood inside the house, smiling kindly at Michelle. Staring at him with a sizable lump in her throat, she could almost feel the past eighteen years fall away. Could almost imagine that she was eight years old, frightened, lonely, despairing of ever seeing her family again. Could almost hear his deep, comforting voice murmuring, "It's okay, Michelle, I'm a friend. You can just call me Vinnie. I'm here to take you home."

She'd never completely forgotten the horror of that time, though she'd tried. Tried so successfully that she *had* almost forgotten how kind her rescuer's dark eyes had been, how safe she'd felt when she'd burst into tears and he'd taken her into his big, strong arms. How he'd carried her out of that terrible place where she'd been held and hadn't let her go again until she'd been restored to her frantic parents. How she'd clung to him as the only good thing that had happened to her in five long, traumatic days. How he'd visited her several times afterward, bringing her little gifts, making sure she was coping with the endless questions of the police.

"Vinnie," she whispered, her eyes filling with sudden tears.

His creased face softened. "Hello, Michelle. It's good to see you again."

And then he held out his arms and she stepped into them without hesitation. And, as had happened on that evening so long ago, she was immediately warmed by a sense of being completely safe, utterly protected.

It had been a very long time since she'd felt that way.

Standing quietly behind them, Tony watched in surprise and rapidly growing fascination as Vinnie gathered Tony's formerly cool, seemingly unflappable client into a fervent bear hug. Other than confirming that he had once handled a sensitive job for the Trent family, Vinnie had refused to discuss the case even with his son, telling Tony that the details would be up to Michelle to discuss if she chose.

It had been Vinnie who'd suggested bringing Michelle here to tell her about the call Tony had received from her attorney. "You're still too mad," Vinnie had said bluntly—and entirely accurately. "You'll only set her back up if you go throwing accusations around about a man she's known nearly all her life."

Brimming with curiosity about Michelle's emotional reaction to seeing Vinnie again, Tony followed impatiently when his exuberant father ushered her inside the house. They entered the wood-panelled den where Tony had spent so many hours in his youth. And then Vinnie turned back to Michelle, studying her flushed face in approval.

"Look at you," he said. "All grown-up and prettier than ever. No wonder your father bragged about you the way he did while you were off at college."

Obviously a bit flustered by her impulsive greeting, Michelle stopped straightening her hair and looked at Vinnie questioningly. "You stayed in touch with my father?"

Tony was as surprised as Michelle by Vinnie's reply. "Your dad and I had lunch together once a month for nearly fifteen years. In fact, I saw him only two days before his heart attack. I came to the funeral. A real crowd turned out, didn't they? Your father had a lot of friends."

"A lot of people claimed friendship with my father because of who he was, not because they genuinely liked him," Michelle answered with a trace of bitterness. And then she gave Vinnie a smile that made Tony fully aware that he'd never received one like it from her. "It must have meant a great deal to him to know you weren't that type."

Vinnie was clearly pleased. "Your dad was a fine man," he said gruffly. "We had some good long talks. I miss him."

"So do I," Michelle whispered huskily. And then she crossed her arms at her waist, making Tony fancy that she'd suddenly gotten smaller and more vulnerable. "I didn't know my father had stayed in contact with you when you stopped visiting us at home."

Tony wondered if the hurt in her voice was as obvious to Vinnie as it was to him. His left eyebrow lifted as he looked toward his father. Vinnie cleared his throat and glanced at his son before looking back at Michelle.

"I wanted to keep visiting you, Michelle," he explained gently. "It was your mother's idea for me to stop. She thought you'd be able to put everything behind you quicker if I wasn't hanging around to remind you. Maybe she was right."

Michelle obviously didn't agree, though it was just as obvious—to Tony, at least—that she was reluctant to criticize her mother's decision. "I felt so safe when you were around," she said instead. "And you always made me laugh. I missed you when you stopped coming by."

Vinnie sighed. "I'm sorry if I unintentionally hurt you. We were all only trying to do what was best for you, of course."

"Yes, of course." Michelle smiled again, her practiced, social smile this time. Tony wondered if it annoyed Vinnie as much as it did him. His curiosity was rapidly growing about the case his father had taken on for the Trent family. Obviously, Michelle had been involved. The most obvious possibility, of course, was kidnapping. The very thought made Tony's blood run cold. He could only hope he was wrong.

Suddenly tired of being left out of the conversation, he cleared his throat. "Why don't we sit down?" he suggested when he had their attention. "Dad and I want to talk to you about a new development in your case, Michelle."

"Where are my manners?" Vinnie scolded himself, immediately taking Michelle's arm to lead her to a deep, comfortable sofa. "Please, sit down. I wish my wife was here to meet you, but she's working on a case this afternoon. Did you remember that she's an attorney with the D.A.'s office? Tony, why don't you get us something to drink. There's iced tea in the refrigerator. Or would you prefer coffee, Michelle? My son makes a decent pot of coffee—taught him myself."

Michelle glanced at Tony with amusement lighting her blue eyes, making him shove his hands quickly into his pockets to keep them from reaching out to her. Damn, but this woman could take his breath away! he thought in dazed amazement. What was it about her that did this to him?

"Iced tea will be fine, thank you," she murmured, drawing her gaze from Tony's with a touch of heightened color in her cheeks.

As he headed for the kitchen, Tony wondered if that faint blush indicated that Michelle could possibly be attracted to him, as well. Or was he being hopelessly optimistic to imagine that these feelings weren't entirely one-sided?

Chapter Four

Oddly shaken by that exchange of glances with Tony, and still embarrassed by her uncharacteristically emotional greeting of Vinnie, Michelle clasped her hands in her lap and looked down at them, her thoughts whirling. Of everything she'd learned in the past few months, discovering that it had been her mother who'd put an end to Vinnie's visits shook her most profoundly.

Michelle had adored the gruff, kind-eyed man who'd rescued her from her kidnappers, had looked forward to his visits with the eagerness only a lonely eight-year-old could have known. She still remembered those visits so clearly—Vinnie had admired her toys, played games with her, brought her funny, inexpensive little gifts, told her stories about his three boys that had made her long to meet them, play with them.

She remembered hearing Vinnie talk exasperatedly about his oldest son, Tony, the ringleader, the one who'd

so carefully planned and executed the pranks his younger
brothers had gleefully followed him into. Funny, she'd
forgotten that until now. Her mouth quirked into a slight
smile as she could almost hear Vinnie sighing and saying, "Don't know what I'm going to do with that boy."

And then her smile faded when she remembered telling Vinnie that she'd love to meet his sons. Vinnie's dark
eyes had softened as they'd rested on the lonely little girl
in her huge, toy-filled bedroom. His hand had been warm
on her shoulder.

"My boys would like to meet you, too," he'd said sincerely. "They'd treat you like a pretty little princess it was
their privilege to entertain. And my wife would just love
to know you. She was always disappointed we never had
a little girl for her to pamper. Maybe you'll join us for
Sunday dinner sometime, okay?"

But that invitation for Sunday dinner had never ma-
terialized, and Vinnie's visits had ended soon afterward.
Now Michelle knew that they'd stopped at Alicia's request. Why? Hadn't her mother known how much
Michelle had enjoyed those visits, how she'd longed to
meet and play with Vinnie's children?

Feeling guilty that the thought even crossed her mind,
Michelle wondered for a moment if Alicia had stopped
the visits precisely for that reason. Alicia had always been
so overprotective of her adopted daughter, so lovingly, if
almost neurotically, possessive. Particularly after the
kidnapping. It had been a long time after that before
Michelle had been allowed out of her mother's presence.
Alicia had even wanted to hire a tutor and pull Michelle
out of the private school she attended, but Michelle's father had firmly vetoed that idea, asserting that the child
needed playmates.

"I was sorry to hear you lost your mother recently," Vinnie said from the nearby chair he'd settled into. "I know the two of you were very close."

Michelle pulled her gaze from her hands to glance up at him, noting the genuine sympathy in his dark eyes. "Yes, we were."

"You doing okay?"

She managed another polite, distant smile. "I'm fine. Thank you for asking, Mr. D'Alessandro."

Vinnie scowled, the expression darkening his usually pleasant face, drawing his heavy, dark brows into a pronounced V. " 'Mr. D'Alessandro?' You called me Vinnie before."

"Michelle tends to hide behind formality whenever she feels that she's losing control of a conversation," Tony said blandly, returning to the room with a tray holding three glasses of iced tea. He smiled when Michelle glared at him. "Just as she's tempted to fire me every time I step out of line."

"Like now," Michelle muttered, refusing to dignify his unrequested analysis of her with the heated denial that obviously trembled on her lips.

"Undoubtedly." He set the tray on the coffee table, then sank onto the sofa beside Michelle, ignoring the vacant chair across from his father. He offered Michelle a tall glass, smiling at her expression. "Tea?"

Innately reserved, properly raised, studiously dignified Michelle Culverton Trent would never have considered dumping a full glass of iced tea over anyone's head, he thought as she accepted the glass. Never, that is, before now. He waited to see if she'd follow through on the urge that was written so clearly on her lovely face. He wasn't surprised when she tilted her chin and gave him a cool nod. "Thank you."

"Don't you just love the way she gets all haughty and royal when she's displeased?" Tony asked his father. "Princess Di couldn't do it better."

Thoroughly irritated, all traces of sadness gone, Michelle frowned at him. He was quite pleased with himself for taking the pain out of her eyes. For some reason, it bothered him a great deal to see Michelle Trent looking sad and vulnerable.

"You had something to discuss with me about my case? Something that involved your father?" she asked brusquely.

"Actually, I don't know if Dad's involved or not," Tony admitted. To Michelle's obvious relief, he stopped smiling so cockily at her and chose to accept her switch to business. "I had a call yesterday afternoon that I thought I should discuss with you. I discussed it with Dad first to get his professional opinion on how this should be handled. I often consult with my father on my cases."

"You had a call? Concerning me?"

"Yes. It was your attorney, Carter Powell."

"Carter?" Looking thoroughly confused, Michelle set her tea glass on a coaster and turned to face Tony more fully. "Why would Carter call you? How in the world did he know you were working for me?"

"That's what I thought I should ask you," Tony explained. "I understood you'd told no one but me of your search for your family."

"Only you and my friend, Taylor Simmons," Michelle confirmed.

"Taylor Simmons?" Tony frowned as he repeated the name. "Would this Simmons guy have talked to your attorney?"

"Taylor is a woman and no, she wouldn't have talked to Carter," Michelle corrected him coolly. "She would never discuss my personal business with anyone, even my attorney."

"A woman, huh?" Tony nodded in approval, though he didn't pause to examine his reasons for being rather relieved by the information. "So why did Carter Powell call and order me to stop working on your case? Why would he be so opposed to you finding your family that he'd resort to threats against me?"

"Threats?" Michelle stared at Tony in disbelief. "Oh, surely not."

"I'm telling you, Michelle, the man threatened me."

"With what? What, exactly, did he say?"

Tony scowled. "They weren't direct threats, of course. He had more discretion than that. It was all implied."

"Then you were surely mistaken. Carter has always been protective of me, particularly since my father died, but he would never threaten anyone."

"Dammit, Michelle, I know when I'm being threatened," Tony retorted heatedly.

"I'm quite sure it's happened often, given your personality, but trust me, this time you're mistaken."

Vinnie intervened when Tony would have told her exactly what he thought of her opinions of him. Looking rather amused by the younger couple's squabbling, Vinnie leaned toward Michelle. "You really don't know how your attorney could have found out about your search for your family, Michelle?"

She shook her head. "I really don't. Unless Tony, during his search, somehow tipped him off?"

"I didn't," Tony inserted curtly. "I know how to do my job."

Vinnie nodded, his lips twitching with the smile he held back. "Then perhaps you should contact your attorney and ask him yourself," he suggested to Michelle. "It's up to you to determine whether the man is exceeding his authority as your attorney in trying to protect you.''

''Yes, I agree. I will certainly contact Carter immediately.'' Michelle shot Tony one quick, so-there look.

''Michelle, is there anyone else who may have cause to feel threatened by your search?'' Tony asked thoughtfully, searching her face for a reaction to his impulsive question.

Puzzled, she asked, ''Why?''

''Humor me, okay? Who stands to benefit if something happens to you?''

She shrugged. ''My uncle, I suppose—my father's brother. He and his wife live in California. I don't see them very often, since they weren't particularly close to my parents. Uncle Richard and his son, Steven, run the California branch of Trent Enterprises.''

''What's your uncle like?'' Tony asked.

''Distant,'' Michelle replied slowly. ''Rather snobbish, I'm afraid.'' Reluctantly, she added, ''He tried to talk my parents out of adopting me. I found out years later, by accident, that he thought they were making a mistake to take in a child who'd been raised for two years by people he considered socially inferior. He warned them that they didn't really know what to expect from such questionable breeding.''

''He told you this?'' Vinnie demanded, looking appalled at such cold insensitivity. Tony's hands had clenched around his tea glass. He knew they would have made fists had they been empty.

Michelle shook her head, an old pain coloring her voice when she explained. ''I found a letter he'd written them in my father's things after Mother died. It...hurt.''

She hadn't meant to add that, Tony realized when she abruptly stopped speaking, looking annoyed with herself. Immediately concealing the vulnerability, she smiled faintly and shook her head when Vinnie would have reached out to her. "I got over it. As I said, I was never particularly close to my uncle, anyway."

But she hadn't gotten over it, Tony decided, not really. Had that old letter given her one more reason to feel alone and lost after her mother's death? Had it been one more reason for her to begin a search for the family she'd once had and lost?

And then she seemed to realize why Tony had asked about her uncle. She looked at him when she spoke again. "As I explained, Uncle Richard is a snob, but I can't imagine him giving you veiled threats through my attorney. It just isn't his style. He would be much more likely to make his objection in person. Forcefully, but openly. He's never been one to mince words or conceal his opinions."

"What about your cousin? Steven, wasn't it?"

"I don't know him very well," Michelle admitted. "We rarely saw each other, since he was raised in California. He's five years older than I am. All I really know about him is that my father called him an irresponsible playboy. I think he has a weakness for pretty, not-very-bright women, even though he's been married for several years."

Tony cleared his throat, wondering how to approach the next subject. "I have one more question."

She gestured in resignation. "Go ahead."

Glancing from Michelle to Vinnie and back again, Tony asked bluntly, "What happened to you eighteen years ago? Why did your father hire mine under such secrecy?"

Michelle flinched. "That isn't relevant."

"How do you know it isn't?" Tony countered. "You don't even know how your attorney became involved in this."

Michelle looked to Vinnie, her expression somewhat pleading. "Is it really necessary to rehash that old case?"

Vinnie sighed and gave his son a look that held both censure and understanding. "Probably not. But my son likes to know all the angles when he takes a case, particularly when problems crop up. I told him it was up to you whether you wanted him to know about that other incident."

Michelle was quiet for so long that Tony was convinced she would refuse to tell him. And then she sighed, pushed back her hair and gave him an annoyed look. "I was—I was kidnapped when I was eight years old. Your father found me and rescued me five days later."

Tony made a massive effort to conceal how appalled he was at having his guess confirmed. He couldn't understand why he so violently hated the thought of Michelle in danger—then or now. "What happened?" he asked, his question more harsh than he'd intended.

Michelle looked down at her hands, seemingly relieved when Vinnie answered for her, as though understanding that she didn't like to talk about that time. "The kidnapper had been a trusted family employee," he explained. "A security guard who'd worked for Harrison Trent for three years. During that time, he befriended Michelle, teasing her and playing with her and talking to her to earn her trust. One day he tricked her away from her family by telling her he wanted to show her a litter of kittens he'd found in the garage. He drugged her and drove away with her in the trunk of his car."

Tony swallowed a string of vicious curses, setting his tea glass down with a thump that splashed liquid over the rim. "I hope you got the bastard."

"I got him," Vinnie confirmed grimly. "Beat the holy hell out of him, too, when we were supposed to be making the ransom drop. Let's just say by the time I was through with him, he couldn't wait to tell me where he had Michelle stashed."

"I was in a closet," Michelle murmured. "for the greater part of five days. It was dark and hot and sometimes I thought I'd smother."

Tony couldn't withstand her lost-little-girl tone. Without thinking, he reached out to her, covering her hand with his own. "I'm sorry," he said, holding her eyes with his when she looked at him in surprise at his action. "I wish I didn't have to make you relive this. But I have to know if there's anyone besides your attorney who has reason to want to stop me from doing my job."

He'd half expected her to snatch her hand from beneath his. It pleased him when she didn't. "I still think you're overreacting to Carter's call," she murmured, though without accusation this time.

"Believe me, Tony, I followed up all leads eighteen years ago. The jerk wasn't working alone, but I was satisfied that everyone involved was apprehended. I checked out Michelle's uncle, but I found no evidence that he'd participated in any way. As for the lawyer—well, all I can tell you about him is that he was Harrison Trent's attorney for years without any problems that I know of."

"I don't like being threatened," Tony grumbled, still angry when he remembered the obnoxious tone the attorney had used during the call.

Michelle did move her hand then, sliding it from beneath Tony's to reach for her tea glass. "I'll let Carter know that I don't appreciate him trying to interfere in my business without my permission," she said. "He won't bother you again."

Tony was far from satisfied, but it was obvious that he'd get no further with Michelle at the moment. After all, she'd known Carter Powell most of her life, and Tony for less than a month. How could he expect her to trust his gut feeling that something just wasn't right with her family attorney?

"I understand Tony's located one of your sisters," Vinnie said, smoothly changing the subject.

Still rather pale from the pain of rehashing her traumatic childhood experience, Michelle nodded. "Yes, he has. She lives in Fort Worth."

"Now isn't that a coincidence? You're practically neighbors."

"Yes."

"I guess you're really looking forward to meeting her."

Tony watched as Michelle moistened her lips with the tip of her tongue. They glistened enticingly and it was with some difficulty that he focused on what she was saying in answer to his father's comment.

"I haven't actually decided whether I should contact my sister," Michelle said vaguely.

Vinnie started to question her further, only to be interrupted when Carla D'Alessandro entered the room. "Sorry I'm late," the slender brunette apologized to her husband. "This Harmon case is such a headache. Hello, darling," she added for Tony's benefit, smiling fondly at him as she sank into the vacant chair.

"Hi, Mom," he greeted her, standing. "You look tired. Want a glass of iced tea?"

"That sounds wonderful. Thank you."

"No problem." He gestured at Michelle. "This is Michelle Trent, a client of mine. Can I get you anything else, Michelle?"

"No, thank you." She looked to his mother as Tony headed for the doorway. "It's very nice to meet you, Mrs. D'Alessandro."

Michelle found it hard to believe this woman was Tony's mother. Slim and attractive, Carla D'Alessandro looked ridiculously young to have a son in his early thirties. But her smile was warm and genuine, her eyes kind. Michelle suspected that Carla was a mother who'd always be available when her sons needed her.

By the time Tony returned with his mother's drink, Michelle had heard about his younger brothers—Michael, an attorney in Austin and Joe, a medical student in Houston—and about the scrapes the three adventurous brothers had gotten into during their youth. As he had years earlier, Vinnie again insisted that Tony had always been the ringleader.

"Don't believe it," Tony refuted mildly, handing Carla her glass along with a loving kiss on the cheek. "I was just the one who always nobly took the blame. To protect my little brothers, you understand."

Michelle gave him a look she hoped fully expressed her disbelief. "Of course."

"And if I *did* come up with the majority of the ideas, it was only because I was the most intelligent," Tony added, dropping back onto the couch beside Michelle.

"I believe your brothers would take issue with that," Carla murmured.

"If you'd had brains, you'd have done like your brothers and gone into respectable professions," Vinnie added sternly. "Instead, you had to follow in my shoes and be an ex-cop-turned-P.I. I tried to talk you out of it, but you never would listen to any advice I had to give."

"Of course I listened to you, Pop. I just didn't always agree with you. And besides, whoever said law was a respectable profession?" He grinned at his mother as he taunted her about her career.

Quite calmly, Carla took off her shoe and lobbed it at him, murmuring something in Italian that didn't sound particularly flattering. Laughing, he caught the shoe deftly, chiding his mother for throwing things at him that could accidentally hit Michelle instead. Smiling as Carla defended her throwing aim, Michelle thought wistfully that this seemed to be a happy, loving family. How she missed the good times she'd spent with her parents. How she longed for a family of her own, despite her lingering fear of taking such a risk.

Michelle waited only a few minutes longer before announcing politely that she really had to go. Both Carla and Vinnie urged her to come back anytime, so warmly that she felt she really would be welcome should she visit again. Not that she expected to do so. After all, why should she?

"How about giving me a lift home, Michelle?" Tony asked casually. "It's not far out of your way."

She couldn't graciously refuse, of course, not in front of his parents. "All right."

Tony managed to hide his amusement at her expression. He knew full well that if it had been up to Michelle, they wouldn't have been leaving together. He chose not to take it personally. He'd already decided that the toughest part of this case would be convincing his beautiful client that he could be trusted—as an investigator and as a man who was growing more personally involved every minute he spent with her.

He kissed his mother, then lingered at the front door with his father for a few moments after Michelle had gotten into her car. "What do you think, Dad?"

Vinnie shrugged. "She obviously trusts her attorney. Maybe you *did* misinterpret the call."

"Carter Powell knows information about Michelle that he shouldn't know. And I didn't misinterpret his instructions for me to drop the case and try to convince Michelle to drop it, as well. Something's going on."

"You may be right, Tony. I'll point out that all you've been hired to do is to locate Michelle's brothers and sisters, but I don't expect you to drop this other thing."

"The problem is that I don't really expect Carter Powell to drop it. I'll hear from him again."

"Then I'll just tell you to be careful."

"I always am, Dad." Tony glanced toward the car, where Michelle waited with apparent patience. "What do you think of her? Did she turn out the way you'd expected she would?"

"She's a lovely, well-mannered, intelligent woman. But in her eyes I still see a lot of the lonely little girl I knew."

"Yeah. Maybe I can do something about that."

Vinnie narrowed his eyes. "What did I tell you about getting personally involved with your clients, boy?"

"You told me it was dangerous and ill-advised," Tony replied without hesitation. "You also told me that if you hadn't done so yourself thirty-five years ago, you never would have married Mom."

Vinnie sighed gustily. "Don't keep the lady waiting, Tony. It's rude."

"Right. I'll call you later, Dad, okay?"

"Mmm. And Tony?"

Tony had already started down the steps. He looked over his shoulder. "Yes?"

"Watch yourself."

Knowing that Vinnie referred to Michelle as well as to her aggressive attorney, Tony nodded. "I will. Ciao, Dad."

Tony waited until Michelle had backed out of his parents' driveway before glancing at his watch. "Damn," he muttered, shaking his wrist as if it would help, "stupid watch has stopped again. I'm going to have to break down and buy a new one." As though it had just occurred to him, he added, "It's getting late, isn't it? Why don't we stop somewhere for dinner?"

"Dinner?" Michelle glanced at him warily. "Now?"

"Yeah. Unless you have other plans?"

"Well, no, but…is there something else about the case you want to discuss with me?"

He shifted in his seat to face her, watching her profile as she drove. "To be honest, no. This has nothing to do with the case. It's purely personal."

He watched as her fingers tightened on the steering wheel. "Personal?" she repeated, as though she wasn't quite sure she'd heard him correctly.

"Yes. Will you have dinner with me, Michelle?"

She moistened her lips as she had earlier. Again, the gesture drew his full attention to her soft, lush mouth, making him wonder exactly how those lips would feel beneath his. "I don't know, Tony. I'm not sure that's such a good idea."

"It's a dinner date, Michelle, not a lifelong commitment. No big deal, right?" It was a big deal, of course, at least to Tony. But he thought it best not to let Michelle know exactly how much her answer meant to him. He didn't want to frighten her away by pushing for too much, too soon.

"I don't think it's wise for us to date while you're working for me," Michelle explained carefully.

"Does that mean you'd go out with me if I *wasn't* working for you?"

Again, she hesitated. "Maybe."

"So what's the problem? I'm not going to stop looking for your brothers and sisters, and I won't suddenly decide to raise my fees. Nor lower them, for that matter. As far as business goes, it's strictly professional. But, after hours, I'd like to get to know you better."

"Why?" she asked bluntly, taking advantage of a red traffic light to look fully at him.

"I like you," he answered simply. And then he smiled. "I don't know why, exactly, but I do. So why don't you give me a chance to try to convince you to like me, too?"

"If I say yes, it's only to dinner," she warned, her fingers still flexing nervously on the steering wheel.

"Of course. That's all I expect." *For tonight, anyway.*

She seemed to reach a sudden decision. "All right. Where would you like to eat?"

He couldn't quite believe it had been that easy. He knew there was still a long way to go before Michelle fully trusted him, but this was one hell of a start. "Ever been to Vittorio's?"

"Yes. It's very good."

"My uncle—Mom's brother—owns the place. There's always a table for me there."

In response to an impatient honk from behind them, Michelle pressed the accelerator, passing beneath the light that had turned green without her noticing. And then she reached for the car phone built into her dash. "I'll just let my housekeeper know I won't be home for dinner," she explained. "She worries if I don't show up when she's expecting me."

Tony settled back in his seat and pretended not to listen while she made the call. He was also trying hard not to think about Michelle's wealth, which only made him nervous when he dwelled on it. His family had been comfortably middle-class, nowhere near Michelle's social or financial standing. But after finding out about bits and pieces of her childhood, he was sincerely grateful for his own normal background. Loving parents, brothers to play with, enough money to provide a few luxuries in addition to the necessities, but not nearly enough to cause his family to live in constant fear of kidnappers or fortune hunters.

At the moment, Tony was feeling considerably richer than Michelle. He wondered if she wouldn't agree with him.

Chapter Five

"So anyway, after he'd begged for weeks to be quarterback, we finally told Joe he could try it for a couple of plays. First pass he made to me sailed right through the neighbor's window. Old lady Winter," Tony added with an expressive grimace. "Meanest old biddy ever to haunt the state of Texas. Not only did she demand that we pay to fix her window, but she refused to give us back our football. And it was a good one, too. Real leather."

Michelle smiled, thinking of the younger Tony's indignation—an indignation that still colored his deep voice. "Did you get into trouble with your father?"

Tony grinned. "Nah. Dad couldn't stand old lady Winter, either. He grumbled a little and told us to be more careful, but we knew he thought it was kinda funny."

That didn't really surprise her about Vinnie. Michelle would have bet he'd have been a great father for a trio of boys. Again, she found herself envying Tony his memories of growing up with his brothers, with whom he was obviously still close.

"Did you always want to be a private investigator, like your father?" she asked.

He shrugged. "Actually, I was a cop first. Dad was a cop, too, you know. He quit the force after being injured on the job—he was shot during a holdup attempt. While he was on medical leave, he started doing some background research on a couple of Mom's cases. He liked it so well he went into the business."

"How old were you when you joined the police department?"

"Twenty-one. Right out of college."

"You didn't like it as much as you'd thought you would?"

"No." Without elaboration, he finished his linguine, then abruptly changed the subject. "So what about you? We've been talking about me ever since we got here. What were you like as a little girl? I'll bet you were a perfect child, right? Never mussed your dresses or lost the bows from your curls. Straight-A student, the kind teachers just love."

Flushing, Michelle looked down at her half-eaten vegetable lasagna. Tony had just pretty well summed up her childhood. She tried to remember an incident in which she'd rebelled against her parents' sometimes suffocating rules. "I did get into trouble once," she remembered. "I was at Taylor's house and I stayed forty-five minutes past my curfew. We'd been watching old movies on TV and lost track of time. My parents were worried sick. I was grounded for a week."

"Forty-five minutes?" Tony repeated. "How old were you?"

"Sixteen," Michelle admitted.

"I see."

Feeling oddly as though she needed to defend her un-adventurous adolescence, Michelle murmured, "My parents were always rather overprotective. Especially after—well, you know."

"Didn't you ever feel the need to cut loose and do something daring? Something your parents wouldn't approve of?"

"I did once," Michelle answered quietly, picturing a young man with a devilishly charming smile and bright, hungry eyes. The problem was that she'd misinterpreted that hunger as a desire for her, rather than for her money. It hadn't helped that her father had been unable to resist the urge to say "I told you so," when the truth had come out.

She'd spent the past five years living carefully, cautiously, pouring her energy into her obligations to Trent Enterprises, her heart into her hospital volunteer work. She'd even managed to convince herself that she was happy—most of the time.

Tony waited a few minutes for her to expand on her answer. When she didn't, he changed the subject. "Why are you having such a hard time deciding whether to contact your sister Layla? I've checked her out, as well as her husband, and they seem like perfectly respectable, apparently likeable people. We know Layla wants to be found or she wouldn't have registered with the reunion service. So why don't you call her?"

"I wouldn't know what to say to her," Michelle admitted, risking total candor. "She may be my biological sister, but she's still a stranger. I don't know her, I don't remember her. What would we talk about?"

"You haven't known me very long, but we haven't had any trouble talking tonight," Tony pointed out with a smile of understanding. "Of course, I've carried the brunt of the conversation, but maybe Layla's a talker, as well. Maybe you'd end up finding a new friend as well as a sister."

"You make it sound so easy," Michelle accused him, pushing her plate away, her appetite gone. "How would you feel if you suddenly discovered that you had brothers and sisters you'd never met, never known about? Would you want to rush out and find them?"

"I've asked myself that question since I took your case," Tony confessed. "And I've decided that, yes, I would want to find them. Maybe they'd be strangers, but there's something special about knowing you share the same ancestry, the same genes. Blood relationship is certainly no guarantee that you'll be close, or even *like* each other, but how can you not make an effort to find out?"

Though she was surprised that it was so easy to talk to this man about something so personal, Michelle realized that she really wanted his opinion. "Sometimes I think I'd really like to meet her," she said, watching Tony as she spoke. "I think about how nice it would be to have a sister, to know my nieces and nephew. But what if we meet and it's awkward and uncomfortable? What if we end up just staring at each other and trying to think of something to say? Or worse, what if one of us has expectations the other just can't fulfill?"

That was one of her biggest concerns, that Layla would expect her to immediately experience some bond, some connection that she may never feel. Ten at the time they'd been separated, Layla probably had memories of her younger sister, whereas Michelle had nothing but half-heard voices from dreams. "I wouldn't know what to do," she murmured, hoping Tony would somehow understand what she herself was struggling to comprehend.

It seemed he did. His smile softening, he reached across the small table and took her hand. "I can see why you'd be nervous. But I think you owe yourself a chance to meet her, just to satisfy your own curiosity. I think that curiosity is going to haunt you until you do something about it. Am I right?"

Michelle sighed, leaving her hand in his, though she refrained from returning his warm squeeze. "Probably."

"If it would help, I'll go with you when you meet her. Maybe it would be easier for you with someone objective along to keep things moving if the conversation drags."

Michelle was surprised by his offer. But she was also pleased, particularly since she sensed he genuinely wanted to help her. Because he cared?

She brought herself up short at that thought, quickly pulling her hand from his. It was much too soon to be thinking that way, she reminded herself sternly. Much too risky to start trusting another man with a charming smile and hungry eyes. To think that maybe this time the desire *was* for her, and not for her wealth.

"Thank you for offering. I'll think about it," she said, stirring sweetener into her freshly refilled coffee to avoid his eyes for the moment.

"You do that."

Tony might have said something more on the subject, but they were interrupted by yet another member of the restaurant staff stopping by to make sure their dinner was satisfactory. And didn't they want dessert?

Tony had explained with a rueful smile that being the nephew of the owner had always guaranteed him very prompt and personal service when he dined at Vittorio's. Sometimes *too* personal, he'd added when his uncle had asked a few pointed, matchmaking questions about Tony's relationship with Michelle.

It amused Michelle to note that the laid-back, Texan-down-to-his-boots private investigator subtly changed when he was with his family. When she'd first met him, she'd thought the only thing particularly Italian about Anthony D'Alessandro was his name. Now she could see that his ancestry was more a part of him than she'd previously suspected. She also hadn't expected that he could switch without hesitation from lazily drawled English to rapid, flawlessly accented Italian, as he did when he spoke to one of the older restaurant employees, who was obviously delighted to be able to converse in her native tongue.

Michelle had found Tony much too attractive when their association had been nothing more than professional. Now, seeing him under more personal circumstances, she was drawn even more strongly to him. Which played utter havoc on her peace of mind. She had no intention of getting personally involved with the man she'd hired to find her long-lost family!

Michelle drove Tony straight to his apartment building after dinner. She was relieved that he didn't press her about contacting Layla, choosing instead to keep the conversation light and amusing. "I enjoyed having dinner with you, Michelle," he said when she parked in a space he'd pointed out by his apartment. "We'll have to do it again."

"Perhaps," she said, still trying to be cautious.

He smiled and slid a hand behind her head. "Definitely," he corrected, his mouth already lowering toward hers.

Michelle stiffened, but it was too late. Tony's lips covered hers deftly, warmly. And she melted into the kiss as though she'd been starving for it.

Tony lingered over the kiss just long enough to make her want more. And then he pulled slowly, reluctantly away. "Drive carefully, Michelle."

He opened his door and had one foot outside before Michelle found her voice. "Tony?"

He glanced over his shoulder. "Yes?"

"I still think it would be wiser to keep our relationship on a professional basis. At least for now," she added a bit shyly.

His smile melted whatever was left of her prudence. "Maybe it would have been wiser," he agreed. "But it's much too late for that now, *cara*. Goodnight."

"I—uh—goodnight." She waited until he'd closed the door behind him before putting the car into reverse and backing out of the parking space.

Cara. The word echoed repeatedly in her mind as she drove home, Tony's husky voice as clear as though he still sat beside her. She spoke no Italian, but she knew that word. Dear. Did Tony toss out such endearments easily, or was he really beginning to care for her, as he'd implied?

And was she being an utter fool to wonder if she'd found more than a chance of locating her long-lost family when she'd stepped into Tony D'Alessandro's office?

Tony lay sprawled on his back in bed, his hands crossed behind his head, eyes focused intently on the ceiling, as though he'd find some answers in the acoustic tiles above him. He chewed thoughtfully on his lower lip, then released it when he fancied he could almost still taste Michelle, though it had been hours since he'd kissed her. Hours since he'd made himself pull away from her when what he'd really wanted to do was to carry her into his apartment and find out everything there was to know about Michelle Trent. Like what it would take to release the passion he sensed smoldering behind her prim-and-proper veneer.

Since thoughts of that nature proved more uncomfortable than productive, he turned his attention to his lingering misgivings about her attorney. Despite Michelle's conviction that Powell had only the best intentions where she was concerned, Tony suspected otherwise. Carter Powell hadn't sounded like a kindly family attorney loyally looking out for the welfare of a valued young client. He'd sounded very much like a man willing to resort to threats to protect his own best interests. Why? What was he afraid of if Michelle continued her search?

In sudden decision, he stretched toward the nightstand beside the bed, snagging the telephone receiver. He punched in a number and waited impatiently for an answer. "Chuck? It's Tony. Sorry I woke you. First thing tomorrow, I want you to turn over your notes on Jared Walker to Cassie. Let her take the search from here. . . .

"No, you haven't done anything wrong. I've got a new assignment for you. I want you to find out everything there is to know about Carter Powell, an attorney here in Dallas. I particularly want to know about his work for Trent Enterprises. Michelle Trent, in particular. And, Chuck—I'm not going to ask a lot of questions about how you do your research. Just get me everything you can find. Soon."

* * *

Michelle hung up her telephone with a sigh of frustration. She'd been trying to reach her attorney for nearly a week—since Tony had told her about Carter's call to him. Each time she'd called, Carter had been in court or in a meeting or out of the office. She hadn't even been able to reach him at home.

Already annoyed with him for calling Tony without her authority, she decided she was going to have to be very firm when she did speak to him. He was going to have to acknowledge that she was an adult now, not the child he'd known since toddlerhood, and that she was quite capable of handling her own personal business. And she didn't appreciate having to go to so much trouble contacting him when she needed to speak to him.

She was working at home that day. Though she'd never been interested in the corporate operation of Trent Enterprises, and had no need to earn a living, she'd wanted something productive to do with her time. It had been her father who'd suggested a job for her, not long after the fiasco with Geoff, when Michelle had been desperately in need of something to do besides brood about the disastrous ending of her first serious love affair.

Since that time, Michelle had taken on all responsibility for the sizable charitable contributions made by Trent Enterprises, Dallas. She was the one who investigated charitable organizations, responded to pleas for funds, approached the board of directors with yearly budgeting proposals and requests for increases as needed during the year. Every week she received stacks of mail containing requests for donations; she diligently read and researched each one. Not only did the task give her something worthwhile to devote herself to, but it also served a legitimate purpose, one she could be quite proud of.

She was reading a form-letter request from a national
charity organization in the home office that had once
been her father's when she heard the front doorbell ring.
Knowing Betty would answer it, she didn't pull her attention from the paperwork until she heard a sound from
the open doorway. She looked up expecting to see her
housekeeper, only to find Tony D'Alessandro leaning
casually against the doorjamb, arms crossed over his
chest, watching her with obvious amusement at her surprise.

"Hi," he said.

"Tony! What are you doing here?"

"I don't suppose you'd believe I just happened to be
in the neighborhood."

She laid the letter on her desk. "Try again."

He dropped his arms and sauntered into the room,
looking around with interest at the rich wood panelling,
the crowded shelves of books, the framed hunting prints,
the comfortable leather furniture, the glossy cherry desk.
"Nice. I've always wanted a study like this."

"You still haven't told me why you're here."

"That housekeeper of yours is quite a watchdog," he
remarked, walking around to her side and resting a hip
on the desk, his jeaned leg only inches from her hand.
"You wouldn't believe what I had to tell her to convince
her to let me in to see you unannounced. I'd already had
a hard enough time getting past the big guy working on
the front gate."

"That's Betty's husband, Arthur. He's been with the
family as long as Betty has. He was my mother's driver,
though now he primarily handles general maintenance of
the grounds and vehicles, since I prefer to drive myself,"
Michelle explained, pulling her hand away to clasp it with

the other in her lap. "Did you find out something new about my family, Tony? Is that why you're here?"

He shrugged and reached out to brush a strand of hair away from her cheek. "There is a lead on your oldest brother, Jared. We've confirmed that he entered the Navy straight out of high school and served for several years. Nothing on his most recent whereabouts yet, but we'll find him."

Her cheek tingling from that all-too-brief contact, Michelle looked up at him. "You could have told me that over the phone."

"Mmm," he murmured in agreement. "But I couldn't have done *this* over the phone." And he leaned over to kiss her, his mouth covering her surprise-parted lips with the same seductive skill he'd displayed the last time he'd kissed her.

He really was going to have to stop doing that, Michelle thought, her eyelids drifting downward. Or else she simply couldn't be held responsible for her actions.

Again, it was Tony who brought the kiss to an end. "I've been wanting to do that again for the past six days," he murmured, touching a fingertip to her lower lip. "Have I mentioned that the shape of your mouth makes me crazy?"

Michelle cleared her throat. "Oh, is that what does it?" she managed to say fairly evenly.

He chuckled. "Are you ever at a loss for a put-down?"

"With you it seems to come naturally." To avoid talking about the kiss, she immediately turned the conversation back to business. "How long do you think it will take you to find Jared?"

The smile in his eyes told her he knew exactly what she was doing, though he answered cooperatively enough. "I've turned the case over to Cassie Browning. She's been working part-time for me for nearly a year," he reminded her. "She's young, but eager. Goes full tilt into any assignment I give her. I think she's got her eye on a partnership. D'Alessandro and Browning Investigations. Or, knowing Cassie, she'd probably prefer top billing."

Michelle tried very hard not to be bothered by the fond indulgence in Tony's voice when he talked about his employee. It was really none of her business if this Cassie had her eye on more than a professional partnership with Tony, Michelle reminded herself sternly. So why was she suddenly feeling suspiciously—almost primitively—possessive?

"I have a few more things to do this afternoon," she said pointedly. "Was there anything else you wanted to discuss with me?"

"I've got a couple of tickets to a play tonight. I know this is short notice for a Friday evening, but how about it?"

Michelle had been momentarily distracted by the chime of the front doorbell. Who was it *this* time? "How about what?"

He sighed his exasperation with her deliberate obtuseness. "Will you go to the play with me tonight?"

That got her full attention again. "Tonight?"

"That's when the play is," he replied patiently. "I'll pick you up at seven, okay?"

"Come on, Michelle, tell the man yes before someone else does. Someone like me," Taylor added, strolling into the room with a speculative look at Tony. She held out her hand to him across Michelle's desk, her smile full of mischief. "Hello. I'm Taylor Simmons. You must be Tony D'Alessandro."

Rising to his feet, Tony briefly took her hand, returning her smile. "As a matter of fact, I am. How did you know?"

"You're the only handsome Italian-type Michelle has mentioned lately," Taylor quipped, grinning unrepentantly at Michelle's groan of embarrassment. "So, Michelle—are you going out with him tonight or not?"

Resisting the urge to hide her face in her hands in the hope that both of them would just disappear, Michelle stood and shoved her hands into the pockets of her full cotton skirt. "I guess I will."

"You'll have to forgive her. She's usually much more courteous," Taylor told Tony with laughter warming her husky voice. "In fact, Michelle cut her teeth on the social graces. So what have you been doing to annoy her, hmm?"

"I seem to do that without even trying," Tony answered.

"That's not so bad. She needs to be challenged occasionally. It wouldn't be good for her to get too complacent, you know?"

"I *am* still in the room," Michelle reminded her friend peevishly.

Taylor laughed. "So you are. Have I annoyed you so greatly that you'd never consent to loan me that great sequined jacket you bought at Neiman's last month? I've got a date tonight and I don't have a thing to wear."

"What? No grubby jeans or safari jacket?" Michelle asked in mock surprise. "This must be someone special."

"Well, no," Taylor admitted ruefully. "But I've been wanting to try that ritzy new restaurant since it opened last month, and this guy just happened to have reservations for tonight."

Tony cleared his throat. "I'll leave you two to your comparisons of notes about your dates tonight. It was nice to meet you, Taylor. See you at seven, Michelle."

"You haven't told me what play we're seeing," Michelle reminded him quickly as he headed for the door. "I won't know what to wear unless you tell me where we're going."

"Robert F. Kennedy High School," he answered over his shoulder. "It's my cousin's senior-class play. A comedy, I understand, though I'm not sure whether the author intended it to be. I think it's safe to assume the dress will be casual."

With that, he was gone, leaving Michelle to stare after him in half-amused disbelief. He was taking her to a high school senior play? That was his idea of a date?

Taylor waited only until Tony was out of hearing before making a fist and jerking it downward in front of her in a sign of approval. "All *right!* Michelle, he's delectable. Why didn't you tell me?"

"I told you he was nice-looking," she murmured, still rather distracted.

"You didn't say he was gorgeous. And you didn't say what a great smile he has, nor how funny he is. I really liked him."

Michelle frowned. "You did?"

Taylor laughed and shook her head. "No, not like that. I liked him, but I don't think he and I would ever have any real electricity. Not the kind I felt bouncing around between *you* and Tony, anyway."

Flushing, Michelle pushed her hands deeper into her pockets. "Don't be ridiculous. I hardly know him."

"So how does he kiss? I'd bet he's damned good at it."

"What makes you think he's kissed me?" Michelle hedged, knowing her deepening flush gave her away.

"There was a smudge of pink lipstick at the corner of his mouth, right beside that cute little dimple. The same color you're sort of wearing, by the way. Unless he's into cross-dressing, there's only one way I can think of that your lipstick ended up on his mouth."

"So he kissed me. It was just a kiss."

"Just a kiss?" Taylor asked, her eyebrows lifting skeptically.

Michelle sighed. "Okay, it was an incredible kiss. An award-winning, bell-ringing kiss. But," she added when Taylor grinned, "that doesn't mean anything else is going to happen between us. I don't intend to rush into anything."

"Nor am I suggesting you should," Taylor replied promptly. "I'm simply suggesting that you give Tony a chance. Forget about Geoff and judge Tony on his own merits, all right? Maybe the two of you will turn out to be perfect for each other. It's been known to happen."

Michelle nodded, unconsciously tracing her lower lip with one fingertip. "I know he's not Geoff, Taylor."

But those old scars couldn't be put aside as easily as Taylor made it sound. It was going to take time for Michelle to decide for herself whether Tony was a man who could be trusted with her wary heart.

Chapter Six

Michelle might have had more fun on other dates than she did with Tony that night. But if she had, she couldn't remember. She might have laughed more some other evening during her life. She just couldn't have said when. She might have had more attentive, more charming, more irresistibly entertaining escorts. If so, those men had long since slipped her mind.

Surrounded by Tony's aunts, uncles, cousins and parents in the high school auditorium, she should have felt shy, out of place. Instead, she felt welcomed and appreciated, part of the group that laughed so good-naturedly at the antics of the enthusiastic young people on stage. And when Michelle commented that Tony's cousin Dominic showed signs of real acting talent, the others were so pleased and flattered that one would have thought the praise had come directly from Steven Spielberg.

It was probably one of the most successful dates Michelle had ever had. Which didn't explain why she grew more nervous and unsettled as the evening drew closer to an end. Nor why, by the time she and Tony lingered over grilled chicken sandwiches at his favorite fast-food restaurant after the play, she'd become quiet and introspective, avoiding his eyes as she pretended to concentrate on her fries.

"Michelle, is something wrong?"

"No, of course not. How's your sandwich?"

"How *was* my sandwich, you mean," he said, motioning toward the empty wrapper in front of him. "I've been finished for ten minutes."

Startled, she realized she'd withdrawn more than she'd been aware. She couldn't even remember the last thing she'd said to him. Had they been talking about the play? His family? The weather?

"Sorry," she murmured, clasping her hands in her lap. "I was thinking about something else."

Like how very much she was growing to like him. How much she enjoyed being with him. How badly she wanted him to kiss her again. And how the very thought of a relationship with him had her breaking into a cold sweat.

Tony rested his elbows on the plastic-laminated table-top, still watching her more closely than she found comfortable. "I've been avoiding talking business this evening, but I did want to ask if you ever talked to your attorney about his call to me."

Michelle shook her head. "I've tried to call him, but he's been hard to reach this week."

"I bet," Tony muttered.

She ignored him. "I left a message for him to call me as soon as possible. I'm sure I'll hear from him tomorrow."

"Mmm." Tony's skepticism was quite obvious in the quiet murmur and the lift of his eyebrow. In response to the look she gave him, he sighed and let the subject of her attorney drop. "Have you thought about my offer to go with you to meet your sister? Would you like me to set up a meeting?"

Her stomach contracted with a new set of nerves. "I don't know, Tony. I—"

"Michelle. Let me call her for you. We both know you want to meet her."

"Do we?" she muttered, giving him a resentful glare. "Since when do you know so much about what I want?"

He didn't answer. Instead, he gave her a smile that held so much cockiness and sympathetic understanding that she couldn't decide whether to squirt ketchup on him or burrow into his arms. Since neither action seemed particularly appropriate at the time, she took a deep breath and said, "Give me more time to think about it. If I decide to take you up on your offer, I'll call you."

"You'll think about it? Seriously?"

"That's what I said, wasn't it?" she snapped. "If you're so convinced this is what I want, why question my decision?"

"I'm well aware that you don't particularly value my advice, but I still think you'll be sorry if you don't do this. I'd hate for you to have any regrets later."

He just couldn't resist getting in a little dig. Why was it that Tony seemed to like her best when she was more than a little annoyed with him?

"Finished with your dinner?" he asked, abruptly changing the subject. "Want a fried apple pie or an ice-cream cone for dessert?"

"No, thank you."

"Then I'll bus the table." He reached for her empty paper cup, giving her a grin. "Can't say I don't take you to the best places, can you, darlin'?"

"I think you look quite natural busing tables," she retorted, doing her best to hide the little shiver that coursed through her at his lazily drawled endearment. "Perhaps you missed your calling."

"I'll keep that in mind if people suddenly stop wanting incriminating photographs of cheating spouses."

Michelle smiled with a vain attempt at cool amusement and handed him her empty French-fry wrapper.

Tony insisted on walking Michelle to her front door when he took her home. With amusingly old-fashioned courtesy, he helped her out of his four-wheel drive and kept one hand at the small of her back as they walked up the four steps to her door.

Keys in hand, she looked up at him with a polite social smile, assuming he would kiss her again, aware that she wanted him to. "I enjoyed the play, Tony. And the meal. Thank you for taking me."

Leaning one shoulder against the door, he touched her cheek, stroking the line of her jaw with one gentle finger. "I enjoyed having you with me. In fact, I think it would be all too easy to become addicted to being with you."

It seemed so easy for him to say things like that. Could he really mean them? She moistened her lips, wondering what to say in return.

Tony drew his finger across her damp lower lip. Her mouth parted slightly in reaction, and he ran the tip of the same finger just along the inside of her lip. She shivered, imagining his mouth on hers, his tongue tracing the path his finger had taken.

"Have I told you that I think you're the most beautiful woman I've ever known?" Tony murmured, sliding his other hand into her hair so that her face was cupped between his palms. She felt his unsteadiness with a sense of wonder. "That I've never met anyone who affected me quite the way you do?"

Her eyes closed when he kissed her, her hands rising tentatively to rest on his chest. The kiss was long and deep and thorough, and Tony was breathing rapidly when it ended. Michelle wasn't sure she was breathing at all.

"Michelle," he whispered, his lips moving against her temple, his arms drawing her closer. "Tell me I'm not the only one feeling these things. Tell me it's not all one-sided."

Her fingers clenched convulsively into his soft cotton shirt. "I don't—I don't know what you want from me," she managed, lifting her eyes slowly to his face. "What you want me to say."

He sighed and rested his forehead against hers. "You really have a problem with trust, don't you?"

"I've had reason to."

"Men who said they wanted you when what they really wanted was the Trent money?" Tony asked perceptively, lifting his head.

She nodded stiffly.

"I could tell you that isn't the case with me. I could tell you I couldn't care less about your money. That it's only you I want—very badly. But I know it's going to take time for you to believe those things. Time for you to get to know me, to know you can trust me. I won't rush you."

"I—" She cleared her throat of a large, near-painful lump. "Thank you."

He shook his head, his smile crooked. "I foresee a lot of cold showers in my future. But, just to hold me over . . ." And he kissed her again, until her knees were weak, her ears buzzing, her lungs burning from lack of oxygen. She clung to the doorknob when he finally released her, not at all sure that her legs would support her without the assistance. "Will you see me tomorrow?" he asked.

"Yes," she whispered, her voice barely audible.

"I'll pick you up tomorrow afternoon—say, two o'clock? Dress casually. You do own a pair of jeans, don't you?"

"Of course," she replied, hoping she was right. When *was* the last time she'd worn a pair of jeans?

He dropped one last, quick kiss on her still-trembling mouth. "Good night, Michelle."

She could only nod in response. He smiled with a mixture of satisfaction and frustration, then loped toward his Jeep. Michelle pulled in a much-needed breath and opened her front door, ready to be inside where she could hide in the security of her bedroom.

By the time Tony picked Michelle up Saturday afternoon, she'd begun to wonder if she'd lost her mind during the evening before. She hadn't acted at all like herself, hadn't maintained any sort of professional distance between herself and Tony. Just the opposite, in fact. She'd encouraged him to believe she was interested in more than a professional liaison with him—and it was much too soon for her to even speculate about anything of a more intimate nature.

Pressing her cool hands to her flaming cheeks, she stood before the mirror in her bedroom, trying not to relive the kisses they'd shared when he brought her home.

Unable to completely block them out of her thoughts. They'd haunted her dreams during the night, replayed themselves over and over in her mind all day—and, desperately as she might try to believe otherwise, she knew full well that she was not only expecting, but *hoping* he would kiss her like that again today.

What had ever happened to that cool, cautious reserve she'd cultivated so carefully during the past five years?

Aware that it was nearly two—the time he'd said he'd be picking her up—she concentrated on the reflection in the mirror again, wondering if she'd dressed correctly. It would help, of course, if she had some idea of where he'd be taking her, but she was already learning that there was no predicting what Tony D'Alessandro might do.

Since he'd suggested jeans, she'd found a pair—though it had taken twenty minutes of searching. She didn't remember the last time she'd worn them, but she'd obviously gained a couple of pounds since. The soft denim fit her like a second skin, molding her slender hips, hugging her thighs, shaping her long legs. They sported a designer label on the back pocket, though she couldn't have said whether that particular designer was the "in" one at the moment. She'd chosen a short-sleeved floral cotton T-shirt and white leather Keds to complete the casual outfit, pulling the top section of her hair into a barrette and allowing the remainder to fall loose to her shoulders. Studying her reflection, she decided wryly that she looked about twelve years old. And she was having severe doubts about leaving this house without changing into something more tailored and respectable.

Downstairs, the doorbell chimed discreetly. Michelle wiped suddenly damp palms on the legs of her jeans and reminded herself that Tony was doing a job for her—but that he had become a friend, in a way. After all, he was the son of a friend of her father's. At least until this search for her siblings was completed, she had no intention of allowing it to go further than that. She was feeling too vulnerable, too unsettled just now. Too susceptible to a brilliant smile and warm masculine charm.

"So watch your step, Trent," she told the denim-clad figure in the mirror. And then she turned on one sneaker and headed downstairs, settling her face into the polite social smile she reserved for employees and casual acquaintances.

Hands in the pockets of his faded jeans, Tony waited impatiently in the antique-filled parlor to which the ever-efficient Betty had directed him. Frowning at the expensive accoutrements surrounding him, he wondered what it would have been like to grow up amidst so much luxury, waited on hand and foot by loyal servants. Having been taught from an early age by his liberated, career-minded mother to make his own bed, iron his own shirts and cook his own meals when necessary, Tony couldn't picture himself in Michelle's place.

Not that he didn't appreciate the nice things around him now. Tony had a healthy respect for money and the luxuries it could provide—he'd just never considered it the primary ingredient for happiness.

Just as well, he thought with a grimace, remembering the current shape of his bank account. Admittedly, the new large-screen TV he'd recently purchased had left a major dent in his finances. But watching the basketball play-offs on fifty-two inches of viewing screen had made the investment seem worth it at the time.

A sound from the doorway made him turn to find Michelle watching him silently. She was wearing jeans, he noted immediately—and, boy, did they look good on her! How he'd love for his hands to mold her hips as caressingly as that soft denim did. But her expression . . .

He almost shook his head in exasperation at the cool smile she gave him. She might as well have been wearing a sign warning him to keep his distance. Whatever progress he'd made on their date last night had apparently dwindled during a night of second thoughts.

Which only meant, of course, that he was even more determined to regain lost ground.

Without giving warning of his intentions, he took two steps toward her and drew her into his arms for a fervent kiss of greeting. "You look great," he said when he drew back, pretending he didn't notice the startled reproval in her expression. "Ready to go?"

The soft hollow of her throat was exposed by the scooped neck of her flowered T-shirt, her rapid pulse clearly visible there—evidence of her reaction to the kiss. Had Tony not been trained to be so observant, he might have accepted at face value her brisk nod and detached tone. "Yes," she said evenly. "Where are we going?"

She was good, he'd grant her that. Indulging himself with one last, quick look at that telltale throbbing in her throat, he took her arm. "How does a picnic sound?"

"It's a lovely day for one," she commented, her arm stiff in his loose grasp. "Very warm for this early in June."

"Yes, it is, isn't it?" His smile mocked her formality, but he didn't push, knowing she still had a long way to go before she learned to trust him the way she should. After all, he counseled himself, she still hardly knew him.

Something he intended to remedy as quickly and as thoroughly as possible during this day together.

It amused Tony that Michelle settled into his Jeep as gracefully as though she were sliding into a limousine, smoothing denim as carefully as she would silk. He told himself it was a good sign that she was behaving so formally—it meant he was making her nervous. Which beat the hell out of being ignored altogether, he decided, whistling between his teeth as he rounded the front of the Jeep and climbed beneath the wheel.

He lifted a friendly hand to the heavyset middle-aged man wielding hedge clippers on the bushes beside the massive front gates of the Trent estate, which Michelle had explained were usually kept open during the daytime, closed at night. The man glared back at him. "I think I'm making progress with Arthur," he commented. "He didn't shake the clippers at me today."

"Arthur doesn't trust strangers easily," Michelle replied.

"Then it seems he has a lot in common with his employer."

She shrugged delicately.

Tony cast her a thoughtful, sideways glance. "Will you tell me about him?"

She returned the look in question. "About Arthur? What do you want to know?"

"No, not Arthur. The guy who hurt you so badly. The one who made you so suspicious of my motives and my interest in you."

Her brows drew downward into a frown. "Oh. Him."

So there had been a "him." Tony had been taking a stab in the dark, half hoping he was wrong. His hands tightened on the wheel. "Who was he? When did it happen?"

She looked out the window beside her, concealing her expression from his searching looks. "He wasn't anyone important. Someone I met in my senior year of college. I was naive, he was smooth. I'd fallen for him before I realized how deeply attracted he was to my money. He didn't even bother to deny it when I finally confronted him about it—as though it amused him that I'd ever thought he'd want me for any other reason. I got over him easily enough, but I'm no longer naive. I suppose I owe him that one."

"What was his name?"

She looked at him then, obviously startled by his harsh tone. "Why?"

"So I can smash his teeth in if I'm ever lucky enough to run across him. I owe him one, myself. Because of that jerk, I've got to somehow convince you that I'm not mentally counting money every time I kiss you, that I don't see dollar signs every time I look at you. I've never had to defend myself against being a gigolo before. I can't say I much like it."

Michelle flushed. "I never said I thought you were a gigolo," she muttered.

"Isn't that what they call guys who court women for their money?"

"It may be," she retorted with renewed spirit. "But that hardly applies here, does it? It's not as if you're... courting me."

He lifted his left eyebrow. "Is that right?"

"You're doing a job for me. I'm paying you to find my brothers and sisters."

He swallowed a curse. "Right," he said coolly. "But that's all you're paying me for, got that? After hours, I'm on my own time. Which means I hope you like hamburgers and pizza, lady, because my budget doesn't often run to chateau briand. *Capisce?*"

To his surprise, she giggled. "You can cool the Italian temper," she said with more genuine emotion than she'd shown since he'd picked her up. "I happen to like hamburgers and pizza just fine."

He didn't quite know what he'd said that had set her at ease, but suddenly she was talking as easily as she had during their date the night before, her smile the real one now, not the fake social expression he'd grown to dislike so intensely. "I don't see a picnic basket," she said, looking over her seat to the back of the vehicle.

Tony was glad he'd spent an hour that morning cleaning the debris out of his Jeep and vacuuming the formerly grubby flooring. "I didn't bring a picnic basket."

"Are we stopping for takeout?"

"No."

Michelle waited a moment, then sighed gustily. "Picnics generally include food," she informed him. "You did say we're going on a picnic?"

"A barbecue, actually. It's at my cousin Paul's house. He and his wife, Teresa, have invited us over for a cookout and softball game with some mutual friends."

"We're going to someone's home?" Michelle repeated. He watched as she plucked discontentedly at her jeans. "I should have worn something nicer."

"Sweetheart, it's a barbecue, not high tea. You look fine." She looked sexy enough to stop traffic, of course, but he didn't see any need to elaborate at the moment.

"I don't remember meeting your cousin Paul last night. Was he there?"

"No, he and Teresa had other plans and couldn't come to the play. They sent Dominic a good-luck telegram before the opening. He got a kick out of it."

"Just how many cousins do you have?"

He grimaced. "Mom's side or Dad's?"

"Combined."

"Heaven only knows. They're spread out from New York to California, not counting the distant relatives still in Italy. Dad's got seven brothers and sisters and they've all got kids—Paul's a D'Alessandro, by the way—and Mom's one of five girls, no brothers. We have a major reunion on one side or the other every two or three years, usually here in Dallas since it's sort of halfway for those at opposite sides of the country. Grandfather D'Alessandro was the one who first settled here—he had some vague dreams of being a cowboy like the ones he'd seen in the American movies when he was a kid in Italy."

"And was he a cowboy?"

"Nah. Ended up selling shoes in a department store. But he never missed the rodeo when he had the chance to go to one. He took me a few times before he died when I was ten."

Michelle looked dazed by the size of his family. "How do you keep up with everyone?"

"The aunts keep us well-informed," he answered in amusement at her expression. "The family hotline's probably been busy all morning about you after last night."

"About me?" she repeated weakly.

He laughed. "Yeah. Aunt Marie probably called Aunt Angelina first thing." His voice changed to an exaggeratedly accented falsetto. *"You should meet the lovely girl Antonio brought to Dominic's play. So pretty. So refined. Much too good for our Tony, of course, but maybe she won't notice until after they're married. He's almost thirty-three, you know. We'd almost given up on him finding a nice girl."*

Though she'd flushed brightly at his mention of marriage, Michelle laughed. "Surely, it's not that bad."

"Are you kidding? It's almost a sin in my family to be single past thirty. Especially for the girls. My cousin Anne-Marie's going on twenty-eight now and still not married. The aunts are spending a small fortune lighting candles for her. Her mother, Aunt Lucia, has stopped nagging her to find an attractive young doctor and started hinting about any single guy with a pulse."

"So how did you get away with being single so long?" Michelle asked, twisting in her seat to look at him. "You've never been married, have you?"

"No. I was involved with someone for a while, but whatever we had wasn't strong enough to weather some personal problems I had a couple of years ago," he replied, wincing as he thought of how badly he'd treated Janice just before they'd broken up.

Angry and embittered with his job at the police department, caught in the midst of a political turmoil, he'd taken his frustration out on her with impatience and emotional neglect. Had there really been anything serious between them, she'd have knocked some sense into him and demanded that he treat her with the respect she'd deserved. Instead, she'd decided he wasn't worth the effort and she left him just before he left the department. He'd been too caught up in his own problems to miss her for long. "She's married now, I hear."

"Does that bother you?" Michelle asked just a little too casually.

"No. It's been over a long time."

"Oh."

Unable to read her tone, he glanced over at her. She was looking out the windshield at the road ahead, her hands clasped loosely in her lap, her beautiful face composed, her thoughts hidden from him. Disliking the distance between them, he reached out and took her left hand in his right one, raising it to his lips. He noted in satisfaction that her breath caught audibly when he flicked the tip of his tongue across her knuckles.

All in all, the day was going quite well so far.

Michelle liked Teresa D'Alessandro from the moment she met her. Dark-haired, dark-eyed, seven months pregnant and unabashedly pleased with her condition, Teresa welcomed Michelle to her modest countryside home, warmly claiming that Tony was one of her favorites of her husband's many cousins. "I'm from a small family myself," she confided to Michelle soon after they'd arrived. "I have one brother and he has only one child. The first few times Paul took me to D'Alessandro gatherings, I was overwhelmed."

"I know the feeling," Michelle confided, glancing around the large, acre-and-a-half backyard of Teresa's home, where some twenty people—more than half of them claiming kinship with Tony—laughed and teased and talked familiarly. Tony was right in the middle of the group, his voice raised as he defended himself against a good-natured gibe of some sort, talking rapidly and with a great deal of gesturing. Again, Michelle noted that he suddenly became very Italian when surrounded by his family. Definitely fascinating.

"I was raised as an only child," she explained to Teresa, trying to keep her mind on their conversation rather than Tony, "and I have only one cousin, whom I don't know very well. I'm not accustomed to such large, extended families, either."

Teresa nodded, then smiled. "You get used to it quickly," she assured her. "The D'Alessandros are a very loving, very supportive clan. Any one of them would be here in a minute if we needed them. It's a nice feeling, you know?''

"I'm sure it is," Michelle replied, though she wondered if Teresa thought her relationship with Tony was more serious than it actually was. Teresa talked as though Michelle, too, would be a part of that clan soon. Michelle considered explaining that this was only her second real date with Tony, that it was much too soon to be thinking seriously about a relationship with him, but then she decided to just let it go.

Some things only got more complicated with explanations.

Breaking away from the group of men with whom he'd been talking, Tony rejoined Michelle and Teresa. "How are you at softball, Michelle? We're about to get up a game, now that everyone's here."

"I've never played," she admitted.

Both Teresa and Tony stared at her in surprise, to her discomfort. "You've never played softball?" Tony repeated. "Ever?"

"No. Never. But don't let that hold you back," she added hastily. "I'll enjoy watching while you play. I'll talk to Teresa."

"No way. It's long past time you had your first lesson," Tony argued flatly. "You're on my team."

Michelle shook her head. "I'm not going to make a fool of myself in front of your friends. Really, Tony, I'd rather just watch."

"Tough," he answered succinctly, his grin daring her to continue arguing with him. "You're playing. We need you," he added. "The teams will be uneven if you don't play, since Teresa's sidelined by her delicate condition."

"Delicate condition, my behind," his cousin-by-marriage retorted indelicately. "If Paul weren't so concerned about the ball hitting me in the stomach or something, I'd show you I could run circles around you—even in my 'delicate' condition!"

Tony laughed and gave Teresa a quick, affectionate hug. "You probably could, but let's not try it today, okay? Paul's nervous enough about his first baby."

"No kidding. The man has all but wrapped me in cotton during the past couple of months," Teresa muttered in exasperation. "He's even fetching his own beers these days."

"That *is* a miracle," Tony agreed solemnly, his eyes smiling.

"You guys aren't talking about me again?" Paul, a few years younger than Tony but very similar in appearance, joined them on the brick patio, tossing a softball from hand to hand. He smiled at his wife, his love for her apparent in his softened expression. "You're not trying to make me look bad in front of Tony's girlfriend, are you, *amore?*"

Teresa slid her arm around her husband's waist. "Of course not, Paul. You usually do that so well yourself."

Paul growled. Michelle laughed, even though she wasn't quite sure how she felt about being referred to as Tony's girlfriend. Not that it seemed to bother Tony. He slid an arm around her waist. "Hey, Paul, Michelle's never played softball before. I think we need to do something about that, don't you?"

"Definitely," Paul agreed enthusiastically. "Hey, everybody! Tony's girlfriend's a rookie! We've gotta show her how this game is played, right?"

Michelle's face flamed as the others immediately and teasingly agreed. Tony laughed, earning himself a poke in the side from her elbow. He grunted in response, but leaned over to brush his lips across her cheek. "Trust me, *cara*. This is going to be fun."

Chapter Seven

" ' T rust me. This is going to be fun.' Hmmph!"

Tony laughed at Michelle's disgruntled mutter, glancing across the console to where she sat in the passenger seat of his Jeep, glaring at the streak of dirt that decorated her clothing from neck to knees. "I never said you had to try to slide home during your first game, Michelle. That was your idea, remember?"

"I wasn't trying to slide home," she retorted. "You know perfectly well that I tripped over my shoelace."

He grinned. "Oh, is that what happened? To be honest, I thought you were starting the slide a little early. After all, you'd just left third base."

"And I would have made my first run if I hadn't tripped," she sighed, remembering her disappointment in being tagged out. She'd been so pleased just to hit the ball and make it to third base. When the next batter had connected, she'd started to run without noticing that her shoelace had come untied during the game.

"Don't worry about it, darlin'. You did fine for your first game. After all, our team won."

She made a wry face. "I really don't think that had much to do with my being one of the team members. But your friends were very patient with me."

"They liked you."

She was warmed by his words, pleased that she'd managed to fit in again with his family and friends. Though she still tended to be rather shy in such large, exuberant crowds, she'd enjoyed herself immensely today. She couldn't help comparing his casual family gatherings to her own past family functions, when a few impeccably dressed relatives gathered for dinner at one home or another. Food served on the finest china and crystal, self-conscious manners, conversations centered around politics or topical events, polite air kisses as opposed to the smacking embraces Tony's family exchanged.

"Do all your family members speak Italian?" she asked to distract herself from more comparisons. She'd been highly entertained by the occasional good-natured squabble during the exuberant ball game, conducted in amusing combinations of Italian and English slang. And again, Tony had slipped into emphatic Italian as easily as his cousins, to Michelle's secret delight.

Tony shrugged. "It's habit to fall into it when we get together. Besides, it pleases the aunts that we haven't completely lost touch with our heritage—or with each other."

Michelle thought fleetingly of her six brothers and sisters—would they have had barbecues and played softball together had they not been separated so young? If she were to contact them now, was there any chance that her children, if she ever had any, would grow up knowing and enjoying their cousins as much as Tony seemed to enjoy his?

"What are you thinking?" Tony asked suddenly, making her look up to find him watching her as he drove.

She pushed a strand of hair away from her face. "I was thinking about my brothers and sisters," she admitted. "Wondering if it's too late to ever feel like a family with them now. Whether they'd even be interested in trying. Maybe they have all the family they need now."

"And maybe they're as lonely as you are, wishing they had brothers and sisters to share their lives with," Tony returned. "Maybe Layla would give anything for a sister to talk to and go shopping with and whatever else sisters do together. Let me call her, Michelle. Let me set up a meeting."

Her throat tightened, her fingers clenching in her lap. "I don't—"

"Say yes."

She took a deep breath. "All right. Set it up."

The Jeep swerved fractionally before Tony straightened it. "Was that a yes?"

"Yes. You'll still go with me to meet her?"

"Of course. If you want me to."

"I want you to."

"Then I will." He waited a moment, then gave her a smile. "Was that really so hard?"

Her own smile felt shaky. "Yes."

He reached over the console to touch her cheek. "I don't think you'll regret it, Michelle. This first meeting was inevitable from the time you hired me to find them."

"I know," she admitted. "But I'm still nervous about it."

"I understand."

Oddly enough, she believed him. It was as if Tony understood exactly what she was feeling, in a way no one else had before him. Not even her adopted parents. Or Taylor. She'd never felt quite as close to anyone else as she did to Tony at this moment. And that realization was as terrifying as it was exhilarating.

Tony walked Michelle to her door, but refused her polite invitation to go in for a drink. "I'd better go. I'm sure you'd like to clean up and get some rest."

"A hot bath does sound nice," she agreed with a smile. "I think I used muscles this afternoon I didn't know I had."

"You'll feel them tomorrow." He rested one hand on the doorjamb beside her head, looming over her as she turned to face him. "I'll give you a call tomorrow, okay? We'll set up the meeting with your sister."

"All right. If she's agreeable, of course."

"Something tells me she will be." He lowered his head to kiss her, his hand still propped above her head. "Did you have a good time today?" he asked when he released her mouth, his head still bent to hers.

"Very much," she murmured, aware that his lips hovered only an inch or so from her own, wanting him to kiss her again. When he didn't immediately move to do so, she took the initiative and lifted her mouth to his.

Tony didn't let her effort go unrewarded. Crowding her against the door, he wrapped both arms around her and kissed her until her ears buzzed, her knees quivered, her heart raced frantically in her chest.

He groaned when he pulled away. "If I'm going to stick by my resolution to give you plenty of time to learn to trust me, I'd better go now. You could tempt a saint, Michelle Trent, and I'm no saint."

No, Tony was no saint. He was a devil in tight denim—and Michelle had never been more tempted in her life. But she sighed and nodded, putting another prudent three inches between them as she stepped sideways and reached for the doorknob. "Goodnight, Tony."

"Buonanotte, tesoro." He touched her cheek as he turned to leave. She opened her door and stepped into the house, uncertain whether her heart had melted in response to his seductive murmur or the incredible tenderness in that fleeting touch of his fingers against her face. She covered her still-warm cheek with her hand as she headed dreamily up the stairs to her bedroom.

Michelle was awakened early Sunday morning by the ringing of the telephone on her nightstand. Still half-asleep, she groped for it, knocking a paperback book to the the floor before successfully finding the phone. Pushing her hair out of her eyes, she croaked, "Hello?"

"Did I wake you?"

"Tony?" She rubbed her eyes and sat up.

He laughed, the low, rich sound making her shiver. "I'm sorry. You must have really been out of it."

"I'm awake now. Good morning."

"Buon giorno, carina."

"I like it when you do that," Michelle murmured, lingering remnants of sleep making her forget to guard what she said to him.

"When I do what?"

"When you speak Italian. Very sexy."

His voice deepened. "In that case, I'll have to speak to you in Italian more often."

"Oh, I think you're quite dangerous enough as you are," she said, coming fully awake with the unmistakable meaning in his tone. "Why did you call?"

"I just wanted to start my day out with the sound of your voice. I couldn't think of a nicer way to wake up."

"Oh." She blushed, though she knew it was silly.

"We'll have to do this more personally sometime."

"Tony..."

He laughed again at her mutter of reproval. "Sorry, *tesoro*. It's not fair of me to take advantage of you when you're still in bed. Um—let me rephrase that. It's not fair of me to take advantage of you when you're in your bed and I'm still in mine."

"You're incorrigible."

"So I've been told. How are those muscles you were complaining about after the ball game? Sore this morning?"

Michelle stretched lazily. "No. They're fine."

"Good. I'll make a ball player of you yet."

"Is that right?"

"Mmm. It was fun, wasn't it?"

She smiled, knowing her smile carried through her voice. "Yes. Very much so. Thank you for taking me."

"We'll have to do it again."

They talked for nearly an hour, chatting about nothing in particular, laughing frequently, until Tony reluctantly informed her that he had to go. He was having lunch with his parents and youngest brother that day and hadn't even showered yet, he explained. He promised Michelle he'd be in touch with her again very soon. She knew from his tone that he would follow through on that promise.

When her doorbell chimed Sunday afternoon, Michelle answered it, half expecting to find Tony on the other side, even though he hadn't said he'd come by. After talking to him that morning, she'd hung up the phone with a dreamy smile and a funny little buzz of excitement somewhere deep in the pit of her stomach. A buzz that hadn't quite gone away since.

She had never been courted quite so intriguingly—nor so successfully.

She hadn't at all expected to find her attorney on her doorstep.

"Carter!" she greeted him. "This is a surprise."

He stepped across the threshold, his distinguished face grave, his faded brown eyes focused intently on her face. In his early sixties, Carter Powell kept himself in good shape, only a hint of a paunch beneath his hand-tailored suit, his hair gray but still thick and stylishly groomed. "Hello, Michelle. I hope this isn't a bad time for you."

"No, of course not. Come into the den. Betty's not here this afternoon, but I'd be happy to make you some of the herbal tea you like."

"No, thanks. I can't stay long."

"You've been very busy the past week. I've tried to reach you."

"Yes, I know. I'm sorry I couldn't get back to you sooner. As you said, I've been busy."

Sitting across from the wing-back chair he'd selected, she dropped the polite chitchat. "You seem to have found the time to check up on me. Why did you call Tony D'Alessandro and ask him to drop my case, Carter? How did you find out that I'd hired him?"

"You know that I've always kept an eye on you, Michelle," Carter returned stiffly, lowering his gray brows in apparent offense at her tone. "I promised your father before he died that I would, and I have done so."

"You haven't answered my questions," she reminded him patiently. "What possible reason could you have for ordering Tony to call off the search for my siblings? And why would you do that without contacting me first?''

He sighed and patted his hair as though to make sure it was still neatly styled. "Perhaps I was out of line not to call you first," he admitted. "It has become such a habit to see to your best interests that I sometimes do so without considering whether you'd approve of my methods. But you have to understand, I was shocked when I found out that you'd embarked on this foolish, dangerous quest. I simply wanted to put an end to it as quickly and as painlessly as possible.

"Foolish? Dangerous?" Michelle shook her head in confusion. "I have no idea what you're talking about, Carter. I'm simply trying to locate the brothers and sisters I was separated from when I was a toddler."

"Michelle, you know nothing about these people, about the way they've turned out, how they've been raised. They're strangers, not family. What could you possibly have in common with them?"

"Genes, for one thing," she replied dryly.

He made an impatient gesture of dismissal. "An accident of birth. The important thing is that you've been raised as a Trent, given the responsibilities inherent with that name. Why would you want to risk being at the mercy of a bunch of strangers claiming a kinship you don't even remember?"

"I don't expect to be at anyone's mercy," Michelle answered calmly, though his words had renewed her own nervousness at the risks inherent in the quest she'd undertaken. "Tony is checking out my brothers and sisters very carefully. The one sister he's already located is a real-estate agent, married to an accountant, the mother of three young children. Very respectable, very safe, apparently."

"You've located one of your sisters?" Carter repeated sharply. "You've already been in contact with her?"

"No, not yet," Michelle replied. "Though I've authorized Tony to set up a meeting with her."

Carter shook his head. "I think you're making a grave mistake, Michelle. How do you know this woman won't expect you to help her put those kids through college?"

"Carter, you're overreacting. I have no intention of supporting any of my brothers and sisters or their families. I only want to meet them. Is that so hard for you to understand?"

"Yes, I'm afraid it is. You have friends, you have family. Why didn't you come to us if you felt something lacking in your life?"

Michelle wondered if Carter had been hurt that she hadn't consulted him before hiring Tony. After all, he had taken care of her for years. "My uncle and cousin live in California, Carter. I hardly know them. And as fond as I am of you, you have your own family, your own very busy life. This decision is already made, the search already started. You're just going to have to accept that. I promise you I'll be very careful. I'm not even going alone to meet my sister. Tony's going with me."

"Is that right? And what's in it for him?"

Michelle bristled at his tone. "Nothing's in it for him. He offered out of kindness when he sensed that I was nervous about the meeting."

"Yes, well, I assume you haven't been billed for his services as yet. I can assure you he isn't motivated entirely by the kindness of his heart. Private investigators don't make their money by offering free babysitting services to their clients."

"Babysitting services?" Michelle repeated slowly. She couldn't believe Carter was talking to her this way. He never had before. And then she realized that this was probably the first time she'd ever gone against his recommendations.

Something in her voice or her expression made Carter clear his throat and hold up a conciliatory hand. "Now, Michelle, I didn't mean to insult you. I simply meant that I think you should be wary of this man and his motives."

"I want you to leave Tony out of this," Michelle snapped. "Leave him alone, Carter. No more calls, no more interference. Is that clear?"

"There's no reason for you to take that tone, Michelle."

"Isn't there?" She stood. "If you'll excuse me, I have several things to do this afternoon. You know the way out, of course. If I have need for your legal services, I'll contact you."

Carter stood, shaking his head, looking unexpectedly amused. "If that didn't sound just like Harrison Trent when he was in a temper. You may have been adopted, but you are very much his daughter. He loved you very much, you know. It was important to him that I promised to watch out for you."

She couldn't help softening. "I know he loved me. I loved him, too," she murmured. "I miss him, and Mother. But I'm perfectly capable of looking out for myself."

"So I see. You've grown up on me, Michelle. It's very hard for me to realize that you're not the little pigtailed girl I used to ride on my knee."

Her temper cooling, Michelle reached out to the man she'd known all her life, touching her fingertips to his arm. "Thank you for being concerned about me, Carter. But trust me to know what's best for me. Believe me, I've learned the hard way about being too naive or trusting. I'll be careful."

"I hope so. By the way, Michelle, how did you find out about these siblings of yours?"

"Mother told me about them in a letter she left me. I found it in her things a few weeks after she died."

"Oh. That surprises me."

Michelle cocked her head thoughtfully. "You knew about them all along, didn't you?"

He hesitated only a moment before nodding. "Yes. From the beginning. And, to be honest, I agreed with your parents' decision not to tell you about them. I couldn't see that there was anything to be gained by doing so."

"Obviously my mother changed her mind."

Again, he nodded, his expression grave. "Yes. I hope she didn't make a mistake." He was almost to the door when he paused and looked back at her. "Michelle, will you do me one favor?"

"What is it?" she asked cautiously.

"Let me look over the final bill from this investigator before you pay it, just to make sure everything's legitimate. Instruct him to itemize. And don't give him any money in advance without a fully detailed statement, all right?"

Thinking half-guiltily of the thousand dollars she'd already paid Tony in advance, Michelle shifted her weight. "I'm sure your concern is unnecessary, Carter, but if it makes you feel better, I'll have you examine the bill before I pay it. I'm convinced you'll find it quite reasonable."

"Yes, well, we'll see. It doesn't hurt to be cautious. After all, you've only known this man a few weeks." *And you've known me twenty-four years,* his eyes added, just a touch of hurt still visible in their depths.

"All right. Thanks for coming by, Carter. I'll talk to you soon."

Michelle waited until she'd heard the front door close behind him before sinking bonelessly back down in her chair. Carter had seemed so utterly convinced that she was making a mistake in contacting her long-separated family.

What if he was right? Hadn't she worried about that for weeks before hiring Tony to find them? Hadn't her concerns been the reason she'd hesitated about contacting Layla once she'd been located?

What if she was only setting herself up to be hurt again?

She chewed unconsciously on her knuckles as her thoughts turned to Carter's warnings about Tony. She desperately wanted to believe Tony's assurances that he was interested in her, not her money. But, as Carter had reminded her, she really hadn't known Tony very long. And he *was* being paid to help her find her brothers and sisters.

Hadn't she known from the beginning that it was unwise to let personal feelings interfere with a professional relationship?

"...so then we piled the guy's intestines onto a tray and reached in—"

"Joe, please!" Carla D'Alessandro protested faintly, looking rather green at her youngest son's gory description of a surgery he'd recently assisted with. "Must you go into such gruesome detail?"

"Oh, sorry, Mom," the handsome young man apologized with a smile. "I didn't mean to gross you out."

From a chair nearby in his parents' den, Tony snorted. "Yeah, right. Like everyone sits around talking about abdominal surgery. You're going to lose a lot of friends if you don't change this new habit of talking shop to civilians, Joe."

"Your brother's going to make a fine doctor," Vinnie put in sternly, looking up from the Sunday sports section he'd been scanning. "You should be proud of him, not criticizing him for his dedication to his work."

"So there," Joe muttered, giving his older brother a smug grin.

"Yeah, well, just keep your needles and scalpels away from this bod," Tony retorted, patting his flat stomach. "I only trust my organs to a guy who knows what he's doing."

"I'd be happy to recommend a good veterinarian," Joe tossed back.

"Now, boys," Carla interceded patiently before Tony could respond. "I'd hate to have to send you to separate corners at your ages."

Tony laughed, knowing that she'd probably do so if she deemed it necessary, even though he was almost thirty-three and Joe twenty-four. Knowing as well that he and Joe would probably go.

Still grinning at the thought of sitting in a corner at his age, muttering and sucking his thumb, he stood and stretched, then tucked his knit shirt back into the waistband of his faded jeans. "Mind if I use the phone in the kitchen? I need to make a call."

"Bet you're calling a girl, right? And we all know your taste runs to blond, busty and borderline bright. So who's the bimbo-du-jour, Tony?"

Tony scowled at his grinning sibling. "Someday someone's going to rearrange that pretty face of yours, Giuseppe D'Alessandro. And it may just be me."

Joe cocked a dark eyebrow and made a show of flexing his biceps. *"Che cosa?"*

"You heard me, *fratello.*"

"Anytime you want to try it, brother."

"Boys," Carla murmured again, not bothering to look up from the business section of the Sunday newspaper.

Chuckling, Tony headed for the kitchen. Though he carried Michelle's number on a slip of paper in his wallet, it wasn't necessary for him to pull it out. The numbers came as easily to him as his own when he lifted the telephone receiver and pressed the buttons. He smiled in pleasure when Michelle, rather than her housekeeper, answered at the other end. "Hi."

"Tony."

Something about the way she said his name made his brows draw sharply downward. "Something wrong?"

"No, of course not. How are you?"

How are you? He frowned quizzically at the receiver, wondering why she'd gone back to the rather distant formality she'd projected the first few times they'd been together. "Okay," he answered cautiously. "I wanted to ask you if you're free tomorrow afternoon."

"I—uh—why?"

"How'd you like to go meet your sister?"

"You've talked to her?" Michelle asked quickly.

"Yeah." He smiled a little as he remembered the other woman's tearful excitement when he'd talked to her not long after he'd called Michelle earlier. "She's really looking forward to seeing you, Michelle. She sounded very nice."

"You're still going with me, aren't you?"

The faint trace of anxiety in the question pleased him. Whatever was bothering her today, at least she still wanted him with her for this meeting with her sister. She wouldn't want just anyone with her at such a personal time—would she? "Of course I am. Didn't I promise I would?"

"Thank you."

"No problem. So what are you doing this afternoon?" he asked casually, hoping for some clue to the sudden change in her behavior since their pleasant, hour-long call earlier that morning.

"Paperwork. And I just had a brief visit with my attorney."

Tony stiffened. "Powell?"

"Yes. He won't be bothering you again."

So that was it. Her longtime attorney had been preying on her old insecurities. "What did he say about me?"

"He's simply concerned about me, Tony. I told you that from the beginning. He's worried that my brothers and sisters will try to take advantage of me, and that..." She stopped abruptly.

Tony had no trouble completing the sentence. "And that I'll take advantage of you."

"He's just overly cautious."

"Did he try to talk you into firing me?"

"Of course not. He knows I intend to make my own decisions. He simply asked to see your final bill before I pay it. Itemized, of course. I assured him that he wouldn't find any problems with it, but if it made him feel better, I'd let him look it over."

Fingers clenching the receiver, Tony swallowed his fury. It wouldn't exactly look good for him to throw a fit over Powell's request to see his bill, he reminded himself. Michelle would wonder if he *was* trying to hide something, when the truth was that Tony was angry that Carter had done so much damage to the fragile trust Tony had established with Michelle during the past two days.

It was all he could do to keep from blurting out that he had no intention of taking money for anything he did for her. Theirs had long since stopped being a professional relationship. She probably wasn't ready to acknowledge that, either.

"All right. When it comes time to bill you, I'll send an extra copy," he forced himself to say evenly.

"Thank you for understanding. And, again, I'm sorry Carter bothered you. He was only trying to protect me."

Was he? Pushing aside his lingering doubts about the attorney's motivation, Tony abruptly changed the subject back to the plans for the following day. "I'll pick you up tomorrow afternoon—say, one o'clock?"

"I have some things to do tomorrow morning," Michelle countered. "I'll pick you up at one at your office."

His scowl deepened at the subtle but unmistakable power play. Why was it so important that Michelle drive tomorrow? he wondered disgruntledly. "Fine," he muttered, deciding to go along with her. For now. Until he had a chance to remind her in person that she had no reason to be suspicious of him.

"I'll see you tomorrow, then."

"Right. 'Bye, Michelle." He couldn't help hanging up with more force than he'd intended.

"Damn," he grumbled, slamming his fist on the kitchen countertop.

"Problems?"

Tony looked up to find his father watching quizzically from the doorway. "Where are Mom and Joe?"

"Your mother is helping Joe pack to go back to Houston," Vinnie replied dryly, rummaging in the refrigerator. "Sure hope that boy finds an old-fashioned sort of girl to marry. Your mother has him badly spoiled. Want a beer?"

"Yeah. Thanks."

"So does this suddenly lousy mood of yours have anything to do with Michelle Trent?" Vinnie asked, handing Tony a cold bottle.

Tony sighed and twisted the top of the beer, taking a long swallow before answering. "Yeah," he said finally. "She's been talking to her attorney today. He's got her questioning everything from my integrity to my fee scale."

"He's a cautious man. We warned you of that."

"Michelle should know by now that I can be trusted not to take advantage of her."

"Tony, she's known you a few weeks. She's known Carter Powell nearly all her life. Don't be too hard on her."

With a resigned nod, Tony set his beer on the counter and stared glumly at it. "I guess I'm just discouraged that I've still got such a long way to go to gain her trust. I thought we'd made some progress. Thanks to Powell, it looks like we're back to the starting line."

"Is it really so important for you to have Michelle's unconditional trust?" Vinnie asked quietly.

Tony looked at his father, trying to decide how to answer. Before he could form the words, Vinnie lifted one heavy eyebrow. "I see that it is," he said.

His face warming, Tony looked quickly away. "I'll admit I'm falling for her. Hard."

"After spending time with her again, I certainly understand why. But—be careful, Tony. She's been badly hurt. You can't rush her into trusting you before she's ready.''

Tony thought of the old fear in Michelle's eyes when she'd talked of her kidnapping, the old pain when she'd mentioned the man who'd wanted her money more than her. Would it be so hard for her to believe that all Tony wanted was to make sure no one ever hurt her like that again?

"I won't rush her," he promised his father. He only hoped he'd be able to keep that pledge.

Chapter Eight

Expecting to go into Tony's office Monday afternoon, Michelle guided her car into a parking space at exactly one o'clock. But before she could even reach for the door handle, the passenger door opened and Tony leaned in. His black hair was attractively wind-tossed, his dark eyes gleaming. He wore a white shirt, a navy-and-burgundy floral tie, a sport coat and jeans. He was probably the most naturally sexy man Michelle had ever known.

"Hi. You really should keep those doors locked, you know. Some weirdo could climb right into the car with you."

"So I see," she replied, watching him slide in and reach for his seatbelt. She hoped her casual tone hid the unexpected burst of excitement that rushed through her at seeing him again. "Perhaps I *should* be more careful."

"Smart aleck," He leaned across the console and kissed her lightly before she'd been aware of his intention. "You look especially nice today. Did you dress up for me or your sister?"

Resisting the impulse to touch the tip of her tongue to her tingling lips, she cleared her throat and restarted the engine, suddenly pleased that she'd selected the becoming jewel-tone print dress. "For my sister, of course. Why should I go to this much trouble for you?"

"More insults, *cara?*" He sounded absurdly pained.

Biting her lip against a sudden grin, she nodded. "I told you it just seems to come naturally around you."

"I'll have to see what I can do about that."

But he didn't sound particularly disturbed, Michelle noted, turning a quick look at him as she guided the car out of his parking lot. In fact, he sounded quite pleased with himself about something. "You know where we're going, I assume?"

"Of course. Your sister gave me very clear directions."

"You wrote them down?" Michelle asked pointedly, looking at his empty hands.

He tapped one forefinger to his temple. "I assure you they're in a safe place."

She gave him a skeptical look. "I hope you mean they're pinned to the inside of your jacket."

He laughed. "You don't give an inch, do you, darlin'? Just drive toward Fort Worth and I'll let you know when to turn."

More relaxed than she'd been since Tony had called to tell her a meeting with Layla had been arranged, Michelle obligingly headed west. Did he know how nervous she'd been when she'd dressed that morning? How her stomach had clenched into knots at the thought of meeting this sister she didn't know? How close she'd come to calling the whole thing off?

"I talked to Bob O'Brien this morning—one of my operatives," Tony added in explanation. "He's got a lead on your sister Lindsay."

"He's found her?" Michelle asked quickly, wondering if she were ready for another meeting so soon.

"No. But we have learned that she was adopted. We think we may even have found the adoptive family's name."

"You don't know where she is now?"

"No," Tony replied again. "Not yet. But there's a strong chance we'll find her with the leads we have now."

"When you do," Michelle said slowly, accepting his ability to achieve the results he promised, "I don't want her—or her family—contacted. Not yet. I don't want anyone pressuring her either for or against meeting me. And... I'd like to wait and see how this meeting with Layla goes before I decide whether to try to make contact with the others," she admitted.

"I understand." He twisted in his seat and draped an arm over the back, his hand dangling close to her shoulder. "Are you nervous?"

"Not as much as I was earlier," she confessed, slanting him a smile that felt just a bit shy. "I'm glad you're going with me."

His eyes darkened in satisfaction. "So am I, Michelle."

Michelle quickly turned her attention back to the road ahead. "Feel free to turn on the radio, if you like," she offered. "Or there are CDs in the console."

Obviously curious about her tastes in music, Tony opened the console and rummaged inside. "Interesting," he murmured a moment later.

She smiled. "Why?" Though, of course, she knew. Her music collection ran from Barry Manilow to Bob

Seger, Prince to Garth Brooks, Rachmaninoff to Miles Davis, Barbra Streisand to Tanya Tucker. Tony wouldn't be the first to point out that it was an eclectic mix, to say the least, and one not generally expected of her.

"Rock, pop, jazz, country, classical, show tunes. About the only types missing are rap and opera."

"I have to draw the line somewhere. No offense to your Italian heritage, of course."

Chuckling, he selected a disc and slid it into the dash-mounted player. "So we have a taste for country-and-western music in common. I didn't expect that. You're just full of surprises, aren't you, *cara?*" His tone caressed her almost as effectively as a physical touch.

She swallowed hard and tried to answer coherently. "I've told you my parents tended to be overprotective when I was growing up. I spent a great deal of time alone with only my dolls and my stereo for company. I wasn't choosy about which stations I listened to, as long as the music was good."

"Bet your mother wouldn't have liked this at all," Tony guessed as Garth Brooks belted into "Much Too Young (To Feel This Damn Old)."

Michelle laughed. "You're right. She hated country. And rock. And pop and jazz. She gave only borderline approval to show tunes, telling me I should enrich my mind with the classics rather than wasting time with popular garbage."

Though he looked as though he would have liked to comment, Tony only nodded. They rode for a few minutes without speaking, yet they weren't uncomfortable. And then Tony asked, "Do you ever think about having a family of your own? You talk about being lonely as a child, but don't you still feel that way sometimes?"

"Sometimes," Michelle admitted cautiously. "I have my work now, of course. And my friends."

"You like kids?"

"I wouldn't spend four or five days a month rocking babies if I didn't," she pointed out.

"Want any of your own?"

She cleared her throat. "Eventually. Being adopted, I used to worry about any medical conditions I might pass along to my children. Now I suppose I'll find out whatever I need to know from the records you've uncovered."

He shrugged. "I didn't see anything in your family history to be concerned about."

"How about my father's alcoholism?" Michelle asked with a bitterness she couldn't quite conceal.

"Lots of people have alcoholism in their families," he reminded her. "There is evidence that the tendency is inherited, but it's not inevitable. After all, you don't seem to have a problem with it."

"No. But I'd be very careful to make sure my children knew there was a possibility they'd inherited the tendency," she added. "My adoptive parents weren't heavy drinkers and they always stressed moderation to me. I would do the same for my children."

"Children? Plural?"

She nodded. "I know from experience how it feels to be an only child."

He touched her cheek, his finger tracing a line down her jaw. "I think you turned out just fine."

She shifted in her seat. "Thanks."

He dropped his hand, though it still rested so close to her shoulder she could almost feel its warmth. "I like big families myself. I've always wanted a houseful of kids, once I found the right woman to have them with."

Since the conversation was becoming a little uncomfortable, and more than a little too personal, Michelle swiftly redirected it. "You'd mentioned that you were planning to spend Sunday with your parents. Did you have a nice visit?"

"Yeah. Joe drove up from Houston, so the only one missing was Mike. He couldn't get away from Austin. The rest of us had a good time, though. Joe's a real clown."

"He's doing well in medical school?"

"Oh, yeah. He's the genius of the family," Tony admitted with unmistakable affection. "Going to make one hell of a good doctor."

"You sound quite proud of him."

"I am. Just don't tell him I said so."

Which, of course, sounded as though Tony assumed Michelle would be meeting his brother. She was having enough trouble dealing with the possibility of getting to know her own family, much less more of Tony's, she thought edgily.

In automatic reaction to the opening piano notes of one of her all-time favorite songs, Michelle turned up the volume.

"'The Dance,'" Tony murmured, indicating he'd recognized the tune, as well. "I like this one."

"It's one of my favorites. Such beautiful accompaniment."

"Nice lyrics, too."

They were quiet during the poignant ballad of a man who looks back at his life and wonders if he would have missed the pleasure to avoid the pain had he been able to predict the future. The song had appealed to Michelle from the first time she'd heard it, had been the reason she'd purchased this CD.

In a country western twang, the singer concluded that life is better left to chance. If anyone's life had been subject to the whims of chance, Michelle figured hers had. The trip she was making now was certainly a prime example.

Michelle parked her car and then sat with her hands clenched around the steering wheel, staring at the house in front of her. Though modest, it was nice, brick-and-vinyl siding with window shutters and flowering bushes just bursting into bloom along the front. The lawn was neatly trimmed. A tricycle and a small red wagon sat under a greening pecan tree at one side. The place was a far cry from Michelle's own impressive mansion, but looked very much like a home.

And inside, her sister waited to see her again for the first time in twenty-four years.

"I'm not sure this was such a good idea," she heard herself saying, her voice sounding rather small.

Tony's left hand covered her white-knuckled right one on the steering wheel. "Everything's going to be fine, Michelle," he assured her quietly. "I don't think you're going to regret doing this."

She took a deep breath and looked at him. "You'll help keep the conversation going if I can't think of anything to say?"

He smiled and leaned over to kiss her lightly. "You bet I will. But if you run out of things to say, you can always start insulting me again. As you've pointed out more than once, that comes naturally for you."

He began to draw back, only to stop in surprise when Michelle reached out to clutch his lapel. "Tony," she whispered, drawing him closer. "Thank you for being here with me."

"Anytime, darlin'," he murmured, and kissed her again, more lingeringly this time.

Rather flustered, Michelle made Tony wait until she'd quickly repaired her lipstick before they stepped out of the car. He took her hand as they started up the walk. She didn't resist.

Tony pressed the doorbell. The door opened before the chimes had faded away inside. Staring at the woman who'd opened the door, Michelle had the oddest feeling that she was looking at an image of herself in ten years or so. She hadn't really expected to see so many resemblances between herself and Layla Walker Samples.

Eyes the same color blue as her own filled with tears as Layla raised one hand to her throat in a show of emotion. "Shelley?"

"Michelle," she corrected, her right hand tightening in Tony's left. "And this is Tony D'Alessandro."

"We spoke on the phone yesterday," Tony said, offering his free hand. "It's nice to meet you, Mrs. Samples."

"Please call me Layla. Come in."

Surreptitiously studying her sister as she released Tony's hand and stepped into the entryway, Michelle noted the strands of gray in thirty-four-year-old Layla's glossy brown hair, the faint lines at the corners of her eyes. Had their mother looked like this when she died? Would the other sister and brothers share so many resemblances to herself?

A comfortably rounded, sandy-haired man who looked to be in his late thirties stood when the quiet threesome entered the inexpensively decorated living room. "This is my husband, Kevin," Layla explained, stepping close to Kevin's side. "The children are playing at the neighbors' house this afternoon, so we can talk."

Michelle glanced at a large studio portrait on one wall. Two dark-haired, blue-eyed little girls sat primly beside a grinning little boy who looked very much like Kevin. "They're very attractive children," she offered tentatively.

Layla smiled and waved Tony and Michelle to a plain blue sofa. "Thank you. Could I get you something to drink? Iced tea? Coffee?"

"No, thank you," Michelle answered, clasping her hands in her lap.

"None for me, either, thanks," Tony seconded. He glanced from Michelle to Layla and said, "It's surprising how much the two of you look alike. Was there a strong resemblance between all the children of your family, Layla?"

Grateful for the opening, Layla nodded and reached for a faded old photograph on the table beside her chair. "This is the only thing I have left from that time," she explained, passing the photograph to Tony. "My foster mother helped me keep up with it, because she thought it was important for me to remember my family."

Michelle hesitated a moment before looking at the photo. When she did, she spotted herself immediately, looking much as she had in the early portraits Alicia had commissioned of her. She was sitting on the lap of a girl of perhaps ten—Layla, obviously. Studying the picture more closely, she saw that Layla still looked much as she had then. An older boy stood behind Layla. His hair was darker, his features less delicate, but the resemblances were there, particularly in the blue eyes. Jared, she thought.

At Layla's left sat a chubby boy of seven or eight, his broad grin showing several missing teeth, his pug nose freckled, his hair lighter than his older brother's, though his eyes were as blue. That would be Miles. Michelle's throat tightened at the thought that she'd never had the chance to know the boy with the mischievous grin. And now she never would.

At the far right of the photograph stood two eerily identical boys in matching clothing, their dark brown hair combed exactly the same, sticking up with the same cowlick in front, their blue eyes fixed on the camera. Only their expressions were different—one serious, the other smiling. Which was Joey, Michelle wondered, and which Bobby?

Finally she made herself look at the woman in the center of the photo, the woman she'd avoided looking at until now. Her mother. A woman who looked older than her late twenties, whose thin face was already lined with weariness, her pale eyes mirroring the hard times she'd known. A baby, no more than eight weeks old, slept in her arms, tiny features indistinguishable from most babies of that age. Michelle realized that Hazel had already been widowed by that time and would live only a few months after the portrait had been taken.

"She won a family portrait in a draw held at the local supermarket," Layla explained softly when Michelle had been silent for several long minutes. "She was hoping for the grand prize of a month's worth of groceries. God knows we could have used them more—but I've treasured this photograph."

Michelle looked up at her sister. "You remember her."

"Yes."

"What was she like?"

Layla hesitated, then moved her hands in a frustrated, vulnerable gesture. "Tired," she said. "Sad. Quiet. But sometimes she laughed at something we said and she looked so different. I always thought she was beautiful when she laughed. And sometimes she sang when she rocked one of you little ones to sleep. She had a lovely voice."

Michelle gazed at the photo and tried to remember being rocked in those arms, longed for just a vague echo of a pleasant voice singing her to sleep. But when she thought of a mother's voice comforting her in the night, it was Alicia Culverton Trent she remembered. Feeling uncomfortable, as though she should apologize to the woman in the photograph, she turned her attention back to her sister. "I didn't know I had brothers and sisters until my adopted mother died a few months ago."

"I know. Tony explained when he called me." Layla tucked a strand of hair behind her ear and sighed. "Maybe it was better for you that way. Better that you didn't remember. It was a long time before I could stop missing my brothers and sisters and get on with my own life."

"Layla wanted so much to find you again," Kevin interceded when his wife's voice broke. "It was my idea for her to register with the service that helps reunite families separated by adoption. We hadn't been married very long and we couldn't really afford to hire someone to search for everyone. And Layla was always afraid to intrude on her brothers' and sisters' lives, worried that they wouldn't want her to show up and remind them of those hard times."

"We don't know if the others will feel that way," Michelle said, glancing again at the photograph. "But we have some leads on them. I think I want to contact them, see if they want to meet us again."

"Oh, I wish you would," Layla murmured wistfully. "I'd love to see them again. Jared and the twins and the baby. If only Miles..." She pressed her lips together and shook her head. "It's so hard to believe he's dead. I still think of him as the happy little boy he was before."

Tony had broken the news to Layla during the call. Michelle was relieved that he'd taken care of that already. Obviously, Layla had taken the news hard. "You haven't mentioned our father," she made herself say, though she wasn't sure she wanted to know. "What was he like?"

Layla made a face. "That's not an easy question to answer. He was gone so much, none of us really knew him. When he was home, he sat in a chair and drank and our mother waited on him hand and foot. I don't know where he went when he left and I don't know why he kept coming back. I don't know why they kept having children together when they could hardly feed the older ones. To be honest, our lives didn't change that much after he died, though Mama got even quieter than she had been before."

"You must have been the one to take care of the rest of us when she worked or when she was sick," Michelle guessed.

Layla smiled a little and nodded. "Jared and I did. Sometimes I felt like the mother of the family. I usually cooked the meals and did the laundry, gave you your baths and tucked you in bed. Maybe that's why I've been so comfortable with my own children—the routine was very familiar to me. I enjoy it."

She smiled at her husband, and Michelle watched with a faint touch of envy. This was obviously a close, happy home, she thought, unable to avoid comparing it to her own big, empty house. She pushed the unbecoming thought away and urged her sister to tell her more about their time together.

Layla cooperated happily, entertaining them with anecdotes of childhood pranks and adventures, obviously remembering those years quite clearly. "You loved jelly sandwiches, Michelle. You asked for them all the time. It was one of the few things we could afford. Do you remember?"

Michelle shook her head, unable to remember ever having a jelly sandwich. Certainly not after she'd gone to live with the Trents. She decided that, though the times must have been hard for the troubled Walker family, there had still been love in the home, and the laughter of children. It was nice to know.

As he'd promised, Tony participated in the conversation, making it easier for Michelle to join in as well. And Kevin was a pleasant, good-natured man with a contagious smile who seemed pleased to meet his new sister-in-law. It was glaringly obvious that he also adored his wife.

"...and there you were, sitting in a rocking chair with the baby in your lap, singing 'Old Mcdonald' while she stared up at you with her big blue eyes," Layla was saying, laughing and shaking her head in remembered exasperation.

Realizing her attention had strayed, Michelle listened more closely.

"I just about had a heart attack. You were so little yourself and you could have hurt her, but you were being so careful. I put her back in her crib and fussed at you for taking her out and you looked up at me and said, 'You was busy, Layla.'"

Startled, Michelle frowned. "But Mother—my adopted mother told me I was a late talker. I was nearly three when she got me and she said I didn't say more than a word or two for the next six months. She even took me to doctors who said there was nothing wrong with me and that I'd talk when I was ready—which, obviously, I did.''

Layla looked puzzled. ''But you talked early, Shel—um, Michelle. By fourteen months you were already using complete sentences. We all thought you were a genius or something.''

''Obviously your silence was in reaction to the changes in your life,'' Tony suggested.

''I suppose so,'' Michelle murmured, unable to remember how long it had taken her to adjust to her new home, her new parents. It seemed now as though they'd always been in her life.

Perhaps that was the reason she couldn't remember anything else of her natural family, she mused. Maybe it had been easier for a confused child to pretend she'd never known a home other than the one she'd ended up in, never known a mother other than the one who read her to sleep every night until she was eleven and pronounced herself too old for the ritual.

A burst of noise from the back door to the house made all four adults look around just as three children scampered into the room. ''We're home, Mama,'' the oldest child, Dawne, announced unnecessarily.

''So I see.'' Gathering two-year-old Brittany into her lap, Layla looked at Michelle. ''These are my children. Dawne, Keith and Brittany.''

Finding herself fascinated by Brittany, who could have doubled for herself at the same age, Michelle smiled. ''Hello.''

''Who are you?'' Keith asked bluntly.

''I'm your Aunt Michelle,'' she answered, turning her smile toward Layla. ''Your mother's sister.''

Her eyes going bright, Layla returned the smile, her own notably unsteady.

* * *

The visit lasted another forty-five minutes before Michelle realized it was time to go. By that time, she was thoroughly charmed by her nieces and nephew, as well as her newly found sister and brother-in-law. She decided to thank Tony as soon as they were alone for persuading her to allow him to arrange this meeting.

"We really must be going," she said, rising from the couch. Tony did the same.

Pushing herself out of her chair, Layla shook her head in admiration. "You're still full of grace," she murmured.

At Michelle's look of puzzled inquiry, she smiled. "You wouldn't remember, of course. It was a family joke that each child was born on a different day of the week. Mama used to recite that poem to us. You know, 'Monday's child is fair of face.' I was born on Monday. Jared loved to make me blush by teasing me about that line."

"Michelle must have been Tuesday's child," Tony commented, smiling at her. "I noted how gracefully and socially correct she was the first time I met her."

Michelle made a face at him, then frowned at her sister. "How could we each have been born on different days of the week? What about the twins?"

Layla laughed. "Joey was born at 11:55 Thursday night, Bobby ten minutes later, which made it 12:05 Friday morning. Jared was Saturday's child, and Lindsay was born on a Sunday. Miles was Wednesday's child."

She paused for a moment, her expression reflective. "The lines of the poem seemed to fit everyone but him. He was supposed to be full of woe, yet he was the happiest, best-natured little boy. . ."

She sighed and shook her head as if shaking off echoes of the past. "I'm so glad you found me, Michelle. I hope we see each other again soon. I haven't stopped missing you—any of you—for twenty-four years."

Michelle took a tentative step toward Layla. "I've always wanted a sister," she said. "I don't intend to lose you now that I've found you."

With a small, choked sound, Layla threw her arms around her, hugging tightly. Michelle returned the hug, her eyes burning, her heart full. She didn't know how it had happened, exactly, but this felt so right, so natural. She had found her sister.

She drew back with a shaky smile. "You'll bring your family to my house for dinner soon? I'll call you."

"We'll be there," Layla promised. She turned to Tony and held out her hand. "I don't know how to thank you."

He took her hand in his larger one. "I'm afraid I can't take credit for finding you. Thanks to your foresight in registering with the service, it only took a couple of telephone calls."

"But you're still looking for the others," Layla argued, "and I think you'll find them. It means so much to me to think that I may get to see them all again after so many years. If Kevin and I can help with the expenses . . ."

"I'm taking care of that," Michelle interrupted firmly, noting Tony's suddenly uncomfortable expression. "I began this search, remember? The expense isn't a problem."

Kevin took Michelle's hand. "You've made my wife very happy today."

She smiled at him. "I'll see you again soon, Kevin."

"Of course. We're family."

The children all politely bade Michelle and Tony goodbye. Michelle's throat tightened when little Brittany raised her chubby face for a kiss and said, "'Bye, Aunt 'Chelle.''

"'Bye, sweetheart." Michelle looked half-pleadingly toward Tony, needing to get away quickly before she burst into tears. He reacted as though he'd read her mind, courteously bringing the visit to an end and escorting Michelle to the car.

"Want me to drive?" he offered as they approached the Lexus.

She nodded and handed him the keys. "Thank you."

Michelle was grateful that Tony didn't press her to speak during the first fifteen minutes of the drive. She needed that time to steady her emotions, to come to terms with the changes that had occurred in her life with this reunion with her sister.

When she did begin to talk, it was about Layla and Kevin and the children, how nice they all seemed, how happy and comfortable their home was, how glad she was to have found them. Tony listened with a satisfied smile, adding little more to the conversation than an occasional agreement.

Over halfway home, Michelle suddenly realized how much she'd been talking. She stopped with a self-conscious laugh, wondering at her uncharacteristic lapse of manners. "I'm sorry. You must be ready for me to be quiet."

"Not at all," he countered without hesitation. "I'm glad you're so happy about the meeting. I'd hoped it would turn out this way."

She nodded. "It could have been so different, of course. We could have been stiff and uncomfortable with each other, found nothing in common, no reason to continue seeing each other."

"True." Tony made a show of wiping his brow with one hand. "You have no idea how I worried about that, since I was the one who nagged you into meeting them."

She laughed and shook her head. "I don't think you lost any sleep over it."

"Don't bet on it," he replied, sounding suddenly so serious that she wondered if he really *had* been as worried as he claimed. Before she could ask, he changed the subject.

Though she went along with the ploy willingly enough, Michelle found herself wondering wistfully if she was really becoming more than just another case to Tony. Or did he give such personal, supportive service to all his clients?

The problem was that he had become so much more than just a business associate to her. He'd become a friend. Maybe more than a friend. And she wasn't at all sure how she felt about that.

Chapter Nine

Tony's emotions were uncomfortably mixed as he listened to Michelle talk about her sister. He was pleased, of course, that the meeting had gone so well. He hadn't entirely been joking when he'd said he'd felt a certain responsibility for the outcome. And he was happy that she and Layla seemed to have the potential to build a lasting, mutually supportive relationship. He never wanted Michelle to be lonely again.

The simple, rather painful, decidedly unbecoming truth was that he found himself jealous of the ease with which Layla seemed to have earned Michelle's affection—and even her trust. With Layla, Michelle had eased down the barriers she kept between herself and everyone else, barriers Tony had only managed to peek through once or twice.

He wanted those barriers between them gone.

Turning into the parking lot of his office, he parked Michelle's Lexus beside his Jeep. "Have dinner with me?" he asked without preface.

She blinked at his abrupt tone, then nodded. "Why don't you follow me home. My housekeeper's baking fish for dinner. There's always enough for a guest."

"Sounds good. I've got a few things to wrap up here first. How about if I see you in—say, an hour and a half?"

"Fine." She reached for her door handle. "Thank you again for going with me, Tony."

He opened the driver's door and climbed out from behind the wheel, not bothering to respond to her repeated gratitude. He waited beside the open door until Michelle rounded the car and joined him there. "Drive carefully."

"I wasn't planning on hot-rodding home."

"See that you don't." He tilted her chin up and pressed a kiss to her smile.

"You seem to be making a habit of that," Michelle observed when he released her.

He studied her expression, unable to quite read her eyes. "Was that a complaint?"

She thought about it a moment, then smiled and shook her head. "No."

"Good. See you later."

All in all, he decided, his hands in the pockets of his jeans as he watched her drive away, the day hadn't gone badly after all.

And it wasn't over yet.

Tony was due to arrive for dinner in less than half an hour when Michelle's phone rang. Thinking it might be

him, she snatched up the receiver of the den extension.
"Hello."

"Hi. It's Taylor."

"Oh, hi. How was the date Friday night?"

"The food was fine. The conversation definitely needed spice. How was yours?"

"We had fun. But I really want to tell you about what I did today."

"Yeah? What'd you do?"

Michelle smiled, anticipating Taylor's excitement. "I met my sister Layla. As well as her husband and her children."

"You met her? Really?"

"Yes. Tony went with me. We spent several hours visiting with them. Oh, Taylor, you'd really like her. She's so nice—and I look so much like her! It was sort of strange at first to look at her and see so much of myself, but after a while it felt really comfortable. And the children are adorable, and so well-behaved. I'm having them over for dinner soon. I'd love for you to meet them."

"Michelle, this is wonderful!"

"I know. I never would have imagined it would turn out like this. I was so worried. Tony kept trying to reassure me it would work out, but I didn't really believe him until I met Layla."

"Layla must have been thrilled to see you again. She remembered you, of course."

It wasn't a question, but Michelle answered it anyway. "Yes. Clearly. She said she would have recognized me right away because of the family resemblances. She told me so many stories about when we were little, in such detail that I almost felt as though I remembered the incidents she described. Tony told me on the way home that he could tell Layla had never really gotten over being separated from her brothers and sisters and that he thinks it meant the world to her for us to contact her."

"So how did it really feel, Michelle? Was it like making a new friend? Or did you really feel as though you were talking to your sister?"

"Both," Michelle answered after a moment of thought. "At first, she was a nice stranger. But the more she talked about the games I enjoyed as a baby and the toys I played with and the foods I liked, the more I felt a real connection, you know? Tony said—"

Suddenly aware of just how often she'd brought Tony's name into the conversation, Michelle paused self-consciously. "Well, um . . ."

"Sounds like things between you and Tony are getting very interesting."

Michelle cleared her throat. "I like him," she admitted. "He's been very good to me since I hired him, gone beyond my expectations of finding my family and reuniting me with them."

"You don't really think he's done that just because he's dedicated to his career, do you?"

"What do you mean?"

Taylor laughed. "Michelle, I saw the way the man looked at you Friday. He's definitely besotted. And you were looking back at him exactly the same way."

"Oh, I—"

"Don't try to deny it. I think it's great. You deserve a relationship with a nice guy for a change."

"It's a little too soon to be talking about a relationship," Michelle said cautiously. "Tony and I have only known each other a few weeks."

"But you're giving him a chance, right?"

"We're . . . seeing each other," Michelle admitted, thinking of his imminent arrival for dinner.

As though in response to her thoughts, the doorbell rang. She knew Betty would let Tony in, but she didn't want him to catch her talking about him with her friend. "I'd better go, Taylor. Betty has dinner ready."

"You wouldn't be evading the issue, would you?" Taylor demanded with mock severity.

"No, of course not. Why don't we have lunch one day this week and we'll talk more."

"I'd love to, but I can't. That's why I called—to tell you I'll be out of town for a couple of weeks. A client wants some fashion shots taken on Galveston Island, and they're flying models in from New York. It's going to be a big job—a little more notice would have been nice. But the client's always supposed to be right, you know. At least, that's what they keep telling me."

"Then we'll get together when you get back in town," Michelle said, smiling at Tony as he strolled into the room. He'd changed, she noticed, into a dark green cotton shirt and charcoal-gray slacks. He looked slim, dark and entirely too handsome for her peace of mind. It was suddenly difficult to keep her mind on her conversation with Taylor.

"I'll call you when I get back," Taylor was saying. "I'd love to hear more about your sister. I can't wait to meet her."

Michelle's pulse shot into overtime when Tony took her hand and raised it to his mouth, his lips warm and soft as they brushed her knuckles. "Oh, yes, of course, Taylor," she said quickly, giving Tony a repressive frown. "We'll talk when you get back."

"Right. Guess I'd better let you go. Sounds like you've got something better to do than talk on the phone."

Michelle tried to speak normally, though it wasn't easy since Tony had turned his attention to her neck. "I—

uh—what do you mean?'' she asked just as he kissed the soft, vulnerable spot beneath her left ear. Her breath caught in her throat.

Taylor's laugh was embarrassingly knowing. Michelle had the strangest feeling that her friend knew her neck was being nibbled as they spoke. ''Tell Tony I said hi,'' Taylor murmured. ''Have fun, Michelle.''

Michelle's cheeks were flaming when she hung up. ''I can't believe you did that!'' she accused Tony, rounding on him.

He stepped back, looking absurdly innocent. ''Did what?''

''Kissed me—like that—right in front of Taylor!''

He laughed, his dark eyes sparkling devilishly. ''Michelle, you were on the phone. I really doubt that she could tell I was kissing you.''

''Trust me. She knew,'' Michelle muttered.

''And would it matter if she did?'' he asked, his tone casual but his eyes suddenly watchful. ''Does it embarrass you to have your friends think you're getting involved with a lowly P.I.?''

''What an awful thing to say,'' she scolded him, planting her fists on her hips. ''As though there's anything wrong with what you do for a living. Or as if I'd be snobby enough to care.''

His smile deepened. ''Then why are we wasting time arguing? How about giving me a real kiss?''

''How about if you...''

Her decidedly indelicate suggestion was muffled into the depths of his mouth. Michelle resisted for all of thirty seconds. And then she put her arms around his neck and kissed him back exactly the way she'd been wanting to all day.

In immediate reaction, Tony tightened his arms around her, pulling her as close to him as physically possible. He deepened the kiss, his tongue slipping between her eagerly parted lips. Michelle closed her eyes and tilted her head back to give him better access.

It seemed like a very long time before Tony lifted his head to give both of them a much needed-chance to breathe. Michelle wondered dazedly if her eyes looked as glazed as his did.

"Whoa," he murmured, his voice husky, his smile shaky. "Now, *that* was a kiss!"

Her arms were still around his neck. Suddenly self-conscious, Michelle dropped them and stepped back. To hide their unsteadiness, she pushed her hands into the pockets of the pleated white slacks she'd worn with a teal silk blouse. "I'm sure Betty has dinner ready. Are you hungry?" she asked, trying to sound somewhat normal. Knowing she failed miserably.

"Honey, I'm ravenous," he answered deeply. It was clearly obvious that he wasn't talking about food.

Her blush deepening, Michelle cleared her throat. "Behave," she ordered him, somewhat desperately.

He laughed. "Yes, ma'am. Maybe we'd better eat. Before I get—um—distracted again."

Betty served dinner with her usual efficiency, coming in frequently to check on them and refill their drink glasses, occasionally giving Michelle a look to signify approval of her guest. "How about dessert?" Betty asked Tony after noticing that his Sevres dinner plate had been cleaned of the baked fish served in her own delicate sauce. "I've made a cheesecake with a mixed fruit topping."

"Sounds good. Thank you." Tony took a sip of the excellent white wine served in Waterford crystal, then smiled across the table at Michelle as Betty hurried away for the desserts. "Do all your guests get such luxurious treatment?"

She met his eyes over the low flowers-and-candles centerpiece artfully arranged on an octagonal beveled mirror. "They do when Betty likes them."

"Then I'm glad I passed the test," he murmured, glancing around at the antique cherry furniture and heavy crystal chandelier. "It wouldn't be hard to get used to this."

Following his gaze, she tried to see the dining room through the eyes of someone who hadn't grown up in the house. She supposed it was quite elegant. But to her it was home, for as far back as she could remember.

Thinking of Layla's much more modest surroundings, she wondered how her sister would feel the first time she saw Michelle's home. She hoped it wouldn't intimidate her. "I really would like to have Layla and Kevin over for dinner soon. Do you think they'd be comfortable here?"

Tony shrugged. "I don't know why not. You and Betty have certainly made me feel welcome tonight." His smile reminded her of the kisses they'd shared before dinner.

Michelle was relieved when Betty entered with their desserts, promising to bring in coffee when they were ready. Not that Michelle had much appetite left. Though normally she would have thoroughly enjoyed the excellent cheesecake, tonight she was all too aware of Tony sitting across the table.

Studying him from beneath her eyelashes, she watched the candlelight dance in his black hair, admired the ripple of muscles beneath his dark shirt when he reached for his wineglass. His firm, beautifully molded lips closed around a bite of the creamy dessert and she had to swallow a low moan as she instinctively imagined those lips on her skin. It wasn't at all hard to imagine herself in bed with him, his dark head bent to her breasts, his tanned, callused hands caressing her body. In fact, at the moment it was very hard to think of anything else.

Tony glanced up to find her watching him. Whatever he saw in her eyes made him stop eating. Very slowly, he set his fork on his plate. Michelle looked quickly down at her own barely touched dessert, though she knew it was too late to hide her reactions to him.

It had never been so difficult before to conceal her feelings. She'd learned early in life to don a protective social mask whenever it seemed prudent to do so. So why couldn't she keep that mask in place whenever she was around this man?

"Michelle?" His voice glided over her like satin—smooth, seductive.

"What?" she whispered without looking up from her plate.

"Would Betty be terribly insulted if we didn't wait for her to serve coffee?"

"I'm—" She stopped to moisten her lips. "No, of course not."

"Then would you mind taking me on a tour of the rest of the house now? I'd really like to see your room," he added huskily.

Her eyelashes flew up, her gaze meeting his across the table. She didn't have to ask what he meant, or to wonder at his sudden interest in her home. It was quite clear that he wanted to make love with her. Now.

Her throat tightened in sudden panic. She knew that all she had to do was say no, or change the subject. Tony wouldn't push her into something she wasn't ready for.

Sometime during the past few weeks, she'd learned to trust him that much.

The real reason she was suddenly trembling, suddenly petrified, wasn't because Tony had indicated he wanted to make love with her. The truth was that she wanted him, too—so badly she could almost taste it—and she simply didn't know what to do about it.

It had been so long since she'd been intimately involved with anyone, so long since she'd trusted any man enough to get that close to her. Was she really ready to take such a step with a man she'd known such a short time?

"Or," Tony said easily, forcing a smile as he picked his fork back up in response to her silence, "we could always finish dessert and have our coffee. Betty's certainly a good cook. How long did you say she'd been with you?"

"Long enough to understand if we don't wait around for coffee." Michelle laid her Irish linen napkin on the table and rose from her chair. For once in many years of caution, she was taking a risk, reaching out for what she wanted. And she wanted Tony—as she had never wanted anyone before.

Tony stood quickly and stepped toward her, rounding the end of the table, his eyes locked with hers. "Michelle?"

She smiled shakily and reached out her hand to him. "You said you wanted to see the rest of the house?"

"I'd like that," he murmured, his fingers closing tightly around hers.

She clung to that large, strong hand as she led him from the dining room.

Michelle's bedroom was large and romantically decorated. A marble-framed fireplace dominated one end;

Victorian chintz chairs and a delicate lamp table formed a sitting area in front of it. A four-poster antique cherry bed was covered with a delicate hand-crocheted spread of antique lace and piled with throw pillows. A matching triple dresser held a silver hairbrush and mirror, photos of her parents in heavy silver frames, and five fragile hand-blown perfume bottles. A heavy, carved armoire hid a television and VCR. Impressionistic prints and paintings adorned the fabric-covered walls.

Michelle noticed that Tony barely glanced around him as they entered the lovely room. His attention was focused solely on her.

"You are so beautiful," he murmured, his hands coming up to frame her face. "I've wanted you since the first time I saw you."

She felt the unsteadiness in his hands and it pleased her to know that he wasn't taking this lightly. She wasn't, either. She covered his hands with her own, giving him a smile that felt decidedly shaky. "Tony."

He lowered his head, very slowly, his lips hovering for just a moment before closing over hers. Michelle tilted her head back and closed her eyes, her entire concentration focused on the kiss. He didn't hurry the embrace, didn't immediately deepen it. Instead, he lingered. He savored. He nipped and nibbled until she clung to him bonelessly, aching for more.

His teeth closed lightly around her lower lip, and then his tongue soothed the nonexistent marks he'd left. He parted her lips with the very tip of his tongue, then drew back just as she opened to welcome him. Growing frustrated with his taunting, she pulled his mouth more firmly to hers and thrust her tongue between his lips, deepening the kiss herself.

Immediately, Tony's arms went around her, crushing her to him as he reclaimed control of the embrace. One hand at the back of her head, he held her still for a sensual invasion and exploration that left her on fire, burning for him as she'd never burned before. She strained against him, arms tight around his neck, breasts crushed against his chest, her hips pressed to his hardened thighs. She wanted—*needed*—him so desperately that she didn't think she'd survive if he stopped now.

She almost cried out in protest when he tore his mouth from hers and lifted his head to stare down at her, his dark eyes glittering, lean cheeks flushed with color. He held her away from him with his hands on her forearms, his hold gentle but firm. "Michelle," he muttered, and his voice was raw, gritty. "Are you sure? Really sure?"

"I want you, Tony," she murmured, touching his hot cheek with her cool, trembling fingers. "I want you so much."

Though he quivered at her words, he seemed to force himself to hold back. "It's been an emotional day for you. I don't want you to confuse your feelings. I don't want you to have any regrets tomorrow."

"You think I'm feeling grateful to you?" she asked in sudden comprehension.

"Yes," he answered bluntly. "And I want it to be more than that."

Touched, she wrapped her arms around his neck once more, rising on tiptoes to bring her face close to his. "It's not just gratitude, Tony," she murmured, letting her sincerity show in her eyes and color her voice. "I don't— I'm not sure what it is exactly, but it's not gratitude. I want you. I've wanted you almost from the beginning."

"Michelle." Visibly shaken, he drew her closer, burying his face in her hair. "Oh God, Michelle. I need you."

"Then why are you waiting?" she whispered.

He made a choked sound deep in his throat. And then he turned to sweep the crocheted spread from the bed, heedless of the throw pillows that tumbled to the floor around them. He lay Michelle on the snowy sheets as carefully as though she were made of fragile glass, and his tenderness brought tears to her eyes.

It must be important to him, she thought hopefully, drawing him down with her. Surely he couldn't look at her this way, touch her this deeply, if it were only casual sex to him.

Though Tony's fingers weren't steady, they were quick. Michelle's clothing seemed to fall from her body as he swept his hands over her, leaving her nude and shy in the light from the crystal bedside lamp. And then Tony shrugged out of his shirt and she forgot to be shy, too caught up in admiration of the perfect male body revealed to her.

His shoulders were broad, tanned, his chest firmly muscled beneath a sexy mat of curly black hair. His stomach was flat, his hips lean, and he slid his charcoal slacks down legs that were long and taut. He paused a moment before removing his black briefs, as though giving her one last chance to change her mind. When she only watched him in silence, he took a deep breath and removed that last barrier between them, revealing himself fully aroused and hungry for her.

Michelle held out her arms.

Gathering her into his arms, Tony buried his face in her neck, planting a string of moist, arousing kisses from the tender spot below her ear to the pulse pounding in the hollow of her throat. Only then did he turn his attention to her breasts, his hands shaping her almost reverently before he lowered his mouth to the pointed, exquisitely sensitive tips. Michelle caught her breath and arched mindlessly when he pulled one pebbled nipple firmly into his mouth, suckling with an intensity that drew an overwhelming hot response from deep inside her.

"Tony! Oh, Tony." She buried her fingers in his thick, wavy jet hair, her smooth legs tangling with his rougher ones.

"Michelle. *Cara.*" Tony slid his hand between her thighs, filling his palm with the crisp curls there, his fingers stroking, inciting. He murmured approval and encouragement in an intriguing mixture of wickedly smooth Italian and sexy Texas drawl. Michelle thought there had never been a more fascinating combination.

And then his fingers moved again and she couldn't think at all.

By the time Tony slipped inside her, she was lost. She'd never known it could be like this. Never experienced such a heady combination of fire and tenderness, giving and sharing. She'd never dreamed that a man's hands could be so clever and so gentle, his lips so skillful and yet so vulnerable. She'd never heard her name murmured with such an entrancing combination of pleasure and pain, demand and request, exhilaration and entreaty.

He was everything she'd ever dreamed of in a lover, sweeping her into passion with a reckless fever she'd never known, yet taking the time to make sure there would be no unwanted repercussions from this glorious interlude.

It wasn't gratitude and it wasn't just desire. It had to be something very close to love.

She cried out against his lips as an explosion of sensation accompanied the disquieting realization, and heard as if from a distance the harsh sound Tony made when he stiffened in her arms with his own release. Afterward, Michelle pushed away any lingering questions about her feelings for Tony, choosing, instead, to give in to the heavy lassitude creeping through her. She burrowed into his chest, his arms snugly around her as she closed her eyes and savored.

She thought she heard him murmur something in Italian as she slid into an exhausted, satiated sleep. She didn't even try to guess what he'd said. At the moment, it was enough to be held close to his warmth, his ragged breath ruffling the damp hair at her forehead, his lips just brushing her skin. His heart beating strongly, reassuringly against hers.

She didn't know how much time had passed when she was roused by Tony's movements as he tried to slip from the bed. "Where are you going?" she asked groggily, her hand tightening on his arm, holding him still.

"It's after midnight," he answered, tenderly brushing her hair away from her face. "You need your rest."

He'd turned off the bedside lamp, she noted sleepily, so that the only illumination came through the lace at the windows, making him look big and mysterious in the deep shadows. Her fingers tightened on his arm.

"Don't go. Stay with me," she murmured. For tonight, she couldn't bear the thought of being left alone in the bed where she'd spent so many lonely nights.

"If I stay," he said, and his voice was suddenly gruff, "you won't get much rest."

She slid her hand slowly up his arm to his shoulder. "Neither will you," she murmured, tugging his head down to hers.

He didn't complain.

Chapter Ten

Michelle's alarm went off at the usual time Tuesday morning. As usual, she groaned, turned off the alarm without opening her eyes and sank deeper into the pillows, stretching lazily beneath the covers. What *wasn't* usual was the solid, hairy leg her toes encountered on the other side of the bed.

Her eyes flew open. "Oh."

Propped on one elbow, the white sheet draped over his hip looking very bright against his tanned skin, Tony watched her with a smile in his dark eyes. "Do you always wake up so reluctantly?"

She smiled. "Yes. But I rarely have such a nice reason to open my eyes."

"Mmm." He bent to brush a kiss against her sleep-softened mouth. "That was a nice thing to say. Careful, Michelle, or you might get into the habit."

She gave in to an impulse to brush a heavy lock of hair off his forehead. "I'm sure you'll give me a reason to insult you again before long. Maybe during breakfast."

"Was that an invitation?"

"You're so bright."

He chuckled. "It's already starting, I see. And I'd love to have breakfast with you, if you don't think your housekeeper's husband will be waiting downstairs with a shotgun."

"I think I'm old enough to have an overnight guest without answering to my staff," Michelle assured him.

"So they don't usually say anything?" The question was asked just a bit too casually.

She avoided his eyes by reaching for the quilted satin robe draped over a nearby vanity chair. "The situation has never come up. I'm not in the habit of having overnight guests here."

"I see." He sounded so smugly pleased with her answer that Michelle was tempted to throw something at him.

"I think I'll take a quick shower before breakfast," she announced, standing and belting herself into the robe, her back to the bed.

His arms went around her before she'd even realized he'd gotten up. "I think I'll join you," he murmured, his lips moving against the back of her neck.

Not surprisingly, it was the longest, most delightful shower Michelle could ever remember taking.

The breakfast table had been set for two. Limoges china, this time, with heavy crystal glassware holding pulpy orange juice. Fresh flowers at the center of the table gave off a welcoming scent, blending with the aroma of fresh-baked muffins in a linen-covered basket, and coffee kept hot in an insulated carafe. Michelle flushed lightly at the raised-eyebrow look Tony gave her.

"Do you always dine so elegantly in the morning?"

"No," she answered with a sigh. "Betty's obviously showing her approval again."

He grinned. "I like her, too."

The door to the kitchen opened and Betty bustled in with a tray, greeting them as naturally as though Tony were a regular at the breakfast table. "Good morning, Michelle. Mr. D'Alessandro."

"Why don't you call me Tony," he suggested, giving her one of his charming smiles as he took his seat.

Betty flushed like a schoolgirl, to Michelle's amusement. "Thank you, Mr. Tony. Help yourself to a muffin. I've got fresh fruit here and bacon, and there's homemade jam on the table if you want it with your muffins. Would you like me to cook you some eggs?"

Tony assured Betty that muffins, bacon and fruit were quite sufficient, explaining that he rarely ate eggs. "Cholesterol, you know."

"Cholesterol," Betty muttered. "Now you sound like Michelle, always counting calories and fats and cholesterol. And not an extra pound on either of you. How are you supposed to put in a good day's work without fueling up at breakfast?"

Dancing with suppressed laughter, Tony's eyes met Michelle's across the table. And held.

Neither of them noticed when Betty suddenly grew quiet and slipped from the room, her own smile tremulously pleased.

Some time later, Tony sighed with audible reluctance and set his drained coffee cup on the table. "I guess I'd better go. I'm expected to make an appearance at the office today."

"And I have a budget meeting at Trent Enterprises this afternoon," Michelle said, equally disinclined to bring the lovely morning to an end.

She walked Tony to the front door, where he kissed her lingeringly. "I'll call you tonight," he murmured, when he finally raised his head and stepped back.

Michelle nodded, and then watched until he'd climbed into his Jeep and started out of the driveway before closing the door behind him. Leaning back against the door, she closed her eyes and allowed herself one long, delicious moment of reminiscing before beginning her usual weekday routines.

Tony D'Alessandro was irrevocably, unresistingly, head-over-heels in love. The utter certainty of the realization should have made him nervous, should have at least had him making an effort to protect himself from the vulnerability of the condition.

Instead, he found himself grinning like an idiot, leaning back in his chair with his hands behind his head, feet crossed on the desk as he replayed every moment he'd spent with Michelle Trent. From the day she'd walked into this very office and annoyed almost as much as she'd aroused him—to the night before, when she'd taken him into her bed and her body with such artless, honest passion that she'd all but brought him to his knees in overwhelming pleasure.

He loved her as he'd never loved another woman. And, at the moment, life looked very good indeed.

"You suppose he's been drugged?" a man's voice asked wryly from the open office doorway.

"Could be," a woman answered with exaggerated concern. "What else could make him look that smug and sappy?"

"Oh, I don't know," yet another man contributed, "he always looks kinda sappy. Don't think I've ever seen him smiling quite that contentedly before, though. Maybe he's brought us all in to fire us."

"Or cut our salaries," the first man mused. "Yeah, he'd like that. More money left for him, you know."

Tony sighed and dropped his arms and feet, straightening in his chair. "Would you jokers knock it off?" he complained to his employees, waving them into the office. "Glad to see you're all on time for our meeting, for a change."

"Tony, there's a call for you on line one," Bonnie announced, standing in the doorway her three co-workers had just vacated.

"Who is it, Bonnie?"

"Mike Halloran."

"Tell him I'll get back to him, will you? And hold all my calls during this meeting..." He hesitated, then added, "Unless it's Michelle. If she calls, put her through."

"Right." Bonnie closed the door to his office behind her as she went back to her own desk.

Tony glanced around to find his staff seated around his desk—and looking at him with identical curiosity. "Shut up," he growled, knowing the effort was futile even as he spoke.

"Michelle, huh?" It was blond, blue-eyed Chuck Johnson who spoke first, his wholesomely freckled face split with a grin. "Who was it told us never to get personally involved with the clients, hmm?"

"So that's why he looked like the post-canary cat when we came in," petite, red-haired, green-eyed Cassie Browning murmured. "Tony's in love, guys."

"Well, hell, I'm half in love with Michelle Trent myself, and all I've seen are her bank statements," Bob O'Brien drawled, his sharp eyes typically cynical.

Tony scowled. "Leave Michelle's money out of this."

Bob shrugged. "You're the one who told me to look into her finances, find out exactly what she's worth and how she's spending it. Just doing my job, boss."

"Yeah, well, keep your opinions to yourself from now on. All I need from you is the information I assigned you to get for me."

"Right." Not noticeably fazed by Tony's tone, Bob tossed a folder onto his disgruntled employer's desk. "There you go."

A second report landed on top of that one. "That's all I could find so far on Carter Powell," Chuck explained. "Other than the mistress he's got set up in Houston, he looks clean enough."

"Mistress?" Tony's left eyebrow rose. "He's married, isn't he?"

"Very. Wife's one of those big-time society types, involved with just about everything. A real asset to his career, if you know what I mean."

"Nothing unusual about a man keeping a piece on the side," Bob muttered. "And what's that got to do with Michelle Trent, anyway?"

"Probably nothing," Tony admitted. And then glanced back at Chuck. "But don't stop yet. Keep digging, okay? If there's anything else to know about Powell, I want it."

"What's this vendetta against the guy? What do you think we're going to find?" Chuck asked curiously.

"Call it a hunch," Tony answered more lightly than he felt. "You know how I hate getting threatening phone calls."

"Speaking of mistresses," Cassie interjected, pulling a manila envelope from a battered briefcase, "Martin Hurley definitely has one, as well. I've got a name, address and photos. *Now* can I work full-time on finding Jared Walker? I've got a lead on a Jared Walker in Tulsa who could be the one we want. And I've got a hunch…"

The three men groaned. Cassie scowled. "All right, I know how you feel about my hunches" she grumbled. "But this time, I'd put money on it. I think I'm close to finding Michelle's brother, Tony. If you'd just put me on the case full-time…"

Tony pulled thoughtfully at his lower lip, weighing the next month's payroll against Michelle's anticipated pleasure in finding her oldest brother. "All right," he conceded finally. "I'll give you a couple months, Cassie. Full-time. But I'll need something more solid from you than a hunch."

"You'll have it, Tony. Soon." Smiling her satisfaction with the small victory, Cassie sat back in her chair.

Tony turned his attention to Bob. "Anything on the twins?"

Bob shook his head. "Nothing. It's like they no longer existed after they ran away at sixteen. For all we know, they didn't."

Tony didn't want to have to tell Michelle that she'd lost three brothers before she'd had the chance to know them. He frowned. "Stay with it, Bob."

"You're the boss."

Uncomfortably aware that Michelle wasn't his only client, Tony directed the meeting into other business matters, though he knew Michelle would never be far from his thoughts. For once, Bob, Cassie and Chuck co-operated easily, as if sensing that they'd teased him

enough for the time being about his obvious feelings for
Michelle Trent.

Tied up with other responsibilities, it was nearly an
hour after his staff meeting ended before Tony had a
chance to open the file Bob had brought him on Michelle's financial status. He took one look at the neatly
typed report and choked on the sip of lukewarm coffee
he'd just taken, the beverage splashing over the rim of his
mug when he set it abruptly on the desk. He blinked, as
though to clear his vision, and checked the numbers
again.

Damn. He ran a hand through his hair, his eyes locked
on the figures. He'd known Michelle was well-off, but her
relatively simple life-style—even considering her luxurious home—had deceived him as to her true worth. Her
father and grandfather had been shrewd businessmen and
clever financial planners. Michelle could live quite comfortably for the rest of her life without ever touching the
principal of her inheritance. No wonder she hadn't found
it necessary to establish a career other than her charity
work.

His hand was shaking a little when he closed the file.
Her money shouldn't make a difference in the way he felt
about her, he told himself—and it didn't, really. But still
he felt the gap widen between them.

He wouldn't lose her, he thought with a scowl of determination. Whatever it took, he wouldn't lose her.

Michelle frowned down at a computer report on her
desk. The figures in front of her represented the monthly
profit-and-loss statement from Trent Enterprises, Dallas. It was simply a formality for her, as major stock-
holder, to look over the reports; the excellent man-

agement staff her father had assembled during his later years ran the corporation smoothly and with little interference from Michelle. Despite her efforts to stay involved with the corporation by monitoring reports and statements and seeing to the responsibilities her father had given her for charitable contributions, she knew she really made little impact on the company's operations.

For the past few years, she'd been content with her part, feeling safe and comfortable in her routines and reclusion. Content with her charity work, her few friends, her rare social functions. Now something was changing. For the first time in years, she found herself wanting more. And more than a little nervous at the thought of the risks inherent in reaching out.

She thought of the risk she'd taken two nights before making love with Tony. Not a physical risk, but an emotional one—opening herself to a heartache infinitely more devastating than Geoff had inflicted. The youthful, infatuated feelings she'd had for Geoff were nothing when compared to the way Tony made her feel. Would she survive this time if their new, so-fragile relationship ended disastrously?

Though they'd talked on the telephone, she hadn't seen Tony since he'd left after breakfast Tuesday morning. He'd explained that he had to work on a case Tuesday night and Michelle had been committed to a civic organization meeting Wednesday evening. Now it was early Thursday afternoon and she missed him so much she ached with it. Should she have allowed herself to get in this deep, this fast? Was she being a total fool?

The telephone at her elbow rang, interrupting her deep musing. Rather relieved at the distraction, she answered it.

"Michelle?"

"Yes?"

"Hi, it's Teresa D'Alessandro."

Pleasantly surprised, Michelle smiled. "Teresa! How nice to hear from you."

"I hope I'm not calling at a bad time. And I know it's short notice, but I have an invitation for you for tomorrow night."

"An invitation? To what?"

"Tomorrow's Tony's birthday. Did you know?"

"No," Michelle admitted. "He didn't mention it."

"That doesn't surprise me. Anyway, he'll be thirty-three, and Paul and his brothers have impulsively decided to give him a surprise party. We want you to help us out."

"A surprise birthday party?" Michelle repeated, intrigued.

"The party's going to be at Vittorio's—we've reserved the private dining room in the back. Maybe you could help us get Tony there without him suspecting anything?"

"I can try," Michelle replied. She'd never been involved in a surprise party before. It sounded like fun.

"Great. I knew you'd want to be involved," Teresa enthused. "We could tell how crazy Tony is about you. Everyone thinks you make a nice couple."

"Well, I—uh . . ." Michelle flushed deeply at the confirmation of Tony's warning that the family had probably already discussed their relationship and given opinions. She wasn't accustomed to having her private life conducted so openly—and certainly not used to the well-intentioned prying of a large, close, demonstrative extended family. And yet, rather than being annoyed, she found herself pleased that the D'Alessandro clan had approved of her.

Teresa laughed in understanding. "I know. I'm starting to sound like a real D'Alessandro, aren't I? Already sticking my nose in. But you might as well get used to it—and keep in mind that we're pretty good-natured about being told to mind our own business."

"What do you want me to do for the party?" Michelle asked, somewhat desperately redirecting the conversation.

"Just tell him you're in the mood to eat at Vittorio's—tell him you're craving Vittorio's linguine, or something—and have him there around eight o'clock."

"But Tony and I don't even have a date for tomorrow night," Michelle protested, feeling rather presumptuous at being involved in the scheme. "What if he has other plans?"

"He won't have other plans," Teresa said confidently.

Michelle hoped she was right. "All right. If I can, I'll have him there at eight. But be prepared with Plan B if this doesn't work out, okay?"

"I'll give you my phone number and Uncle Vinnie's, just in case," Teresa promised. "This is going to be so much fun. Paul and Joe and Mike have been wanting to do this forever. No one's ever managed to catch Tony by surprise before—but this time, we're getting him! We're hoping by getting it together so quickly there won't be time for anyone to spill the beans."

"I hope you're right. I think I'd like to see Tony caught by surprise," Michelle murmured, smiling in anticipation.

Michelle was still smiling several minutes after her conversation with Teresa ended, feeling as though she'd found another new friend. She thought of all the people who'd probably be at the birthday party, some of whom she'd already met, others she hadn't. She'd certainly found a lot of people she hadn't expected to when she'd hired Tony D'Alessandro to find her brothers and sisters, she thought rather dazedly.

A sudden chill ran through her as she pictured going back to a life of lonely days and even lonelier nights. And, again, she wondered if she'd made a mistake in trying to change her safe, insulated life.

Tony and Michelle had made plans to see a movie Thursday evening. Tony called twenty minutes before he was due to arrive and said he'd gotten tied up at work and was running late. "Would you mind if I pick you up on my way home and then stop by my place to change?" he asked.

"Of course not," Michelle assured him. "In fact, if you're too tired tonight, we can—"

"Don't even think it," he ordered gruffly. "I've been looking forward to seeing you all day. I'm showing signs of severe Michelle withdrawal."

"Guess we can't have that."

"I knew you'd understand. See you in a few minutes, honey."

Michelle was waiting by her front door when he arrived ten minutes later. He pulled her into his arms and kissed her as though it had been two years rather than two days since he'd last seen her.

"Whew!" he said, when he finally released her. "Just made it. Another few minutes without a kiss from you and I'd have been a goner."

Breathless and disheveled, Michelle laughed at his foolishness and reminded him that they were going to have to hurry if they were going to have time for him to change before the film began. Tony took her hand and hustled her to his Jeep, teasingly complaining about having had to wear a sport coat and tie for a professional meeting that day, making her laugh at his exaggerated distaste for the clothing.

She couldn't remember ever beginning a movie date with more eager anticipation.

"You look very nice this evening, by the way," Tony informed her when they were underway.

She smiled, automatically smoothing the taupe slacks she'd worn with a delicate short-sleeved eggshell silk sweater. "Thank you."

"Did I ever mention that you're the classiest lady I've ever dated?" he asked, still in the teasing tone he'd greeted her with.

"I'm not sure I know how to take that," she replied with wry humor.

He chuckled. "It's just that you wear your jeans like silk and the casual clothes you have on now like an evening gown. There's something about you that's—well, classy. Maybe it's because of that poem Layla was talking about—you know, full of grace. You're like that."

Michelle flushed and squirmed self-consciously in her seat. "You're embarrassing me."

"Sorry. It was meant to be a compliment."

"Then I'll thank you and change the subject. How was your day?"

"Busy," he admitted. "I've spent the past two years complaining because the business was building so slowly and now all of a sudden I've got more work than I can keep up with. I'm thinking about putting Cassie on full-time, maybe hiring another part-time apprentice."

"That's good, isn't it?"

"Oh, sure. As long as it doesn't interfere with seeing you," he added, catching her hand to give it a squeeze.

"I'm not one of those workaholics who puts the job ahead of personal relationships."

"That's nice to hear," she murmured, caught off guard.

He released her hand and guided the Jeep into the parking lot of a large apartment complex. "This is where I live."

Michelle looked around curiously. The complex was big and professionally landscaped, one of those sprawling, midpriced areas planned for working-class singles and young marrieds. The parking lot was filled with economy cars and pickup trucks, the identical buildings marked with large metal numbers. Tony parked in front of building number twelve.

"I'm in apartment B," he explained, opening his door. "Come on in. It'll just take me a few minutes to change."

The apartment was furnished in "early department store"—boxy blue-and-green-plaid furniture, wood-veneer tables, brass-plated lamps. A pair of dark socks lay on the floor beside an empty Pepsi can, an untidy stack of newspapers scattered close by. The adjoining kitchen was similarly cluttered. Tony cleared his throat. "I—uh—wasn't expecting company when I left this morning."

She smiled. "Don't worry about it. It looks just the way I'd expected it to."

He frowned. "I'm not sure how to take that."

She gave him a little shove. "Go change. We'll be late for the movie."

"Yes, ma'am. Make yourself comfortable. I'll be right back. There are canned drinks in the fridge if you want one, but don't touch the fuzzy green things in the plastic bowls. I'd swear one of them snapped at me this morning."

Laughing, Michelle wrinkled her nose, hoping he was exaggerating. He disappeared into the apartment's only bedroom, leaving her to look around the living room, curious about the personal things he'd set around. A framed photograph of his parents, another of Vinnie and Carla surrounded by three teenaged boys. Michelle touched a finger to Tony's face in the photo, entranced by the glimpses of the man he'd become in the youth he'd been.

There was a sport trophy on the table with the photographs. Football, she noted. Most Valuable Player. Judging from the year engraved into the metal, Tony would have been a senior in college when he'd earned the award. She hadn't even known he'd played football.

A built-from-a-kit bookshelf beside the couch overflowed with paperback novels. Michelle noted without surprise that Tony's taste ran to adventure and thrillers. On top of the bookshelf, two goldfish swam lazily in a bowl decorated with blue aquarium gravel and a plastic pirate skeleton.

Framed posters hung on the wall—colorful, tasteful, unusual. Michelle studied them with interest. They weren't inexpensive. Neither was the large-screen television, nor the state-of-the-art VCR and stereo system. Despite his off-the-rack clothing and department-store furniture, Tony didn't scrimp on things that were important to him, it seemed.

Two strong arms circled her from behind, startling her. "Okay," Tony said into her ear, "so the place won't ever be featured in one of those ritzy decorating magazines. But I've got big plans for moving up someday."

"Is that right?" she asked, turning in his arms to drape her own around his neck. He'd changed into soft-washed jeans and a short-sleeved, band-bottomed white pullover that contrasted appealingly with his dark coloring. His ebony hair was slightly mussed, as if he'd hastily combed it with his fingers after donning his shirt. He looked wonderful.

"Tony," she whispered, lifting her face to his. "Kiss me."

He made a sound somewhere between a laugh and a groan and pulled her closer. "it would be my pleasure," he murmured, just before his mouth covered hers.

The first touch of their lips seemed to enflame both of them. Tony pulled her roughly against him, crushing her breasts to his chest as he deepened the kiss, claiming her mouth with painstaking thoroughness. Michelle didn't protest his sudden intensity, but threw herself whole-heartedly into the embrace, as hungry as he for more.

His hands swept her body, stroking down her back, cupping her bottom, pulling her tightly against him. She felt his arousal, hard and swollen against her stomach, and she trembled in reaction. She buried her fingers in his hair, holding his mouth to hers. The kiss grew frenzied, feverish, his hands avid, demanding.

His groan came from deep in his chest, reverberating against her. "Michelle," he grated, his voice hardly recognizable, his lips still moving against hers. "How badly do you want to see that movie?"

She closed her eyes and took a quick breath when his mouth moved to her throat. "What movie?" she whispered.

The words had hardly left her before she found herself caught into his arms, being carried swiftly through the living room toward the open bedroom door.

Tony dropped her without ceremony onto the unmade bed, following without hesitation to cover her mouth and her body with his own. She gathered him into her arms, their legs tangling, her mouth moving hungrily beneath his lips. Their breathing had grown harsh, rapid, their movements frantic, clumsy with need. Michelle's formerly neatly coiled hair tumbled around her face, the pins lost, unnoticed. Her tailored clothing fell carelessly on the floor, followed immediately by Tony's jeans and pullover.

His mouth was hungry at her breasts, his fingers searching out the tender, swollen skin between her legs. He murmured broken words of desire, of need. Of love. Incapable of answering, Michelle held him more tightly, silently urging him on. And when he thrust inside her, she cried out, his name trembling on her lips, her love for him swelling inside her until she shuddered with a release more powerful, more devastating than anything that had come before it.

And still he drove her on, shifting, rocking, stroking until she exploded again, sobbing with the incredible beauty of it. This time he was with her, his lips at her ear, his voice raw and husky and tender. "Michelle. Oh, love."

And then he, too, was unable to speak coherently for several long, heart-stopping moments.

Chapter Eleven

Muffling their giddy laughter, Michelle and Tony slipped furtively through the front door of her house, well aware that the night was more than half over. "I've got to go," Tony murmured between kisses as they lingered in the entryway. "You need your rest."

"I'll miss you," she murmured, holding his face between her hands as she returned his kisses.

"I'll miss you, too, but I have an early meeting in the morning."

"It *is* morning," she reminded him, nibbling lazily at his lower lip.

"Mmm." He kissed her, then set her resolutely away. "Go to bed, Michelle."

She sighed. "If you insist."

"Sorry about missing the movie."

She smiled wickedly. "I'm not."

His eyes warmed, but he managed not to reach for her again. "Let me make it up to you tomorrow—uh, tonight. We'll try again."

Michelle suddenly remembered the assignment his family had given her. She moistened her lips, hoping she didn't ruin their scheming. "Um—would you mind if we went back to your uncle's restaurant for dinner?" she asked, her fingers twisting behind her back. "I really enjoyed eating there last time."

Tony looked surprised, but pleased. "Of course. Uncle Vittorio will be delighted to see us. I'll call him and make sure he has a table ready for us."

"All right." She knew his uncle would handle his part much more smoothly than she had hers. "Good night, Tony."

He risked one last, quick kiss, then stepped back with a sigh. "Good night, Michelle. Sleep well."

"You, too."

He grimaced ruefully, one hand on the doorknob. "I'd sleep better if you were in my arms," he murmured. And then he laughed quietly. "Then again, maybe I wouldn't sleep at all."

"Maybe you wouldn't," she agreed huskily, her eyes locked with his.

He groaned and opened the door. "You could test the willpower of a monk, *tesoro*. Good night."

The door closed with an abrupt click behind him. Michelle automatically turned the lock, then brushed her tousled hair away from her face and walked dreamily toward the stairs, feeling very much like a woman in love.

Michelle checked her appearance in her purse compact, frowning as she patted a stray hair into place in her neat chignon. She touched the corner of her mouth with her little finger, making sure no lipstick was smudged there. She hoped the jewel-toned floral silk dress she wore was appropriate for the evening.

Tony sighed gustily from behind the steering wheel. "Michelle," he said, drumming his fingers on the wheel, "you look beautiful. *Bellisima. Perfetta. Now* can we go eat?"

Michelle flushed and put the compact away. She was really lousy at this surprise party bit, she thought ruefully. She'd been so nervous ever since Tony had picked her up that he'd asked twice if something was wrong.

"Sorry," she said, reaching for her door handle. "It's just that I know we'll be back on the family hotline tomorrow, and I want to look nice for the inspection."

Tony laughed, accepting her explanation as logical. "You're the one who wanted to eat at my uncle's restaurant tonight," he reminded her, climbing out of the Jeep.

"Yes, I was, wasn't I?" She took a deep breath as he caught her hand in his to escort her inside.

Tony seemed puzzled when his uncle immediately ushered them to the private dining room. Michelle was watching his face when what seemed to be hundreds of people called out in unison as she and Tony were led into the room. *"Buon compleanno,* Tony!"

His eyes wide, his face split with a grin, Tony looked to Michelle. She smiled back at him, pleased that he'd obviously been caught off guard. "Happy birthday, Tony."

"You were involved with this?" he demanded, sliding an arm around her shoulders as they were surrounded by laughing, chattering members of his family.

"I was just assigned to get you here," she answered.

"Which you did very well," Teresa complimented, giving Tony a hug, made awkward by her pregnancy. "Were you surprised, Tony?"

"Are you kidding? I can't believe you guys did this!"

"Hey, *old* man!" A dark-haired young man who had to be one of Tony's brothers punched Tony's arm. "Got you!"

"Yeah, you did. Now I owe you one, *fratello*. Joe, this is Michelle Trent. Michelle, my youngest brother, Joe. He's not real bright, but we're fond of him, anyway."

Smiling, Michelle held out a hand to Joe. "Don't worry, I never believe anything he says. You're the doctor, aren't you?"

"I'm working on it," he replied, leaning over to kiss her cheek as naturally as if he'd known her for years. "Nice to meet you, Michelle. The family's been telling me nice things about you."

Michelle sighed faintly, then smiled and shook her head. Apparently she was starting to get used to the D'Alessandro clan. It didn't even particularly bother her anymore to know that she and Tony were the topic of so many family conversations.

Tony was practically engulfed by family members—his brother Michael, his parents and cousins—all of whom wished him a fond happy birthday, then turned to include Michelle in their midst. A tiny, very old woman was led to Tony by a solicitous relative whom she waved aside as she kissed the cheek Tony leaned over to offer her. She spoke to him in a rapid spate of Italian. He answered easily in the same language, his tone soft with affection. And then he glanced at Michelle.

"*Ah, scusami, Tia Luisa. Ti presento Michelle Trent.* Michelle, this is my father's aunt Luisa Sanducci. She keeps the rest of us in line."

"I only try," Luisa retorted, the words heavily accented but clear. Her faded dark eyes warm, she patted Tony's arm with a frail, spotted hand. "With this one, it is difficult. *Mio Dio,* he is such a handful!"

"*Io?*" Rounding his eyes in mock innocence, Tony placed a hand on his chest as though shocked at the accusation. "*Tia,* you wound me."

Luisa chuckled and shook her head, looking at Michelle with a wry smile. "You see? He is incorrigible."

Tony laughed and hugged the older woman. "*Ti amo, Tia Luisa.*"

"*Anch'io ti amo, caro.* Now stop wasting your time with me and enjoy your party."

The next two hours passed in a blur of laughter and teasing and affection that was almost visible between the people in the room. On the rare occasions when she wasn't involved in pleasant conversation, Michelle watched in delight as the others traded good-natured insults and swapped bits of gossip. A heated political quarrel broke out between two of Tony's uncles, swiftly and efficiently interrupted by their wives. Minutes later, the same two uncles stood side by side and toasted Tony's birthday with yet another new bottle of wine.

As always, it fascinated Michelle to watch Tony with his family. He was so different with them, she mused, watching his hands fly as he gestured to illustrate something he was saying to his brothers. So Italian. So utterly irresistible. And she was rapidly beginning to love his close-knit family almost as much as she was beginning to love him.

As the hour grew later, Tony was led to a table holding a pile of gifts in brightly colored packages. While he opened them and exclaimed over each one, Michelle nervously pulled a square package out of her purse, her heart pounding. She'd spent all morning looking for the right present for Tony, and now she questioned her choice.

Was it too much? Should she have chosen something less expensive, less personal? Yet they were lovers, deeply involved in an affair that was growing more important to her with each passing day. Did that make her choice more appropriate?

Tony's eyes met hers and held as she handed him the package. The rest of the family watched avidly when he tore off the silver paper to reveal the jeweler's box beneath. Tony caught his breath at his first glimpse of the thin, elegant gold-and-steel watch.

"Michelle," he said, looking from the watch to her flushed, anxious face. "This is beautiful. Thank you."

"Well—you needed a new one," she reminded him, uncomfortably aware of the many eyes focused on them. "I hope you like it."

He'd already removed it from the box to discover the words engraved on the back. "'Happy birthday, Tony.'" It was dated and signed only "Michelle." She had been tempted to have the jeweler add "With love," but knew it was much too soon for that.

"I love it," Tony murmured, taking her in his arms without regard for their audience. "Thank you, Michelle." And then he kissed her, lingeringly and thoroughly, to the obvious approval of his family.

Michelle was totally embarrassed when he released her, but couldn't manage to be annoyed with him. She felt oddly comfortable with Tony, with his friends and family. For the first time in so very long, she wasn't at all lonely, didn't feel like an outsider.

Even as the thought warmed her, an ominous frisson of warning slid down her spine.

You're getting in too deeply, Michelle. You're setting yourself up for heartbreak.

Pushing the depressingly pessimistic thought away, she resolved to enjoy every minute of the remainder of the party. She refused to let her cowardice ruin such a wonderful evening.

Tony's hand was in her hair, his body warm and heavy against hers. Limp and pleasantly exhausted from their lovemaking, Michelle lay beside him, her eyes closed, her slightly swollen lips curved into a contented smile. She felt his lips graze her temple and opened her eyes to look at him, savoring his smile. "I thought you'd fallen asleep."

"No." He dropped another tiny kiss on the end of her nose. "Just recuperating."

She ran a hand up his chest, fingers burrowing into the crisp dark hair. "I understand the stamina begins to go as you get on in years," she murmured commiseratingly. "You really should get some rest, poor dear."

Tony choked on a laugh and tugged her into his arms. "Witch," he muttered with mock ferocity. "Give me five more minutes and I'll show you stamina."

"Gee, I don't know, Tony. I wouldn't want you to strain yourself."

"You didn't have many spankings when you were growing up, did you, *cara?*"

"I was shamelessly spoiled."

"I noticed." He nuzzled her hair. "So how did you manage to turn out so perfectly, hmm?"

"Oh, I wouldn't say perfect."

"I would," he murmured, no longer teasing. His lips moved against hers. "Perfect." And then he kissed her, almost reverently, the beauty of the embrace bringing a lump to her throat.

They held each other in silence for several long moments after the kiss ended. And then Tony drew back, only to stop immediately when she winced at a sharp tug on her scalp.

"Oh, sorry, honey. My watchband caught a strand of your hair," he explained, gently extricating it. "There. Better?"

"Better," she assured him.

Supported on his right elbow, he lifted his left wrist to admire the watch again. "It's a beautiful watch, Michelle. Thank you again."

"You really like it?" she asked, oddly shy.

He smiled. "I really do. You shouldn't have been so extravagant, of course, but I appreciate the gesture."

Had she spent too much? Michelle wondered with a fresh surge of anxiety. Was Tony concerned about her motives in buying the watch?

"I wanted to get you something you needed," she explained seriously. "And I wanted to get a good watch that wouldn't wear out too quickly. It's not as if I couldn't afford it, Tony."

"Michelle, it's a great watch," he repeated firmly. "And I know you could afford it."

She searched his face gravely. "Does that bother you?"

He hesitated, then shrugged. "Sometimes," he admitted. "I worry that you'll think I'm like that jerk you knew before—the one who only wanted you for your money. That's not true this time."

Touched, she pressed her fingertips to his cheek. "I know you're not like Geoff, Tony. You're nothing like him."

"No." He caught her hand and pressed a hot kiss in her palm. "Oh, Michelle, I—"

He broke off whatever he'd intended to say to kiss her hand again. Unnerved by the sudden intensity of the moment, Michelle spoke quickly. "Tell me how to say 'Happy birthday' in Italian," she requested. *"Buon...?"*

"Buon compleanno," he completed, seemingly as relieved as she to ease the tension between them.

"Buon compleanno, Tony," she repeated carefully.

He smiled at her accent. *"Grazie."*

"Teach me something else."

His left eyebrow rose wickedly. "All right. Repeat after me. *Ti desidero."*

"Ti des—Ti desi—" Michelle paused and looked at him in question. "What am I trying to say?"

He pulled her closer, his legs tangling with hers, and she realized that he'd grown hard and aroused again. He covered her breast with his hand, his slow kneading making her swell into his palm in heated response. "You're telling me you want me," he murmured, his lips moving against hers.

She wrapped her arms around his neck, arching into him. "Then let me say it my way," she whispered. "I want you, Tony. I want..."

His mouth covered hers, smothering the unnecessary words.

"Dad? Dad, are you out here?" Tony looked around his father's large backyard late Saturday afternoon, searching among the many flowers, bushes and vegetable plants with which Vinnie had amused himself since his retirement.

Vinnie's gray head popped up from behind an enormous azalea bush he'd been pruning. "Tony! I wasn't expecting to see you this afternoon. What's up?"

Holding two cans of beer he'd brought out from the kitchen, Tony waited until his father approached him, then motioned toward a couple of wrought-iron lawn chairs and matching table. "Got time to sit down a minute? I need to talk to you."

"Sure." Vinnie set his gardening tools on the table and took one of the beers. "Thanks. I was just about to stop for a cold drink. Already getting hot, isn't it?"

"It tends to do that around this time of year," Tony replied, settling into one of the chairs.

"Mmm." Vinnie tilted the can for a long swallow before lowering it to look at his son. "Okay, now. What did you want to talk about?"

"Michelle."

"Why doesn't that surprise me? You've gone and fallen in love with the girl, haven't you?"

Tony flushed and cleared his throat. "Well, yes," he admitted. "But that's not the problem."

"Good. I wouldn't mind having her for a daughter-in-law. I picked her out for you a long time ago, you know."

"So why didn't you do something about it long before this?" Tony demanded with a skeptical grin.

Vinnie shrugged expressively. "If I'd introduced her to you, you'd have resisted her just to prove you didn't need me interfering in your love life."

Tony snorted, looking down at his opened but untouched beer. "I doubt it. Even if I'd tried, I'm not sure I could ever have resisted Michelle."

Vinnie smiled reminiscently. "That's the way I felt about your mama."

"Yeah. I know." Tony only hoped his own love affair worked out as successfully as Vinnie and Carla's.

"Chuck called me at home a couple of hours ago," he said, getting to the real reason for his visit. "He's found something on Carter Powell that disturbs me. I'm not sure what to do about it."

"It concerns Michelle?" Vinnie demanded, straightening abruptly in his chair.

"Very much so."

"Have you talked with her?"

"No. I don't have any proof yet, Dad. I'm afraid she wouldn't believe my suspicions. After all, she's known the man most of her life."

"Then get your proof."

"That's why I'm here," Tony agreed grimly. "I need some professional advice from the best on how to go on from here."

Vinnie set his beer down, all business now. "Okay, son. Start from the beginning. What have you got?"

Michelle hummed beneath her breath as she turned her car through the gates of her driveway Saturday afternoon. After Tony had left that morning, she'd dressed and headed for the hospital to spend time with the babies, their tiny bodies cradled in her arms as she'd rocked them and crooned to them. At one point she'd found herself daydreaming about rocking an infant of her own, picturing it with silky ebony hair and mischievous dark eyes.

She'd caught herself short, sternly chiding herself for throwing away all caution in her infatuation with Tony, but still the fantasy had enchanted her.

Her contented smile faded when she saw the car parked in front of her house, one she recognized immediately.

Carter Powell. There'd been a time when she'd enjoyed his visits; now she worried that they'd only quarrel again over her involvement with Tony and the search for her remaining brothers and sister.

"I'd given you another five minutes before I left," Carter said without preamble when Michelle joined him in the parlor where Betty had served him tea and cakes.

"I'm sorry, Carter. Did we have an appointment for this afternoon?" Michelle waved him back into his chair as she seated herself near him.

"No," he admitted gruffly, setting his teacup and saucer on a convenient coaster. He reached down to the floor, where he'd set his Italian leather briefcase. "I have some things to show you."

Her stomach tightened, as if in forewarning that she wouldn't like what he was going to tell her. "What is it?"

He held out a manila folder. "This is a copy of a report that Tony D'Alessandro requested from one of his employees. He received it this past week."

Mechanically, Michelle took the folder, though she didn't immediately open it. "What is it? And how did you get it?"

"How I got it doesn't matter," Carter replied coolly. "My job is to watch out for your welfare the best way I know how. As for what it is, I suggest you see for yourself."

Very slowly, Michelle opened the folder and looked down. The numbers printed on the pages made her catch her breath. "I don't understand—"

"I see you know what you're looking at," Carter said with audible satisfaction.

She stared at the pages, dazed by their implications. "It's a financial statement of some sort. On me."

"Yes. Everything you're worth is printed on those pages, Michelle. Bank accounts, stock holdings, investments, assets. It's all there."

"And you say Tony asked for this?" Michelle asked, raising her eyes to his, knowing their expression begged to give her a reasonable explanation for what she'd seen.

"That's right. You wouldn't think it would be necessary for him to have this information if all he's interested in is finding your brothers and sisters, would you?"

She swallowed. "I'm sure Tony thought there was a good reason..."

"Like what, Michelle?"

She couldn't come up with even one possibility. "I don't know."

"He's not the first man to look into the future benefits before making a commitment to you, is he?"

She gasped. "Carter! That's a terrible thing to say!"

His face softened. "I'm sorry, Michelle. Very sorry that I have to handle this in such a manner. But I can't stand back and watch you be hurt again by a fortune hunter."

"Tony's not a fortune hunter," Michelle protested. "He's not interested in my money."

"I understand the two of you have been seeing a great deal of each other during the past few weeks."

"You've been checking up on me?" Michelle asked indignantly.

"I've been keeping an eye on you," he replied without apology. "Just as I promised your parents I would. I keep my word."

"You're wrong about him, Carter. You don't know Tony, you don't know what he's like."

"What has he told you, Michelle? That he cares for you? That you mean more to him than your money? That he's not like any of the men you've known before?"

She clenched her fingers around the folder, unable to answer.

"Other than that fiasco with Geoff Mansfield, I've never thought you to be a particularly naive young woman. Do you really believe D'Alessandro fell in love with you at first sight? That he didn't ask for this report because he wanted to know the full extent of your worth before making a commitment he couldn't get out of? He even orchestrated your reunion with your sister as a ploy to attach himself to you when you're at your most vulnerable. He *did* hold your hand during your meeting with her, didn't he? And I'm sure you were properly grateful."

"You're wrong about his motives," Michelle repeated dully. "I know you are."

"I hear you spent quite a bit on a man's watch yesterday. Did he turn it down when you gave it to him? Or was he touchingly pleased by the gift?"

Temper exacerbated by pain brought Michelle to her feet. "You overstep yourself, Carter! How dare you have me watched that closely."

He only looked at her without getting up. "I'd say keeping an eye on your recent purchases was relevant to my questions about D'Alessandro's motives. Did he take the watch, Michelle?"

"It was a birthday present," she snapped back, beginning to pace in agitation. "He told me it was too extravagant, but he couldn't graciously refuse the gift."

"I'm sure he had no intention of trying. The man's no fool. Tell me, dear, did you know he was fired from the police department two years ago?"

"Fired?" Michelle whirled to face him, her heart stopping. "No. He quit."

"He told you that?"

"He—" She tried to remember. "No. We haven't really discussed it. But I was sure..."

"You don't have to take my word for this, you know. It's easy enough to check his employment records with police headquarters. Why would I lie to you when I know you can do so?"

Her knees felt weak. She sank back into her chair. "Why was he fired?"

"That I don't know," Carter returned grimly. "Whatever it was was covered up—probably because his father left the force with honors and his mother's a respected attorney with the D.A.'s office. Give me a few more days and I'll find out the whole story."

Desperately needing to be alone to think, Michelle lifted her chin and looked at her attorney, determined to hide her confusion and hurt. For now, anyway. "Was there anything else you wanted to tell me?"

"Your sister, Layla Samples, and her husband have two mortgages on their home. Through sheer stupidity, they got into some financial trouble three years ago and are still trying to bail themselves out. I suggest you keep that in mind should you decide to maintain contact with her."

"You really have done your homework, haven't you, Carter?" Michelle asked dully, bitterly.

He inclined his head. "That's my job. I've always believed in being thorough."

"I'm sure you'll understand that I'd like to think about the things you've told me. I'd like to be alone."

"Very well." Carter rose and straightened his expensively tailored suit, every inch the composed, efficient attorney. "Just keep in mind that I've told you these things for your own good, Michelle. Just as I've always watched out for your best interests, from the time you were a very young girl. Your father trusted me, you know, as did your mother. I never gave them any reason not to do so."

"I know that, Carter." She started to thank him for his concern, but the words wouldn't leave her throat. How could she thank him for breaking her heart?

"We should talk further, but I know you need time. I'll call you early next week. Perhaps we'll have lunch."

She nodded, already lost in her own thoughts. She was hardly aware when Powell left after one long, searching look at her.

Had she really done it again? she asked herself when she was alone, her eyes locked blindly on the now-crumpled folder. Had she fallen again for an attractive face and pretty words? Had she so easily forgotten the hard-earned lessons of her past?

Had Tony been using her?

Everything within her cried out in protest at the thought. Not Tony. Surely not Tony.

And yet...

She was suddenly haunted by some remarks he'd made, comments that had meant little at the time, yet seemed so ominous in retrospect. *"It wouldn't be hard to get used to this,"* he'd said, looking around her dining room the night they'd made love for the first time. And a few days later, after disparaging his apartment, he'd added, *"I've got big plans for moving up someday."*

She'd thought he'd been teasing at the time. But maybe he hadn't been. Maybe those plans of his had something to do with the folder resting so heavily in her lap.

And yet...

She remembered the trembling in his hands when he'd made love to her, the tenderness in his eyes when he'd smiled down at her and assured her that he didn't care about her money. Only about her. Could he have looked at her that way and lied? Could anyone be that skillful at deception? Geoff had never looked so sincere; it had simply taken her a while to notice the duplicity in his handsome face. But Tony had seemed so utterly, honestly trustworthy.

Had he only been telling her what she'd wanted to hear?

Her knuckles went white as her grip tightened on the file. How had he gotten this information? There were details included in the report that even Taylor, her closest friend, had no way of knowing. If he really wasn't interested in her money, why had Tony wanted these figures? As Carter had so coolly, yet accurately pointed out, Tony had no need of this information to find her siblings.

And had he really been fired from the police department? She knew he'd deliberately led her to believe his leaving had been by his own choice. Why hadn't he told her the truth—about that, or about his feelings for her?

"Oh, Tony," she whispered, her throat tightening against the tears she refused to shed just yet. "What have you done?"

Chapter Twelve

Tony knew something was wrong the moment he saw Michelle when she opened her door to him Saturday evening. "What is it?" he demanded, his eyes searching her strained face as he stepped through the door. "What's wrong?"

She stepped back when he would have reached for her, her arms crossing defensively at her waist. "I'd like to talk to you."

His hands fell to his sides. "All right."

What could have gone this wrong since the time he'd left her bed only a matter of hours before?

She turned to lead him into the front parlor in which he'd waited for her the first time he'd visited her home. Not the more comfortable, less formal den, he noted with a frown, sensing some meaning behind her choice of rooms.

What the hell was wrong?

Michelle didn't sit when she entered the parlor, but turned in the middle of the room to face him, still standing in a position that effectively warned him not to get too close to her. "I had a visit from my attorney this afternoon," she began.

Tony muttered an expletive beneath his breath. "So that's what this is about. What did he say to make you look at me like this?"

"Several things, actually," she replied, her beautiful face as coolly expressionless as it had been on that afternoon two months earlier when she'd entered his office to hire him.

As it had before, her attitude made him feel annoyed and defensive. He linked his thumbs in the loops of his jeans, his feet spread in a wary stance.

"All right, let's have it," he ordered. "What did he say? And you'd better have a damned good reason to believe him if that's why you're suddenly treating me as though I've got some sort of contagious disease," he added roughly.

Her chin went even higher at his tone. "Why shouldn't I believe what my attorney tells me?" she asked. "After all, I've known him for twenty-four years."

"And you've only known me for two months," he added smoothly, quietly. "But I'm the one you've been to bed with, aren't I, Michelle? I'm the one who made you go wild in my arms. I thought that meant something pretty damned important to you. It sure as hell did to me."

"Of course it was important to me!" she snapped, her cheeks darkening at his words. "*Too* important, perhaps. I'd hate to think I'd been that much of a fool twice."

"Twice?" His fists clenched as her meaning set in. "You're comparing me to that Geoff guy again? *What did Powell tell you, Michelle?*"

In answer, she snatched a manila folder off a low cherry table, thrusting it into his hands. "He brought me this. And I hope you've got some explanation for it other than the one he suggested, because I sure as hell can't come up with one!"

At least he'd managed to stir her into a temper, Tony thought with grim satisfaction. He'd rather deal with her temper any day than that icy condescension she'd mastered all too well.

Slowly lowering his eyes from her flushed face, he opened the folder. At first glance, he knew exactly what it contained, as well as why Michelle would now be questioning his motives. "Well, hell."

How had Carter Powell gotten his hands on the report Bob had turned in only a few days before?

She laughed shortly, without humor. "Funny. That's pretty much what I said when I saw it."

"This isn't what it looks like, Michelle."

"No?" She cocked her head, her tone sarcastic. "You mean it *isn't* a full, minutely detailed accounting of my financial affairs?"

He winced and cleared his throat. "Well, yes, it is that, but..."

"Then it's exactly what it looks like."

Tony closed the folder and viciously tossed it aside. "Look," he said, trying to keep his tone even and rational. "Let's sit down and I'll explain."

"I don't want to sit down," she refused stubbornly.

He exhaled gustily. "Fine. We'll stand. But the least you could do is hear me out. I assume you gave Powell that courtesy," he added caustically.

Still standing very straight, very stiff, as if holding herself in control by sheer willpower, she made a short, go-ahead gesture with one hand.

Tony ran a hand through his hair in frustration. What the hell was he supposed to say? How could he explain the suspicions he'd harbored when he'd requested this information without the evidence he needed to prove his half-formed theories?

Carter had evidently preyed expertly on Michelle's old insecurities, reminding her how long and how well he'd served her family. In contrast, Tony had nothing but his word—the word of a man she'd known only a few weeks—to convince her of his sincerity.

Part of him was hurt and furious that Michelle didn't automatically trust him, that she'd even consider doubting him after all they'd become to each other. Yet the more rational side of him knew that she'd been hurt too many times in the past for it to be that easy. And he was going to have to ask her to trust him once again. Until he had proof that Carter wasn't the well-intentioned friend he pretended to be, Tony couldn't explain the investigation he was conducting on his own time. For her.

He only hoped he wasn't expecting too much from her. *He wouldn't lose her, damn it. He couldn't.*

"Michelle, please," he said, wondering how to begin. "Sit down."

She stood where she was for another long, taut moment, as though torn between pride and logic, and then nodded stiffly and perched on the edge of a chair. Relieved that he'd won even that small victory, Tony chose a seat close to her.

"Do you remember that I told you your money wasn't important to me? That it was you I cared for, not your wealth?"

"I remember everything you told me," she agreed stiffly. *I just don't know if I can believe you,* her eyes added.

"It was true, Michelle. It still is." He took a deep breath before speaking again, knowing he risked everything with his words. "I love you."

A visible tremor coursed through her. Her knuckles went white against the arms of her chair. "Don't say that," she whispered.

"It's true."

She shook her head, refusing to look at him. "I don't want to hear it. Not now. I want to know about this file. Did you assign one of your employees to get this information for you, Tony?"

"Yes."

Her eyes closed briefly at his stark reply, then opened again though she still stared at her lap rather than at him. "Why?"

He swallowed a groan. "I can't explain exactly. Not yet."

She glanced at him then, suspiciously. "What do you mean, 'not yet'? Why can't you explain?"

"It's part of an investigation," he replied. "But I don't have everything I need yet. Next week, maybe, I can explain everything to you."

"I want to know *now!*" she cried, looking pleadingly at him. "What does this have to do with your search for my brothers and sisters? Why did you need to know these things about me?"

"It doesn't exactly apply to my search for your family. It's . . . something else. Something I can't really discuss with you yet. I don't have the proof, Michelle."

"Proof?" she repeated, frowning. "Proof of what?"

He remained silent, more frustrated then he could ever remember being in his life. If only he could explain, if only he could hope she'd believe him without any evidence other than his word. *And what if he was wrong?*

She made a choked sound, as though his silence only confirmed her worst suspicions. "Then maybe you can answer this," she said, her voice strained. "Why did you leave the police department, Tony?"

"I quit," he replied, his fists clenching on his knees.

"You quit? Or were you fired?"

His jaw tightened, but he held her gaze evenly. "Does that matter to you?"

"Of course it matters! Don't you think it should?"

"Not if you trust me."

She only looked at him.

Tony sighed heavily. "Yeah, right. That's the real problem, isn't it?"

He rose to pace restlessly around the room, his hands in his pockets. Maybe to keep them from reaching out to her. "I quit the police department, Michelle. My choice."

"Carter said—"

"My choice," he continued as if she hadn't interrupted, "was to quit or be fired. Is that what you wanted to know?"

"What did you do?"

He shot her an angry, fuming look. "You automatically assume it was something I did?"

"Isn't that why most people are given those options?" she whispered, looking as miserable as he felt.

He tried to harden his heart against the look in her eyes, reminding himself that he was the one on trial, the one being unjustly accused of more than one sin, but all he really wanted to do was to take her in his arms and tell her how much he loved her. That he'd never hurt her. Beg her to trust him, whatever the evidence against him. His hands clenched in his pockets.

"It wasn't what I did," he said curtly. "It was what I wouldn't do. At the time, the administration was made up of political game players. There were certain unwritten rules to be followed, certain occasions when we were expected to look the other way rather than to do our jobs. I couldn't go along with that. I didn't cooperate with their games, and I wasn't what they called a 'team player.' I was too impatient to wait for the reforms that were already in the works and I got myself embroiled in an ugly situation. It was best for me to leave when I did, to go into business for myself. To make my own rules."

"Is that the whole truth?"

The quiet question had him whirling furiously on her. "*Dammit,* Michelle!"

"I'm sorry!" she snapped, raising her hands to her temples as though to soothe a vicious pounding there. "I just don't know what to think right now. When Carter showed me that file . . ."

"You automatically assumed the worst about me," Tony finished bitterly.

She dropped her hands to her lap. "You invaded every corner of my personal life, reduced my entire existence to a series of numbers on a computer printout," she accused him brokenly. "You've told me repeatedly that you don't care about my money, and yet you assigned one of your employees to pry this intensely into my affairs. You've admitted this report has nothing to do with the job I hired you for, yet you refuse to explain why you requested it. What am I supposed to think, Tony?"

Wearily, he closed his eyes. "I know how it looks to you," he admitted reluctantly. "Maybe I expected too much . . ."

Opening his eyes, he pulled his hands from his pockets and faced her squarely. "I can only tell you again that I love you, Michelle, and that everything I've done was done for a good reason. I'll get the facts I need to make you understand, but it's going to take me a few more days. Now it's up to you. You can fire me . . . or you can trust me just a little while longer."

"You promised you'd find my family," she whispered.

"Yes. I still intend to do so."

"And this other thing—this 'investigation' that has something to do with me? Will you stop prying into my personal affairs if I ask you to?"

He hesitated, wanting to promise her anything, heavily aware that he couldn't let go of his investigation until he'd proven his suspicions about Carter Powell. "I can't promise that, Michelle. I'm sorry—but please believe I have your best interests at heart."

"I don't know what to believe," she murmured, dropping her eyelashes to hide her expression from him. "I'm really tired, Tony. I'd like you to leave now."

He made a move of protest, vaguely hoping he could convince her of his innocence if she'd only give him a little more time with her. If he could only touch her, hold her.

"Please," she said, her voice barely audible.

He sighed, defeated. "All right. I'll go. I'll call you tomorrow."

"Call me when you have something to show me."

A muscle twitched in his cheek, but he nodded shortly. "Fine. Good night, Michelle."

She didn't answer.

Swallowing a curse, Tony turned and strode out of the room before he did something he'd only regret. Like throw her over his shoulder and carry her to her bedroom, to hold her there until she'd finally learned to trust him. If he thought it would work, he might even try it. But he knew she'd only fight him.

He drove away from her big, walled-in house with a desperate tightness in his chest. She'd hurt him with her lack of faith in him, her willingness to believe that he was only after her money. Hurt him worse than anything had ever hurt him before. But he wouldn't give up on her. He couldn't. He loved her.

He'd provide the proof she needed, he told himself on a sudden surge of reckless determination. And then he'd continue to chip away at those defenses of hers until she finally learned to trust him. To love him the way he loved her. Whatever it took.

For the first time in his stubborn, uncompromising lifetime, Tony D'Alessandro found himself willing to beg, if necessary. And even though the realization shook him, he knew it was true.

So this was love. Why hadn't anyone warned him how much it could hurt?

Unable to sleep, Michelle prowled around her room long after midnight, her hands tangled in her hair, her thoughts whirling, moods swinging. She couldn't forget the look on Tony's face when she'd implicitly accused him of being more interested in her money than in her. He'd looked so... hurt. Betrayed. Sincere.

I love you, he'd said. And she'd come so very close to melting, holding out her arms to him and begging him to make her understand. Even now, hearing the echo of his deep, rich voice saying those three words, she wanted nothing more than to believe him, to trust that he'd never do anything to hurt her.

She loved him so much. She couldn't imagine losing him now. Never sleeping in his arms again, never spending time with his family, to whom she'd begun to secretly hope to belong someday. He'd seemed so honest when he'd looked into her eyes and promised he wanted only her. She wanted so desperately to believe him.

And then she turned in her pacing and her eyes fell on the crumpled manila folder lying at the foot of her bed.

I love you, he'd said. But other people had said those same words, when it hadn't been her they'd loved at all.

In a sudden surge of anguished frustration, Michelle swung her arm to sweep the file from the bed, its contents scattering across the floor. And then, for the first time since finding Carter Powell waiting for her that afternoon, she wept.

"I don't want to hear excuses, Chuck! I've told you what I suspect about Powell and now I want you to get me the proof!" Tony snapped into the telephone receiver gripped tightly in his fist. "Whatever it takes, whatever you have to do...I want that evidence. If Powell picks up a quarter from the sidewalk, I want to know it, you got that?"

"Tony..."

He gestured curtly at Bonnie, who stood hesitantly in the open doorway to his office, trying to get his attention. "And, Chuck—I want to know where Powell got that report on Michelle. Make that a priority, understand?"

He hung up the phone, then glared at his secretary. "What is it, Bonnie?"

She didn't flinch at his tone—the same one he'd been using all morning, to his regret. He shouldn't be taking his pain out on his employees, he told himself wearily. He owed them more than that.

"I'm sorry," he said, before she could answer his question. "I didn't mean to snap."

"That's okay." Her dark eyes were sympathetic. He hadn't told her what had been eating him today, but she seemed to sense that he was hurting, and to care. "You've got a call on line two."

"Who is it?" he asked without a great deal of interest, rubbing his hands across his face. He'd hardly slept since he'd left Michelle's house Saturday evening—nearly forty hours ago. As tired as he was, he wasn't sure he'd ever sleep soundly again—not without Michelle at his side.

"It's Carter Powell. Want me to take a message?"

Tony's hands fell to the desk, his head snapping up. "Carter Powell?"

"That's what the secretary said."

Tony reached for the phone. "Close the door, will you?"

She nodded, slipping out of the office and closing the door behind her.

"D'Alessandro."

A woman responded. "Just a moment, please."

There was a click and a moment of silence. And then a man's voice. "You don't take advice very well, do you, D'Alessandro?"

"Not without considering its source. Or the motives behind it," Tony murmured. "What do you want, Powell?"

"I want you to leave Michelle Trent alone. She's out of your league, D'Alessandro. You may have turned her head at first, but I'm sure that's about to change."

"Thanks to you?"

"As her attorney, it's my responsibility to protect her from unscrupulous opportunists. She's not quite the un-protected innocent she must have appeared when she showed up in your office looking for her long-lost family."

Knowing he was being deliberately baited, Tony man-aged not to respond in temper, though it was a wonder the plastic receiver didn't disintegrate within the vicious grip of his fist. "You don't really think she's going to stop looking for her brothers and sisters, do you, Powell? Nor turn her back on the sister she's already found."

"At the moment, you're my primary concern for her welfare," the attorney replied smoothly. "You didn't waste any time romancing her, did you? Some might call your behavior less than ethical—certainly far from pro-fessional. Considering your career background, I sup-pose I shouldn't be surprised."

"My relationship with Michelle has nothing to do with you."

"Relationship? Oh, I think that's rather strong a word. How much is she paying you for your investigation on her behalf, D'Alessandro?"

"That's none of your—"

"Whatever it is, I'll triple it if you'll take yourself off her case. Tell her whatever you like—that you've got too heavy a caseload or find that you've been mistaken in your so-called feelings for her. It's a generous offer, D'Alessandro. I'd suggest you take it."

Tony spoke from between clenched teeth. "I've got a few suggestions for you, Powell. Like exactly what you can do with your 'generous offer.'"

"You're making a mistake if you think you'll have it all. Michelle was almost taken in by a fortune hunter be-fore, but she's no fool. She won't let it happen again.

And as a long-time friend and trusted associate of her father, I'll do my best to make sure she's protected from you."

Heated accusations trembled on Tony's lips, so strongly that it was all he could do to hold them back. Instead, he managed to say evenly, "We'll see who's protecting Michelle, won't we, Powell?"

"Don't do anything stupid, boy. You really don't want to take me on. Trust me in that, if nothing else."

"Yeah, right."

"If this is the way you want it—"

"This is the way it's going to be."

"Fine. But when it's over—when your career falls down around your ears for the second time—remember that you were warned, will you?" The subtle threat ended with a click and a dial tone.

"Son of a—" Tony slammed his own receiver down without regard for the condition of his telephone.

He was more convinced than ever now that Carter Powell had something to hide. Though the man was careful with the wording of his threats—a tape of the conversation would most likely have sounded as though Carter was doing nothing more than overzealously protecting a valued client's interests—Tony would have bet it wasn't Michelle whom the attorney was trying to protect. He had his suspicions—his convictions—but he needed the proof. And, whatever it took, he would have it.

He reached for his jacket, threw it over his shoulder and strode toward the door. Jerking it open, he passed through the reception area without pausing, speaking to Bonnie on his way past her desk. "I'll be out most of the day. Use the beeper if you need me."

"All right. I'll see you . . ."

But Tony didn't wait around to hear the rest. Jaw set in determination, he headed for his Jeep. He was about to begin the task of clearing his name with the woman he loved.

Michelle spent Tuesday afternoon trying to concentrate on problems more important than her own. She was halfway through a letter requesting funds for a charity organization Trent Enterprises had contributed to on previous occasions when her telephone rang. She looked at it for a long moment before answering, both afraid and hopeful that Tony would be on the other end of the line.

She forced herself to pick it up on the third ring. "Hello."

"Michelle, I'm glad I caught you. I need to talk to you."

Though he didn't identify himself, and though she'd talked to him only a handful of times in the past few years, Michelle recognized the voice. "Uncle Richard? What's wrong?"

"I had a call from Carter Powell this morning."

Michelle tensed.

"The man's concerned about you, Michelle, and I'd say he has justification. What in blazes is going on with you?"

"You'll have to be more specific, Uncle Richard. What exactly did Carter tell you about me?"

"That you've begun a reckless and potentially dangerous search for a bunch of strangers you haven't seen in twenty-four years. And that you're having an affair with the private investigator you hired, a man who is quite obviously interested in more than the investigation you hired him to conduct. Carter told me the man had financial information about Trent Enterprises that no one outside the corporation should have access to. You're aware of this?"

Michelle took a deep breath. "Carter showed me the report Tony apparently requested. And I'm looking into it, Uncle Richard. I've given a copy of the report to Charles Major, in case there was any information in it that he considered potentially damaging to the corporation."

The mention of the CEO of Trent Enterprises, Dallas, seemed to mollify Richard Trent only marginally. "I don't like this at all, Michelle. Whatever possessed you to get into this?"

"Mother left me a letter telling me about my brothers and sisters. I wanted to find them, wanted to at least meet them. They're my family, Uncle Richard. Can't you understand that?"

"Frankly, no, I can't. The Trents became your family the day you were adopted. You were raised with affection and financial and social advantages you would never have had otherwise. These other people are strangers to you, raised God only knows how. I'm sure they'll be delighted to claim kinship with an extremely wealthy young woman, but I can't for the life of me understand what you expect to get in return."

Michelle was tempted to reply that her brothers and sisters wouldn't be much more strangers to her than this man she'd been raised to call "Uncle." She bit the words back. "I just want to meet them, Uncle Richard. I assure you I'll be careful."

"As you've been with this private investigator?" he asked skeptically.

Her eyes narrowed. "My relationship with Tony has nothing to do with this. I'm neither a child nor a fool, Uncle Richard. I'm quite capable of forming my own judgments, once I have all the information in front of me. Believe me, Carter has made sure that I know about Tony's free-lance investigation into my financial affairs.''

"You should be grateful that your attorney is so dedicated to your welfare. Obviously my brother knew what he was doing by asking Powell to watch out for you."

Again, Michelle had to bite her lip against words that could serve no purpose other than to antagonize Richard.

"Listen, Michelle, it's obvious that you've been lonely since your mother's death," Richard continued, trying to make his tone more conciliatory. "I'm sorry I haven't been more available for you, but you're aware, of course, that Trent Enterprises, California, has been going through a major restructuring and has required a great deal of my time."

"I understand, Uncle Richard." *You were never here for me before—why should I have expected you to be now?* She kept that thought to herself, of course.

"Your Aunt Lydia and cousin Steven would like very much to see you. Why don't you fly out to spend a few weeks with us? Your charity duties can be delegated for a time, and I think it'll do you good to get away from Dallas for a while. Steven has several single friends—men of distinguished backgrounds and impeccable reputations—who'd enjoy meeting you. I'm sure they'd be willing to overlook—well, you know."

"My adoption, Uncle Richard? My less-than-blue-blooded background?"

He sighed audibly at her cutting tone. "Now, Michelle, don't get defensive. You know I think Harrison and Alicia did an admirable job of raising you. You've made a place for yourself in society and in the corpora-

tion, and you've conducted yourself quite properly."
Until now, his tone added.

"You don't need to go out looking for a family, my dear," he continued with an unnatural-sounding jocularity. "You have us. I agree that it's certainly time you set up your own household, had some children to occupy your time and affections. That's why I think it would be advisable for you to let us introduce you to some nice young men. I'd be happy to take care of all the travel arrangements. Shall we expect you late next week?"

"No." She forced herself to speak politely. "Thank you very much for the invitation, but I really have too many responsibilities here to take time off just now."

"Michelle, be reasonable. You—"

"Excuse me, Uncle Richard, but I have a meeting this afternoon and I really should be going," she lied without regret. "Thank you for calling. Give my best to Aunt Lydia and to Steven. I'll talk to you again soon."

She hung up, leaving him in midsputter.

She was really getting tired of people trying to tell her what to do, she thought, her temper growing. People who claimed to be acting in her best interests. Carter, Richard—even Tony, who'd tried to convince her that he was looking into her finances for reasons that concerned her, but that he couldn't discuss with her. Even if it were true—and she refused to make that judgment without further evidence—he had no right to treat her as a mindless fool who couldn't take care of herself.

It was true that she'd met him at a time when she was vulnerable, that she'd leaned on him perhaps more than she should have during that traumatic reunion with her sister. But she *was* capable of watching out for her own best interests, dammit, and it was time other people acknowledged it!

She was also fed up with being discouraged from finding her brothers and sisters. They were her flesh and blood, separated only by accidents of fate, and she had a right to know them, to judge for herself whether they'd grown into adults she could respect or even love. Whatever else he may have done, at least Tony had never tried to keep her from finding her family. He and Taylor had been the only ones who'd encouraged her to do so.

Taylor. Michelle sighed as she thought of her friend. She'd be so glad when the photo assignment in Galveston was finished and Taylor home. She needed very badly to talk to someone who'd always been on her side, whose motives were completely open and above suspicion. She needed a friend.

Or a sister.

Michelle pulled her lower lip between her teeth as her gaze turned slowly toward the telephone. She *had* a sister, she thought with a sudden wave of longing. Layla, who'd been so touchingly pleased to find her again, who'd loved her and cared for her as a baby. Who shared her eye color and hair color and the shape of her face. Whose adorable children called her Aunt Michelle.

Nervously moistening her lips, she reached for the telephone and opened her address book. She didn't need Richard's insincere claims of affection, his obligatory efforts to fulfill what he considered to be his duty to his late brother's adopted daughter. And she'd never really belonged to Tony's close-knit clan, no matter how warmly they'd welcomed her among them. She had a family of her own, she thought with renewed determination.

It was long past time to get to know them.

Chapter Thirteen

Michelle looked into the full-length mirror in her dressing room on Wednesday evening, anxiously inspecting her appearance. She wasn't quite sure what was proper for a dinner at home with her sister and brother-in-law, so she'd dressed conservatively in a black silk jumpsuit and simple gold jewelry, her hair swept into a neat chignon.

She checked her makeup, noting that even the skillfully applied cosmetics hadn't completely hidden the effects of four nights of very little sleep. Nor did eye shadow and dark mascara disguise the pain visible in her blue eyes. She could only hope Layla and Kevin wouldn't notice.

She'd been pleased when Layla had accepted her dinner invitation on such short notice. Though the invitation had been extended to the entire family, Layla had insisted on leaving her children with a baby-sitter, explaining that she'd like to have a bit more time with her sister without the distractions of three busy, curious children.

"We still have so much to learn about each other," she'd added, sounding as though she were eagerly anticipating the evening.

Even though Michelle, too, looked forward to being with her sister again, her pleasure would have been much greater if she wasn't still tearing herself up about her feelings for Tony—and her questions about his feelings for her.

If only she could bring herself to accept Carter's assertion—and evidence—that Tony had been using her in the same way Geoff had used her. But, logical though the probability seemed, she simply couldn't believe it. Not entirely. Something inside her—somewhere in the vicinity of her heart—kept trying to convince her that Tony simply wasn't capable of treating her that way. That he couldn't possibly have deceived her so cleverly.

She hadn't heard from him since he'd left Saturday. She'd told him not to call until he had whatever proof he'd claimed to be searching for to justify the report Carter had given her. Obviously he didn't have that proof yet, if it had ever existed at all. But, oh, how she missed him. How she would have loved to have him with her tonight during this dinner with Layla and Kevin.

She heard the doorbell chime downstairs and took one last glance at the mirror. The smile she affected looked natural enough to fool anyone who didn't know her very well—perhaps it would work with her guests. Wishing there was something she could do about the anguish in her heart, she turned and left the bedroom.

Layla and Kevin were waiting in the den, where Betty had been instructed to escort them. The moment she joined them, Michelle could tell that something was bothering them. Kevin wore a sport coat and slacks and tugged uncomfortably at his tie; Layla had on a cotton shirtwaist dress that she smoothed with stiff hands. Holding on to her smile, Michelle held out her hands to her sister. "Layla. I'm so glad you could be here tonight."

Layla's hands were cold. "Thank you for asking us, Michelle."

"Please, sit down. Did Betty offer you drinks?"

"Yes, but we really didn't want anything right now." Layla and Kevin perched side by side on the edge of the oversized couch, looking as though they were being interviewed for a job, Michelle thought in dismay. They hardly looked as though they were comfortable.

Layla cleared her throat. "Your home is lovely."

"Thank you." Michelle wondered if it made her sister uncomfortable to compare the Trent home with her own modest frame house in Fort Worth. "I grew up here," she explained casually. "My parents left the house to me."

"What did your father do?" Kevin asked, looking around the massive den.

"He and his brother were joint owners of Trent Enterprises. Daddy ran the Dallas division while my Uncle Richard handles the California business."

"Do you run the company now?" her brother-in-law asked curiously.

Michelle smiled and shook her head. "I was never really interested in the corporate world, despite my father's encouragement to learn more about it. I handle the charitable contributions for the corporation—budgeting yearly donations, researching and choosing the organizations to benefit from those donations, requesting additional funds from the board of directors when necessary. It's been a very fulfilling job for me, though a demanding one at times."

"You live in this big house all alone?" Layla asked.

"Betty and Arthur, her husband who works for me as general handyman, live in the back wing, but except for them I've lived here alone since my mother died earlier this year."

As though in response to the mention of her name, Betty carried in a tray of fragrant hot appetizers. Relying on signals developed through years of familiarity, Michelle let Betty know that she'd like dinner served very soon. Unfortunately, the evening hadn't started out as well as she'd hoped.

Oh, she wished Tony was there! He'd know what to do to keep the conversation moving.

"How are the children, Layla?" she asked in another desperate attempt to break the ice. She was pleased when Layla's eyes brightened at the question. Like most mothers, she seemed to enjoy talking about her children.

Layla and Kevin had just started to relax a bit when Betty announced dinner. Stepping into the dining room, with its elegant chandelier and exquisite table settings, seemed to make them withdraw even more than before. They sat very stiffly in their chairs, eating the food set in front of them in near silence broken only by Michelle's futile efforts to keep the conversation going.

Fighting an urge to burst into tears, Michelle wistfully compared this awkward family dinner with the D'Alessandro gathering for Tony's birthday. There'd be no embarrassing silences in his family, she thought sadly, no uncomfortable pauses fraught with tension. Tony's family would be more likely to speak their minds about whatever was bothering them, rather than hiding behind polite niceties.

Which suddenly seemed like a very good idea to Michelle.

She set her fork down with a thump, making Layla start and Kevin look up curiously from his dinner. "Layla, is something wrong?" Michelle asked boldly, searching her sister's face across the table. "You seem so uncomfortable. Is it something I've done?"

Layla looked quickly at her husband, then sighed and shook her head. Following Michelle's example, she set her own fork down and folded her hands in her lap. "It's nothing you've done, Michelle."

"Then what's wrong? We talked so easily last week, but tonight we're having to struggle over each word."

"Last week we were in *our* home," Layla explained quietly while Kevin flushed at the words.

"I don't understand," Michelle confessed, looking in bewilderment from Layla to Kevin. "Why should that make a difference?"

"I think what my wife is trying to explain," Kevin began diffidently, "is that we didn't realize when we met you that you were this—well, wealthy."

Not that again. Half-tempted to scream in sheer frustration, Michelle spread her hands beseechingly. "Does that really make a difference? I happened to be adopted and raised by a wealthy couple, but that doesn't change where I came from or who I am. Layla, you're my sister."

"I don't want you to be ashamed of us," Layla admitted. "Or to consider us one of the charity cases you work with all the time. I want us to have things in common—but I'm not sure that we do, considering."

"I am *not* ashamed of you! If I were, would it be so important to me to get to know you both better? And as far as charity, I hardly consider my family as a charity case!"

Kevin reached out to take his distressed wife's hand. "We don't mean to insult you, Michelle. It's just that— well, we don't know many people who live this elegantly. Security fences and servants and houses big enough to hold two or three families. Most of our friends are doing pretty well just to pay their bills."

Michelle's fists clenched in her lap. "I don't have to worry about paying the bills," she admitted, her eyes filling with the tears that had hovered so close since she'd sent Tony away. "But other than that, I'm no different from anyone else. I feel pain and fear and sometimes I get so very lonely. Because of my parents' money, I've been kidnapped and isolated and hurt. I have people guarding me from those who would be tempted to use me to get to the money, and I never really know whom to trust.

"I want to know I have someone who doesn't care about the money, someone who loves me just because of who I am. Someone who remembers me as a little girl who liked horsey rides and jelly sandwiches. Is that so much to ask?" she finished in little more than a broken whisper.

"Oh, Shelley, of course it's not." Layla had left her seat to kneel beside Michelle's chair, her expressive face distressed. "I'm sorry, I didn't mean to hurt you. It just...well, it just took me off guard to see this house and everything. I was being a fool. Can you forgive me?"

Michelle swallowed a sob and tried to smile. "Of course. I'm sorry I unloaded on you like that. I've—I've had a rough week," she admitted.

Kevin pushed back his chair and held out his hand to her. "Think we could start over?" he asked. "We'll try to forgive you for being rich if you can forgive us for being reverse snobs."

Standing beside her sister, Michelle gave a watery chuckle and took Kevin's hand. Then impulsively kissed his cheek. "I'd like to start over," she told him warmly. "I think having a family is worth working for."

"Yeah. So do I. Now can we get back to our dinner? This is the best veal I've ever tasted."

Still smiling, Michelle dashed at her eyes with the corner of her napkin. "I'll be sure to tell Betty you said so. She's very proud of this dish."

Looking far more relaxed than she had earlier, Layla returned to her seat. "Would it help to talk about your rough week, Michelle?" she offered in concern. "Does it have something to do with Tony?"

Michelle's eyes widened. "Why do you ask that?"

"You haven't mentioned him even once this evening," Layla pointed out. "And I could tell when you visited us that there was much more between you than employer and employee."

"Yes," Michelle admitted, "I'm just not sure what at the moment."

"He's not one of the guys who's after your money, is he?" Kevin demanded, looking up from his veal with a scowl that looked suspiciously big-brotherly.

Everything within her wanted to immediately deny that Tony was like that. She made herself answer more cautiously, "I don't know, Kevin. It's...possible."

Frowning, Layla shook her head. "Oh, I find that so hard to believe. He seemed so nice—so concerned about you. Are you sure you aren't misinterpreting something, Shelley?"

As she knew Layla had simply fallen into old habit calling her by her childhood name, Michelle made no effort to correct her. She rather liked it. "My attorney warned me that Tony's been showing undue interest in my finances," she explained when it occurred to her that she would like other opinions. She told Layla and Kevin about the report Carter had brought her.

"How did your attorney get the report?" Kevin asked.

Michelle shrugged. "He wouldn't say."

"You trust him?"

She started to answer that of course she trusted Carter. And found herself hesitating. "He's never given me reason not to trust him," she temporized.

"Sounds like he's going overboard in his responsibilities," Kevin murmured. "Has he made it a practice to keep you from forming outside relationships without his approval?"

"It—hasn't really been an issue before," Michelle answered slowly, thinking back. "My mother was ill for some time before she died and I spent a great deal of my time with her. I have one very close friend that I've known for years and a few other social friends, but I haven't been closely involved with anyone else for some time."

She added carefully, "He did advise me against finding my brothers and sisters. He said he was concerned about me."

Layla made an annoyed sound. "I'm glad you didn't listen to him. I can't imagine you have anything to worry about from our brothers or our little sister. And, trust me, Kevin and I don't expect anything from you but your affection."

"You already have that," Michelle replied with a smile.

Layla returned the smile, then suddenly frowned again. "I just thought of something you said earlier. That you'd been used and hurt and . . . kidnapped?"

Had she really said that? Michelle bit her lip, surprised at her indiscreet outburst. "It happened a long time ago."

Layla insisted on hearing the whole story. When she'd been told, she sat in white-faced horror, her eyes big and wet. "Oh, Michelle, how horrible for you. No wonder you've learned to be so careful. I don't know how you survived it."

"My parents were wonderful to me afterward," Michelle explained. "Overprotective, perhaps—particularly Mother—but loving and caring and very supportive. It helped, though it was a long time before I stopped having nightmares."

"And no wonder." Kevin's brow was creased with his fierce scowl. "I'd like to have gotten my hands on the guy."

"Actually, Tony's father took care of that," Michelle murmured and then, of course, had to explain the connection.

"I still think you should give Tony a chance to prove he's not after your money," Layla declared afterward. "He's a nice guy from a nice family. And he'd be a fool not to love you for yourself."

"I saw the way he was looking at you at our house," Kevin seconded. "Those weren't dollar signs in the guy's eyes, Michelle. He looked crazy about you."

Michelle wanted to believe them more than she'd ever wanted anything in her life. The very depth of her longing made her even more cautious. "I just need time to be sure," she said. "Time—and something more substantial than words."

Kevin and Layla didn't stay long after dessert, claiming they needed to get home at the time they'd told their baby-sitter. The evening passed much too quickly for Michelle, once they'd gotten past the initial intimidation the couple had felt at the luxury of her home.

"Our place next time," Layla announced as they were leaving. "We'll have a cookout, or something. Let you get to know the kids."

"Lord help you," Kevin murmured, earning himself a laughing punch on the arm from his children's mother.

"That sounds wonderful," Michelle assured them. She kissed Kevin, then hugged and kissed her sister. "Good night, Layla. Call me soon, okay?"

"I will. I promise." Layla followed Kevin out the front door, then hesitated on the walk and looked back over her shoulder at Michelle. "Why don't you call Tony? If you *have* misjudged him, he's got to be hurting as badly as you are."

"I'll think about it," Michelle promised. "Drive carefully."

She closed the door with a tired sigh, relieved the evening hadn't been a total disaster, despite its unpromising beginning. And she was thoroughly intrigued by Layla and Kevin's certainty that she'd misjudged Tony's motives. True, they didn't know him, not even as well as Michelle did . . . but they'd seemed so convinced that he wasn't the type who'd use her for her wealth.

Oh, how she hoped they were right!

It was nearly midnight when Michelle finally gave in to an urge that had been plaguing her ever since Layla's parting words. Her hand shaking, she perched on the edge of her bed and picked up the telephone. Even then, she sat for a long time with the receiver in her lap, wondering if she had the nerve to dial the number.

Would Tony be sleeping? Would he be angry with her for sending him away as she had? Had he missed her as desperately as she'd missed him, spent their nights apart remembering what it had been like to lie in each other's arms?

Did he really love her? Or would she be playing right into his hands to give him her trust, when she wasn't entirely sure he'd proven he deserved it?

She closed her eyes and saw his face, heard his deep voice teasing her, laughing with her, murmuring to her as he'd made love to her. She could see him with his family, the warmth and affection that had softened his dark eyes when he'd looked at his mother and his father, his brothers and his dear, elderly aunt. She'd convinced herself she saw that same warmth when he looked at her.

Could she have been so foolishly mistaken?

She loved him. Oh, how she loved him! And right now, in the darkness and silence of her room in the middle of a lonely night, she couldn't seem to convince herself that he had ever lied to her, that he didn't deserve her love.

Taking a deep breath, she punched the numbers quickly, before she changed her mind. She wasn't sure what she intended to say. That she missed him? That she wanted so badly to believe in him? That she trusted him, despite all the evidence to the contrary?

On the fifteenth ring, she finally conceded that Tony wasn't home. It didn't matter what she would have said, he wasn't there to hear it. Her eyes closed, she replaced the receiver on its cradle, wondering where he was at this hour. Who he was with.

And she feared she'd get no more sleep that night than she had during the four long, painful, lonely nights preceding it.

Tony entered his dark apartment and kicked the door closed behind him, so tired he ached all the way down to the heels of his boots. He didn't bother to turn on the living room lights, but headed straight for the bedroom, shedding clothing as he went.

It was two in the morning, he hadn't eaten since breakfast, had been on the run for the past eighteen hours, needed a shave and a shower almost as much as he needed sleep—but his efforts had paid off. He and Chuck had obtained exactly what Tony had expected to find. As well as an unpleasant surprise that had left him with a bitter, dispirited taste in his mouth.

He crawled naked into bed and buried his head in the pillow as though to block out every unpleasant thing that had happened to him in the past few days, from the moment Michelle had confronted him with the file to his more recent firing of an employee he'd trusted.

He'd been tempted to head straight for Michelle's house with the evidence he'd collected, regardless of the hour. Lingering hurt from her lack of faith in him prodded him to shove the facts in her face and demand that she acknowledge how cruelly she'd misjudged him. His piqued ego suggested he make her crawl a little before he forgave her—and he would forgive her, of course, despite his disappointment.

Yet even as those thoughts crossed his weary mind, he knew that all he really wanted to do was take her in his arms and hold her. Bury himself in her softness, her sweetness. Tell her how very much he loved her. Maybe now that he had the proof he'd needed, she'd understand that it was safe to love him in return. That he'd never hurt her, nor would he let anyone else.

Tomorrow. Sinking more deeply into the pillow, he let the first tendril of sleep soothe his troubled mind. Tomorrow he'd be with Michelle again.

Chapter Fourteen

Michelle stepped out of the shower and wrapped herself in a thick terry robe before winding a towel around her dripping hair. On most Thursday mornings, she'd have been up and dressed long before ten o'clock, but today she'd slept late, exhausted from several restless nights and tense, miserable days. She'd awakened to thoughts of Tony this morning—prompted, perhaps, by a night of dreaming of him.

Would she see him today?

She'd just taken an outfit from her closet when a tap on her bedroom door drew her attention. "Yes?"

Betty opened the door just far enough to stick her head inside. "Phone call for you. It's Mr. Tony."

Michelle's stomach knotted, her breathing going shallow. She tried to hide the instinctive reactions from Betty, though she suspected she wasn't entirely successful. "Thanks, Betty. I'll take it in here."

Betty nodded and closed the door, though not without first giving Michelle a look that all but ordered her to be nice to the man on the telephone. Michelle thought in exasperation that she wished it was as easy for her to give Tony her unconditional trust as it seemed to be for everyone else.

Her hand wasn't quite steady when she picked up the phone. "Hello."

"Hi. Were you busy?"

"No, I was just—" Her left hand tightened on the lapels of her robe, as if he could somehow tell that she wore nothing beneath it. "No."

"I need to see you today, Michelle. I have something to show you. Something important."

"I'll come to your office. What time?"

He paused a moment, then replied. "I'd rather come there, if you don't mind. It's something you'll want to hear in privacy—something you'll have to decide how to handle. Will you be in this afternoon?"

She thought about arguing—it seemed so much safer to meet in his office, rather than her home. And then she told herself she was being foolish. "Yes, I'll be in. Three o'clock?"

"Right." He hesitated again, then asked more softly, "How are you?"

I'm miserable. I miss you. I want to be with you, to burrow into your arms and have you make the pain go away. "I'm fine, Tony."

"Good," he answered, though he sounded oddly disappointed with her answer. "I'll see you this afternoon, then."

"Yes. Goodbye."

He didn't respond, but disconnected without another word.

Staring blankly at nothing, Michelle held her receiver until a persistently annoying beeping reminded her to hang it up.

Michelle tapped her pencil rhythmically on her desk, echoing the nervous tattoo of her heart. Tony was due to arrive any minute. She'd instructed Betty to usher him to the office she maintained at home, deciding the relative formality of the setting would make it easier for her to listen objectively to whatever he had to tell her.

She'd thought she was prepared to see him, that she had her emotions fully under control. Yet when he stepped into the room, looking dark and handsome and utterly masculine in a black shirt, black denims and black boots, her heart leaped into her throat. The pencil fell from her nerveless fingers. She tried to speak, then found that she couldn't.

Tony cleared his throat, as though he were struggling with the same problem. "Hi, Michelle."

"Hi," she managed in a reasonable semblance of her normal voice. She waved to the leather chair across the desk. "Sit down. Would you like a drink?"

He shook his head, apparently impatient with the formalities. Dropping into the chair, he set a large envelope on her desk.

She looked at it, strangely reluctant to touch it. "What is this?"

"It's what I want to talk to you about. I have something to tell you, Michelle. I'm sorry, but it may be painful for you."

She drew her lower lip between her teeth, waiting for him to explain.

He took a deep breath. "It's about Carter Powell. I assume you'd guessed that."

She nodded, not at all surprised.

"This envelope contains proof that he's been skimming money from your accounts for the past three and a half years—ever since your father died. Powell's been building his own private stash from the trust funds he and your father set up for you. He's been very clever with it. I've had a couple of friends, both accountants, tracing his path through your records. It took them nearly a week, but they found it. The proof is all there, in the envelope."

Michelle swallowed hard. "How did you get my records?"

He hesitated, then sighed. "One of my friends is sort of a computer genius. There's not much he can't find out when he puts his mind to it."

"A hacker."

"Yes."

The thought that not only Tony, but total strangers, had had access to the most intimate details of her private financial affairs made her feel sick. "Why did you do this, Tony?" she whispered.

He frowned. "I told you from the beginning—I don't like being threatened. That first call Powell made to me was a mistake. Had he been genuinely concerned about you, he wouldn't have asked me to lie to you about being unable to find your brothers and sisters. I suspected even then that he had something to hide."

"Why should he have cared about whether I found my family?" Michelle asked in bewilderment. "What would that have mattered to what he was doing?"

"Oh, I'm sure he was genuinely concerned that your family would take advantage of suddenly finding a wealthy sister. He probably realized that his own machinations would come to light if anyone started looking too closely at your finances. You've obviously trusted him to handle things during the past few years, so until now there's been no reason for Powell to worry about being caught.

"Bringing the report to you last weekend was a calculated risk. He probably knew what I was looking for, but he hoped to make you distrust me enough to fire me before I could come up with anything solid. He thought he could easily convince you that I was just another fortune hunter. He didn't expect you to give me a chance to prove I was working in your best interest, rather than my own."

"I just don't understand," Michelle murmured, pressing her fingertips to her temples. "Carter is a wealthy man in his own right. He didn't need to steal from me."

"He's made a good living," Tony corrected, "but it wasn't enough to support both his wife and his mistress in the manner to which they'd become accustomed. Nor would it ensure him the comfortable retirement he was probably planning with your money."

"His mistress," Michelle repeated blankly, thinking of the many times Carter and his wife of many years had dined with her own parents. "You have proof of that, too?"

"Yes."

Though it was a warm day in late June and the temperature in the house was efficiently regulated, Michelle suddenly felt cold. She rubbed her hands slowly up and down her forearms, trying to reduce the chill. "So the financial report Carter brought me was connected to your investigation of him."

"Yes. And by the way, I found out how Carter got his hands on the report. He'd gotten to one of my operatives—Bob O'Brien. Paid him a hell of a lot more than I could to keep him informed about the progress of my work for you. Bob no longer works for me."

Michelle heard the pain of betrayal in his voice, but at the moment she was having too difficult a time struggling with her own similar feelings to offer sympathy. She'd known Carter Powell since she was two years old. She'd trusted him, as her parents had trusted him before her. She hadn't bothered with monitoring his every movement on her behalf, believing him to be one of the few people she could trust with her money, her best interests.

It seemed she'd been wrong again.

"Feel free to look over the evidence I've brought," Tony said, breaking into her dispirited thoughts. "I've brought more than enough to convince you that I'm telling the truth."

"That's not necessary," Michelle replied dully, not meeting his eyes. "I believe you."

"I'm sorry, Michelle. I know this has hurt you."

She took a deep breath, feeling strangely numb. "I must be getting used to it," she mused quietly. And then she reached for her telephone.

"Who are you calling?"

"Carter." She pushed the first familiar button.

Tony's hand covered hers on the telephone, warm against her icy skin. "Michelle . . . are you sure you want to do that?"

"No," she whispered, without putting down the receiver. "But I think I should let him know I'm going to call the police. It would be less embarrassing for both of us if he quietly turns himself in."

"You're pressing charges?"

"Yes." She met his eyes then, letting her anger show for the first time. "He betrayed me and he betrayed my father. He's not getting away with that."

Tony released her hand. "Good."

Michelle finished dialing the number. "This is Michelle Trent," she said a moment later. "Put me through to Carter. Tell him I strongly advise him to take my call."

Ten unpleasant minutes later, Michelle hung up the phone, her expression stricken. Tony had listened to her side of the conversation, but he wasn't sure what Powell's parting shot had been to turn her face so white. It was all he could do not to reach out to her, to offer comfort he wasn't sure she'd accept from him yet.

"What did he say?" he asked when she continued to sit so very still and quiet in her chair. "When you asked him why he'd betrayed your father's trust—what did he say?"

"He told me it had never seemed quite fair to him that a girl from a low-class, impoverished family should step into all the Trent wealth and power," she answered in a heartbreakingly flat voice. "It wasn't even as if I'd been born a Trent, he said. He agreed with my Uncle Richard that adoption was hardly the same as pure breeding."

His fists clenching on a surge of pure, primitive fury, Tony fought the urge to leap from his chair and go in search of Carter Powell. How he'd love to shove his fist into that shallow, deceitful, arrogant face!

But to do that, he'd have to leave Michelle. And, judging from her pale, listless appearance, she needed whatever support he could offer at the moment.

"You should have told me," Michelle whispered, her blue eyes big and lost in her colorless face. "You should have let me know what you suspected. I had a right to know."

"I couldn't tell you, Michelle. Not without some evidence to verify my suspicions. I could have been wrong, though my gut feelings all told me I was right. And you wouldn't have believed me, anyway, without proof."

Her eyelashes flicked in reaction to the faint trace of bitterness he couldn't quite keep out of his voice. And then she straightened and lifted her chin, as though dragging her emotions back under rigid control. "I'll pay you for the hours and expenses you've incurred in this investigation, of course, as well as your search for my family. If you'll make up a bill, I'll . . ."

Tony didn't even try to swallow the vicious curse that leapt to his lips. He slammed his hands down on her desk as he shoved himself to his feet to loom over her. Michelle jumped at his reaction and stared up at him as though he'd lost his mind.

"I know you're hurting and I know you feel betrayed," he said, his voice low, deadly serious. "But I'll be damned if I'll let you take it out on me."

"I don't know what you mean," she bluffed, her eyes focused somewhere around his Adam's apple. "I simply said—"

"I heard what you said." Deliberately, he rounded the desk. Standing in front of her chair, he reached down to grasp her forearms, pulling her to her feet with a gentle, inexorable pressure. "Now look at me, dammit."

Her wary gaze met his. "I don't appreciate—"

"Tough," he interrupted succinctly. "I haven't appreciated being treated like a money-hungry opportunist during the past week. I haven't appreciated being ordered to provide irrefutable proof that I haven't lied to you or tried to use you. I haven't appreciated sleeping alone the past five nights because the woman I love doesn't trust me enough to believe that I don't give a tinker's damn for her bank accounts! On the whole, I think I've been very patient with you, Michelle. But my patience just ran out.''

"I only offered to pay you for your work," she said in a very small voice.

"I didn't do it for pay," he answered gruffly, his pulse reacting to being so close to her again for the first time in so many long days. "I did it because I love you, and because I hated the thought that someone was using you, taking advantage of your trust."

"I did trust him," she whispered, her voice throbbing with pain. "I thought he cared about me. I thought he was a friend. And all the time, he thought...he only..." Her voice broke.

Tony groaned and pulled her roughly against him, his arms going tightly around her. She felt so small, so vulnerable, bringing out every latent protective instinct within him. "I know, Michelle," he murmured. "I know."

Her breath caught on a sob. She stiffened and started to pull away. "I'm sorry. I—"

"No." He held her more tightly. "You're not alone now, Michelle. You don't have to hide your feelings from me."

She resisted only for another moment. And then she burrowed into his shoulder and gave in to the tears she'd been fighting back. Tony bent his head over hers, cradling her to his aching chest. He deeply regretted that in protecting her, he'd had to hurt her. No one, he thought with reckless determination, would ever hurt her like this again.

Michelle didn't cry for long. Swallowing the last of her sobs, she raised her head. He had his handkerchief ready to gently wipe her face.

"Thank you," she murmured.

"Anytime," he replied, smoothing a strand of hair away from her damp, flushed face. "Feel better?"

"Yes," she whispered, her wet eyes darkening as they met his.

His stomach tightened. "Michelle..."

Her arms crept around his neck.

Tony groaned and lowered his head, his mouth covering hers as hungrily as though he'd been starving for her. Probably because he had been. And Michelle returned the kiss with the same desperate intensity, her lips parting in invitation. An invitation he accepted eagerly.

He drew back with a gasp when the kiss strained the boundaries of his willpower. Finding himself dangerously close to taking her right there on her desk, he tried to regain control. It was a close call, but he managed.

"Let's go to your bedroom," he suggested, his voice raw-edged.

Michelle's eyes flew open. "I don't—"

He kissed her again, smothering the words he wasn't sure he wanted to hear. "I want you," he murmured against her lips. "I've missed you."

Her lips moved beneath his, her hands sliding into his hair. He kissed her deeply, thoroughly, persuasively. "Let's go to your bedroom, Michelle."

She hesitated only another moment before drawing back and offering him her hand.

Feeling as though they'd just avoided a potential crisis, Tony closed his fingers around hers, staying close beside her as she turned and led him toward the stairs to her room. It was going to be all right, he told himself

confidently, his blood racing through his veins in anticipation. Michelle was learning to trust him again. He
didn't intend to let up until she'd learned to love him as
much as he loved her.

Tony noticed that Michelle was unusually quiet as she
locked her bedroom door behind them and turned to
him. Assuming her silence was a result of the emotional
stress she'd been under that afternoon, he spoke soothingly, tenderly to her as he undressed her and then himself. Words of love, of need, of desire. Mostly in English,
but occasionally in the so richly expressive Italian language.

He drew her down to the bed, stringing kisses down her
throat, caressing her breasts, stroking her silky thighs.
"Michelle," he whispered, fitting himself between her
legs. "I love you. *Ti amo.*"

Still she said nothing, though her hands were as busy,
as avid as his own. She drew him to her, her arms tightly
around him, her body arching beneath him. And she
cried out in pleasure when he slipped into her, eagerly
lifting to his thrusts. When she cried out again, he caught
the sound in his mouth, his lips covering hers even as the
explosion began for both of them.

When their tremors at last died away, Tony cradled her
against his shoulder, unwilling to release her. He stroked
her hair with one unsteady hand, his lips against the top
of her head.

"I love you," he murmured, closing his eyes to savor
the pleasure of having her in his arms again.

Though he hadn't intended to sleep, Tony woke with a
start some time later, realizing that the past few sleepless
nights had caught up with him. Judging from the shadows in the bedroom, he'd slept more than an hour. He

turned his head on the pillow to see if Michelle was still sleeping—only to find the bed beside him empty.

"Michelle?" he said huskily, immediately pushing himself upright.

She was sitting in a chair across the room, wearing a heavy, dark robe, her legs drawn up within the circle of her arms. She hadn't turned on the lights, but sat in a shadowed corner, looking alone and distant.

"Michelle?" he asked again.

Her head turned in his direction. "Yes?"

"Are you okay?"

"I'm fine."

Watching her closely, he swung his legs over the side of the bed and reached for his pants. He shoved his feet into them. "You're thinking about Powell?"

She shrugged, the motion hardly visible in the shadows. "I was trying not to think at all."

Tony snapped on a light, making her blink. She looked pale and tousled and still sexy enough to make his blood heat in his veins. Wearing only his slacks, he sat on the end of the bed, deciding they needed to talk more than he needed to act on his renewed arousal. "You're being very quiet."

She tightened her arms around her knees, the pose making her look very young and vulnerable. "I didn't want to disturb you. You looked as though you needed your sleep."

"I'm awake now. Ready to talk?"

"About what?" she asked warily.

"About us. I love you, Michelle. I've told you that several times now. You haven't responded."

Her eyelids fell, hiding her expression. "I...don't know what to say."

He fought down the pain. "Do you believe me?"

She didn't respond, other than seeming to curl more tightly into her chair.

"Dammit, Michelle, answer me! Do you believe that I love you? You—and not your money?"

"I—I want to believe it," she said at last, her eyes damp when they slowly lifted back to his.

His fists clenched on his knees. "What more do I have to do to prove it?" he demanded harshly. "How many tests do you have to put me through? I've offered you everything I have. I want to make a life with you, start a family with you, but you have to know you're all I want. I'd sign prenuptial agreements, promise never to touch a penny of your money, whatever I had to do. If I'd met you as Shelley Marie Walker rather than Michelle Culverton Trent, I'd still want to marry you.

"In fact," he added grimly, "I rather wish that's the way it was at the moment. It would be a hell of a lot easier to prove myself to you."

Her hand fluttered weakly in the air, her expression a curious combination of regret and trepidation. "I don't want to hurt you, Tony," she whispered. "I'm not trying to put you through tests. I just . . . need more time."

He muttered a curse between clenched teeth and abruptly stood, reaching for the rest of his clothes. "Right. More time. More proof. More guarantees."

He thrust his arms into the sleeves of his shirt. "I love you, Michelle," he said flatly. "I'll always love you. But the next move is yours. I won't stop looking for your family, but we can't have a personal relationship if you can't bring yourself to trust me. If you decide what we have is worth taking a few risks, you know where to find me. If I don't hear from you, I'll give you a call whenever I find something on your family."

To his bitter disappointment, she didn't call him back when he turned and left the room.

His revelations about Carter Powell hadn't strengthened Michelle's trust in him, he realized with a sinking feeling in his bruised heart. This latest betrayal had only bolstered her fear of trusting others. And at the moment, he wasn't sure he'd ever be able to break through the protective wall she'd built around herself. Wasn't even sure he had the energy to try.

He climbed into his Jeep, shoved the key into the ignition and turned the wheels toward the massive front gates of the Trent estate. He needed rest, needed time to get over this new hurt she'd inflicted on him. And then he'd probably be back, armed with every emotional weapon he could think of for storming invisible defenses. Because, God help him, he didn't think he could ever walk away from her for good.

Tony had intended to head straight home for about sixteen hours of uninterrupted sleep. He wasn't even sure when he'd changed his mind. But he found himself pulling into the driveway of his parents' home, needing very badly to be with people who loved him and had always believed in him.

He found his father in the den, drinking a beer and watching a baseball game on the cable sports channel. Carla, apparently, was still at work, or Vinnie never would have risked the cigar smoldering in an ashtray at his elbow. "Hi, Dad. Better spray some air freshener before Mom gets home or there'll be hell to pay."

Vinnie nodded at his son and held up a blue spray can. "Got it covered," he said. "I figure I've got a sixty-forty chance of getting away with it this time."

Tony smiled—or tried to.

Vinnie took one look at that weak excuse for a smile and rose to his feet in concern. "Tony? What is it, son?"

"Mind if I get a beer and hang around here awhile?" Tony asked, gesturing toward the television. "We can watch the rest of the game together."

"Of course I don't mind. I'd like that."

Tony nodded and turned toward the small refrigerator installed in a wet bar in one corner of the comfortably furnished room. Vinnie was still standing, still watching him, when he came back with his beer.

"Want to talk about it, Tony?"

Tony shook his head. "Not yet."

Never reticent about showing his feelings toward his family, Vinnie put an arm around his son's shoulders and gave him a bracing hug. "When you're ready, I'm here."

Tony swallowed the lump in his throat. "I know, Dad. Thanks. I may need to take you up on that offer."

"That's what family's for, son. Let's sit down and get comfortable."

"Let me get this straight." Sprawled in an oversized blue leather armchair, Taylor tented her fingers in front of her and looked thoughtful as she spoke for the first time in nearly half an hour of listening to Michelle's garbled rantings.

"Tony says he loves you and wants to marry you. Without being paid or thanked for his efforts, he went to great lengths to expose a man who has been taking advantage of you for years. Tony was even willing to temporarily put up with your suspicions that he may be a calculating gigolo because he didn't want to make accusations against your attorney without evidence, just in case his instincts were wrong. He forgave you for thinking the worst of him and is willing to sign prenuptial agreements promising not to touch your money if you marry him.

"Frankly, Michelle, he sounds like a madman to me. I think he should be shot at sunrise."

Stopping her restless prowling of Taylor's Southwestern-decorated living room, Michelle whirled on her friend in frustration. "I thought you said you'd listen objectively if I'd talk to you about what's been bothering me!"

"I *did* listen objectively," Taylor returned evenly. "I heard every word you babbled. I'm furious with Carter Powell for what he did to you and I think you're entirely right to press charges against him so he doesn't ever try anything like this again. I understand you're hurting and that you think you've been given even more reason not to trust people. What I *don't* understand is why you feel Tony deserves your distrust. Everything he's done has been for your sake."

Michelle moistened her lips and shoved her hands into the pockets of her denim skirt. "I didn't say I don't trust him."

"You didn't say you do trust him, either," Taylor returned.

Michelle couldn't argue with that. She'd spent the past twenty-four hours trying to untangle her feelings about Tony.

"Do you love him?"

Michelle's pulse leaped nervously in response to Taylor's question. "I—"

"Truth, Michelle."

She sighed in surrender. "Yes. I love him."

"So what's the problem?"

"I'm scared," Michelle admitted quietly, looking to Taylor for understanding. "I'm afraid of being hurt again. What if something goes wrong? What if we can't make it work out?"

Still looking deeply thoughtful, Taylor reached up to ruffle her short, dark hair in her habitual gesture. "Remember when you talked me into giving country-and-western music a try, even though I was a hard-core rock-and-roll fan?"

Frowning at the apparent non sequitur, Michelle nodded slowly. "Why?"

"Well, I like it. And I keep thinking of a song that was popular last year...'A Leap of Faith' by Lionel Cartwright. Remember it?"

"Um—yes."

"It seems rather appropriate at the moment. The lyrics point out that you can't always tell what kind of problems you'll encounter in your life, but that real love will always find a way to overcome them. It says that even though your heart's been broken before, you have to take a chance—a 'leap of faith'—and put your trust in someone again."

"It's only a song, Taylor."

"Mmm. But it's true. He says the first step's always the hardest."

"It makes a nice song," Michelle murmured defensively, sinking into a chair that matched the one Taylor sat in, "but real life isn't always so easy. Tony could hurt me, Taylor, worse than Geoff ever could have. That scares me."

Taylor was quiet for a long moment, her eyes curiously blank, as though focused on something Michelle couldn't see. And when she spoke, her voice throbbed with a low, old pain. "The hardest thing I've ever had to face was losing Dylan. Sitting in that hospital waiting room alone, remembering everything we'd found, reliving the moment when that car came out of nowhere and took him away from me—I wasn't sure I'd survive losing him.''

Michelle bit her lower lip, distressed by the extent of the suffering Taylor had never revealed so clearly to her before. "Oh, Taylor..."

Taylor drew a deep breath, as though to ward off tears she had no intention of shedding. "For a long time after they told me Dylan had died on the operating table, I was as angry as I was devastated. I was so damned mad that I'd met him only to lose him after only a few short weeks together. I thought it was horribly unfair that those three weeks would haunt me for the rest of my life, that I'd never stop comparing any man I met to the one I couldn't keep. I lay awake nights wishing I'd never turned that corner and walked into him, that he'd never picked up my packages and smiled at me. That I'd turned him down when he offered to buy me a drink. That I'd never fallen in love with him.''

And then she shook her head, her expression clearing as she turned her gaze back on her unhappy friend. "You know what helped me then? It was another country song. Garth Brooks's 'The Dance.' It made me think about whether I really would have missed knowing Dylan if given a choice, whether I'd trade my memories of those three perfect weeks with him for anything. And I realized that I wouldn't. Whatever I had to go through afterward was worth having the privilege to know him, be with him, love him and be loved by him. And I wouldn't have missed it for anything.''

"But can you ever risk loving again, risking that pain again?'' Michelle asked in a tearful whisper, her hands gripped so tightly in her lap that her fingers ached.

"I hope I'll love again someday," Taylor admitted, "if I can ever find anyone who makes me feel the way Dylan did. I don't want to spend the rest of my life alone. I'd like a family someday. Maybe.

"And what about you?" she asked, turning the questioning to Michelle. "Don't you want children, someone to love? Are you going to spend the rest of your life hiding in that big house of yours, guarding your money and your heart? Or are you going to accept the risks that are simply a part of being alive?"

Michelle caught her breath at the wording. She'd taken a chance at finding her family, and she'd found Layla and Kevin and the children. She'd also found Tony and his lovable, close-knit family, who'd welcomed her so warmly among them.

She'd been willing to work at her relationship with her sister... shouldn't she be willing to work even harder at holding on to the man she loved with all her heart?

She'd long since grown tired of guarding the wealth that didn't really matter to her at all. She was tired of being lonely, tired of being afraid. She wasn't a vulnerable eight-year-old now, but a grown woman, competent and experienced and perfectly capable of taking care of herself. Wasn't she also intelligent enough to know when to put her faith in someone else?

"It's your call, Michelle," Taylor said as though she'd read her friend's thoughts. "Is Tony worth the risk?"

Chapter Fifteen

"That's right, Cassie, I've got to pull you off the Jared Walker investigation—temporarily, at least," Tony confirmed into the telephone. "With Bob gone, we're shorthanded until I can find someone to replace him. I need you on the Grayson Industries security report... Yeah, you can follow up any leads you get on Walker in the meantime. But remember that Grayson's a priority right now."

He was already flipping through his Rolodex file for another number when he hung up. He had a stack of calls and responsibilities to get through on this Monday morning. Not that he minded. He'd just as soon work as spend another day moping around his apartment, missing Michelle.

He'd regretted pulling Cassie off the full-time search for Jared Walker. He would have liked to have been able to provide Michelle with her oldest brother's whereabouts as soon as possible. The problem was, he had other cases to handle, other clients to consider. And Cassie had admitted that she wasn't getting anywhere fast finding Walker. Every time she thought she had a lead, the trail grew cold long before she ran it down.

He had gotten more information on Lindsay, but hadn't yet obtained her current whereabouts. As for the twins—he'd come up cold on every angle he'd tried in searching for them.

He'd wanted to give Michelle her family, even if she wouldn't accept anything else he wanted so badly to offer her.

He cursed when he failed to find the number he was looking for in his file. Damned if he could find anything today! Disgruntled, he punched the intercom. "Bonnie—get me Stu Grayson's number, will you? And have you got those letters ready to go out yet?"

"They're almost ready for your signature, Tony."

"Good. Bring them in with Grayson's number. I've got a couple of other calls I can make first." He took his finger off the button and reached for his card file again.

This call didn't take long; he hung up the phone at the same time the door to his office opened. Without looking up from the paperwork littered across his desk, he held out his hand. "You found Grayson's number?"

A slip of paper was placed in his hand. He glanced at it, noting the number printed neatly in Bonnie's familiar handwriting. "Thanks. Got those letters ready for me to sign?"

"Bonnie said she'll have them ready for you in a few minutes. I told her not to hurry. You're going to be busy for a while."

Tony's head jerked up, his eyes rounding. "Michelle!"

With uncharacteristic clumsiness, he nearly fell over his desk when he stood, kicking his chair from beneath him, his eyes locked on the smiling face of the woman he loved. His heart thudded in sudden hope in response to the look in her eyes. He prayed with everything inside him that he wasn't misreading her expression. "What are you doing here?"

Michelle took a deep, bracing breath in response to Tony's question. The expression on his face when he'd looked up to find her standing there had brought a giant lump to her throat. Why, until now, had she allowed her fears to blind her to the love in his eyes? And how could he still look at her that way when she'd treated him so very badly?

"You're busy," she murmured, suddenly shy. "Maybe I should have waited until after business hours."

"I'm never too busy for you," Tony assured her huskily. He walked around the end of the desk, never taking his eyes from her face. He gestured toward the sofa against one wall. "D'you want to sit down?"

"Not yet," she replied, too nervous to sit, her fingers locked tightly around the papers she held in her left hand.

"All right." Stopping close beside her, he crossed his arms and stood at apparent ease, though there were lines of strain at the corners of his mouth. "What is that?" he asked, nodding toward the papers she held. "Something you wanted to discuss with me?"

"Yes." She cleared her throat, then called on every ounce of courage she possessed. "This...this is a pre-nuptial agreement, Tony. I had my attorney—my new attorney—draw it up. It's legal and binding."

His eyes narrowed. "A prenuptial agreement?" he repeated slowly, looking from the papers to her flushed face. "You're considering my marriage proposal?"

"Does the offer still stand?" she whispered.

His face softened. "Yes," he replied simply. "Nothing's changed about my feelings for you."

The utter sincerity of his words brought tears to her eyes. Her voice trembled. "I don't deserve you, Tony."

"Just tell me you love me," he answered a bit unsteadily, "and I'll sign anything you like. All I've ever wanted is you, Michelle."

In response, she lifted the papers and very calmly ripped them in half. And then in half again. Her fingers opened, allowing the ragged shreds to fall around their feet.

Tony seemed stunned by her actions. "Why did you do that? What are you telling me?" he demanded.

Her tears blurred his face when she looked at him. "I love you, Tony. I trust you. I was a blind, cowardly fool not to trust you from the very beginning. Can you ever forgive me?"

"Michelle. Oh, God." Without hesitation, he reached out to pull her into his arms. "I love you. There's nothing to forgive."

Her arms going tightly around his lean waist, Michelle shook her head against his shoulder, feeling the tears escaping the corners of her eyes despite her efforts to hold them back.

"I should never have doubted you, Tony. You were always on my side, always trying to help me, and I still treated you so badly. I'll spend the rest of my life making it up to you, I promise."

"I understood, you know," he told her quietly, stroking her hair with one unsteady hand. "It hurt, but I always understood. You'd been hurt before, and you kept getting hurt. You had every reason to be cautious."

She lifted her wet face from his shoulder to look up at him. "I've learned that being so cautious is a very lonely way to live. I don't want to be alone anymore, Tony."

He dried her tears with gentle fingers. "You won't ever be lonely again, *tesoro*. I'm going to fill your life with more love, more family than you'll know what to do with. Your brothers and sisters and nieces and nephews. My family, who already love you almost as much as I do. And our own children, however many you'd like. As soon as you want to have them."

"Oh, Tony." She tugged his head down to hers for a long, lingering kiss. "I love you," she said when he finally released her mouth.

"I love you, too, *cara*."

She nibbled at his lower lip. "Tell me in Italian."

He smiled and kissed her. "*Ti amo*."

"*Ti amo*," she repeated.

"*Anch'io ti amo*. I love you, too. *Ti adoro*. I adore you. *Ti amo, e ti amero per tutta la vita*. I'll love you for the rest of my life."

He punctuated the impromptu language lesson with progressively longer kisses.

Emerging flushed and breathless from one particularly enthusiastic embrace, Michelle smiled up at him. "I'd like you to teach me Italian. I want to know everything that's being said at your family gatherings."

"*Our* family gatherings," Tony corrected her. "You'll be a D'Alessandro, too, God help you. And I'd be happy to teach you Italian. In fact, I'd be willing to spend the rest of my life teaching you."

"It may just take that long for me to learn," she murmured, tightening her arms around his neck.

"Does that mean you'll marry me?"

"I thought we had that settled. Of course I'll marry you. It's what I want more than anything in the world."

He kissed her deeply, then drew back just far enough to speak. "About the prenuptial agreement, Michelle. I want you to get another copy for me to sign. I never want you to have cause to doubt me again."

"No." She shook her head stubbornly, utterly determined on that point. "I want *you* to know that I trust you implicitly, that I don't need papers or legalities or anything but your word. I love you, Tony. And I believe in you. Let me prove it to you the only way I know how."

Twin fires flared in his dark eyes. He drew her closer, his hand sliding savoringly down her back. "I'm sure we can come up with some other way for you to show me how much you love me."

She smiled in anticipation. "I'll do that, too," she murmured. "But that will have to wait until we're alone. Your place or mine, but not in your office with your secretary right outside."

"We could lock the door," he suggested, looking absurdly wistful.

She laughed and kissed him, then pulled away. "Later," she said firmly. "I have things to do this afternoon."

"Oh? Like what?" he challenged her.

"I have a wedding to plan," she replied happily. "I have to call Layla and Taylor to help me get started. I'm warning you, my love, it's going to be a major event. I want all your family there."

"*All* of them?" he asked in exaggerated dismay, though he didn't look particularly reluctant.

"All of them," she replied firmly. "Adults, children and babies. All my life I've wanted to belong to a big family. Now you've granted that wish for me."

"You plan our wedding any way you want it," Tony told her recklessly. "Just make sure you don't take more than a month to get it together."

"A month?" she gasped. "But, Tony..."

"Six weeks," he compromised. "That's as long as I intend to wait to make you my wife."

"Then I'd better get started immediately," she said unsteadily, turning toward the door. And then she stopped and turned to throw herself back in his arms for a long, fervent hug. "I love you," she said fiercely. "And I'm going to make you the happiest man alive."

His arms locked around her. "You already have, *tesoro*," he assured her huskily. "Trust me. You already have."

Epilogue

Teresa and Paul D'Alessandro had offered their big backyard as a location for the early afternoon wedding. The acre-and-a-half lawn was filled to capacity with folding chairs, colorful tents, tables of food, masses of flowers. And people. Aunts, uncles, cousins, in-laws, friends.

Taylor served as maid of honor, Layla and another long-time friend of Michelle's were bridesmaids. Vinnie stood as his son's best man, brothers Joe and Mike serving as groomsmen. Layla's son, Keith, proudly carried the rings, while tiny Brittany made an adorable flower girl. Not to be left out, eight-year-old Dawne distributed bags of birdseed to be thrown at the departing bridal couple.

It was a noisy, joyous, haphazardly organized affair. And Michelle wouldn't have changed a minute of it.

"It was the most beautiful wedding anyone's ever had," she enthused, dancing around a plush hotel room much later that evening. "Absolutely, positively, indisputably perfect."

Pouring champagne into two beribboned stem glasses, Tony smiled indulgently at his still-hyper bride. "Perfect?"

"*Perfetto.*"

He managed not to laugh at her accent. "Even when Kevin asked Father Bailey why he had his shirt on backward? Layla nearly melted in embarrassment."

"The kid's been raised Methodist. How would he have known? And Father Bailey thought it was cute."

"Was it perfect when cousin Angelo's two boys got into a fight and spilled the punch bowl all over the skirt of Aunt Lucia's dress?"

"It was an accident," Michelle replied firmly. "Everyone laughed, didn't they?"

"Everyone but Angelo and Aunt Lucia. And the boys weren't laughing when their father got through with them, either."

Michelle made a dismissive gesture with the hand in which he'd just placed a glass of champagne, sending a wave of the expensive, bubbly beverage over the rim to splash at her feet. "Accidents happen."

His eyes laughed at her euphoria. "Is that what you call Teresa going into labor halfway through the reception? An accident?"

"That was a happy coincidence," Michelle replied. "Now we'll always remember little Bianca's birthday—the same day as our wedding anniversary."

"I'm only sorry we couldn't find the rest of your family in time to invite them to our wedding," Tony murmured, setting his half-emptied champagne glass aside.

Michelle shook her head, refusing to let even that dim her pleasure in the day. "Layla and Kevin and the children were there. If we never find the others, I'll always be grateful to you for helping me find my sister."

"I'll find the others," Tony said, his jaw set in determination. "No matter how long it takes."

Suddenly serious, Michelle lifted her free hand to his face, all her love in her eyes. "I know you won't stop trying, Tony," she assured him. "You promised, didn't you? And you always keep your promises, if it's humanly possible to do so."

"You're taking a pretty big chance being so confident in me," he murmured, covering her hand with his own.

"No. I don't think I'm taking a chance at all," she whispered. "I love you, Tony. And I trust you. With all my heart."

His eyes flared. "I love you, too, Michelle. And I'll never do anything to make you regret trusting me."

"I know you won't, darling. Besides," she added with a smile, "you're the one who taught me to swing a baseball bat, aren't you? Just remember that when you're tempted to stray."

"Threats now." He sighed deeply and shook his head, his fingers going to the fastenings at the back of her dress. "I can tell I'm going to have my hands full with you."

Her dress slipped down her shoulders. "In a moment, you certainly will," she agreed, giggling.

"Any complaints, *tesoro?*"

She stepped out of the gown, leaving her clad only in filmy, delectably sexy underthings, and draped her arms around his neck. "Not a one, my love."

He'd caught his breath at the sight of her pale flesh beneath sheer lace and satin. When he spoke, his voice was hoarse, his breathing shallow. "I love you."

She pressed her lips to his, then drew back only far enough to whisper, "Show me how much."

"That's going to take a while," he murmured, lifting her high against his chest and turning toward the bed behind him. "The rest of our lives."

Her smile was blissfully happy. "That's all I could ever ask."

He followed her to the bed, his lean body pressing her deliciously into the mattress, and she lifted her mouth to his, knowing the time for words had passed.

She knew that Tony's love was everything she'd ever longed for. Whatever life brought them from now on would be faced together. Michelle Walker Trent D'Alessandro would never be lonely again.

* * * * *

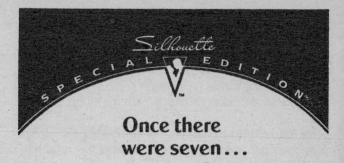

For all those readers who've been looking for something a little bit different, a little bit spooky, let Silhouette Books take you on a journey to the dark side of love with

SILHOUETTE
Shadows

If you like your romance mixed with a hint of danger, a taste of something eerie and wild, you'll love Shadows. This new line will send a shiver down your spine and make your heart beat faster. It's full of romance and more—and some of your favorite authors will be featured right from the start. Look for our four launch titles wherever books are sold, because you won't want to miss a single one.

THE LAST CAVALIER—Heather Graham Pozzessere
WHO IS DEBORAH?—Elise Title
STRANGER IN THE MIST—Lee Karr
SWAMP SECRETS—Carla Cassidy

After that, look for two books every month, and prepare to tremble with fear—and passion.

SILHOUETTE SHADOWS, coming your way in March.

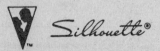

SHAD1

Take 4 bestselling love stories FREE

Plus get a FREE surprise gift!

Special Limited-time Offer

Mail to Silhouette Reader Service™

P.O. Box 609
Fort Erie, Ontario
L2A 5X3

YES! Please send me 4 free Silhouette Special Edition® novels and my free surprise gift. Then send me 6 brand-new novels every month, which I will receive months before they appear in bookstores. Bill me at the low price of $2.96* each—a savings of 43¢ apiece off the cover prices, plus only 69¢ per shipment for delivery. I understand that accepting the books and gift places me under no obligation ever to buy any books. I can always return a shipment and cancel at any time. Even if I never buy another book from Silhouette, the 4 free books and the surprise gift are mine to keep forever.

335 BPA ADMQ

Name   (PLEASE PRINT)

Address   Apt No.

City   Province   Postal Code

This offer is limited to one order per household and not valid to present Silhouette Special Edition® subscribers. *Terms and prices are subject to change without notice. Canadian residents add applicable federal and provincial taxes.

CSPED-93   ©1990 Harlequin Enterprises Limited

Silhouette Books
is proud to present
our best authors,
their best books...
and the best in
<u>your reading pleasure!</u>

Throughout 1993, look for exciting books
by these top names in contemporary
romance:

CATHERINE COULTER—
Aftershocks in February

FERN MICHAELS—
Whisper My Name in March

DIANA PALMER—
Heather's Song in March

ELIZABETH LOWELL—
Love Song for a Raven in April

SANDRA BROWN
(previously published under
the pseudonym Erin St. Claire)—
Led Astray in April

LINDA HOWARD—
All That Glitters in May

When it comes to passion,
we wrote the book.

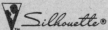

BOBT1R